Breaking Ground

by William D. Andrews

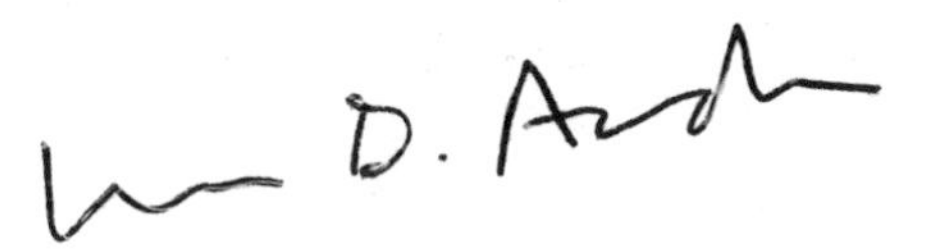

Islandport Press

ISLANDPORT PRESS
P.O. Box 10
Yarmouth, Maine 04096
www.islandportpress.com
books@islandportpress.com

First Islandport Press edition published in June 2011

ISBN: 9781-934031-38-4
Library of Congress Card Number: 2011922198

Book jacket design by Karen F. Hoots / Hoots Design
Book designed by Molly E. Charest for Islandport Press
Publisher Dean L. Lunt

Also from William D. Andrews:

Stealing History

Also from Islandport Press:

Old Maine Woman: Stories from The Coast to The County
by Glenna Johnson Smith

Where Cool Waters Flow
by Randy Spencer

Contentment Cove and *Young*
by Miriam Colwell

Windswept, Mary Peters, and *Silas Crockett*
by Mary Ellen Chase

My Life in the Maine Woods
by Annette Jackson

Shoutin' into the Fog
by Thomas Hanna

Nine Mile Bridge
by Helen Hamlin

In Maine
by John N. Cole

The Cows Are Out!
by Trudy Chambers Price

Hauling by Hand
by Dean Lawrence Lunt

down the road a piece: A Storyteller's Guide to Maine
by John McDonald

Live Free and Eat Pie: A Storyteller's Guide to New Hampshire
by Rebecca Rule

Not Too Awful Bad: A Storyteller's Guide to Vermont
by Leon Thompson

A Moose and a Lobster Walk into a Bar
by John McDonald

Headin' for the Rhubarb: A New Hampshire Dictionary (well, sorta)
by Rebecca Rule

At One: In a Place Called Maine
by Lynn Plourde and Leslie Mansmann

Dahlov Ipcar's Farmyard Alphabet
by Dahlov Ipcar

The Cat at Night
by Dahlov Ipcar

My Wonderful Christmas Tree
by Dahlov Ipcar

These and other New England books are available at:
www.islandportpress

Acknowledgments

Right after the publication of *Stealing History*, many friends and many more folks I met at book signings and talks asked if a sequel was in the works. It was, and *Breaking Ground* is it. I hope those who asked for the sequel will enjoy it. I want to thank those who helped, some who read and commented on this book, and some who more generally encouraged me to keep my fingers on the keyboard when a long trek on snowshoes had more appeal: Al Cressy, Bruce Edwards, John Jebb, Jeff Newsom, Francis Richardson, Kathy Richardson, Saranne Taylor. A small mystery surrounds the question of whether my wife, Debby Andrews, has read *Stealing History*. That's best left to Julie Williamson to solve, but I express again my thanks to her, along with my guess that, no lover of mysteries, she'll skip this one.

At Islandport Press, Amy Canfield repeated her performance as a sharp-eyed and supportive editor, and Trudy Price arranged promotions and signings both cheerfully and efficiently. Warm thanks to them.

My friends on the staff and board of trustees of the Bethel Historical Society suffered the odd delusion that they could find parallels between that organization and the Ryland Historical Society. To them I say, give it up. More seriously, I also say hearty thanks—for all they do to advance the Bethel Historical Society, and for giving me the chance to be part of that vital and fun cultural institution. Ryland should be so lucky.

Prologue

The excavation site looked colorful, festive. Like a mother sheltering her children, a dark green tent spread its top and its partially furled walls over the patch of grass where construction stakes with small orange flags marked the outline for the digging. Also under the tent were chairs and a small table, and leaning against the table were shovels, each decorated with a bright red ribbon. The red ribbons contrasted colorfully with the green of the tent and the yellow of a backhoe that sat off to the side, with its long arm that ended in a toothed scoop turned down and tucked underneath like the neck of a sleeping swan.

Closer up, at the edge of the wood, just barely within the shade of the tent on the recently mown ground, was another splotch of red, but this red was not sharp and confined like the ribbons. Instead, it pooled around the head of a body crumpled and lying facedown in the grass.

Blood. So colorful. Not so festive.

Chapter 1

Julie Williamson considered it positively absurd to quarrel about how many shovels to use at the groundbreaking for the Ryland Historical Society's Daniel Swanson II Center.

Similar disagreements had occurred over the past year, during which, as the historical society's director, Julie had been overseeing final planning for the project. Of course she understood that Mary Ellen Swanson, as the principal donor, had every right to express her opinions and expect them to be listened to. And Mary Ellen exercised that right at every meeting of the board of trustees and its building committee and, in what seemed to Julie, her daily—and rarely announced—visits to Julie's office. As she fell asleep at night, Julie could still hear Mary Ellen's questions in her head:

Should the main entrance door be wood or metal? If wood, should its color match or contrast with that of the facade? Should the door have windows? Should it open to the left or the right?

Was the color of the library walls perhaps just a bit too dark? Wouldn't a nice cream be better?

Should the signs on the restroom doors say "Gentlemen" and "Ladies"? Wouldn't "Men" and "Women" be more, well, up-to-date?

And on and on Mary Ellen went, questioning choices, suggesting alternatives, raising hypothetical issues. The problem wasn't really that she was trying to impose her will; the problem was that she didn't *know* her will. She had as many questions as there were details in the building plan, and she insisted on trotting them all out and subjecting everyone around her to the endless stream of doubts, thoughts, insights, and suggestions.

Now, just a day before tomorrow's July third groundbreaking, Mary Ellen was at it again. About the number of shovels! Because she was the major financial backer and because the new building would bear her late husband's name, Mary Ellen Swanson was the obvious person to take a ceremonial scoop of earth and declare the ground broken. But last Friday, Mary Ellen had dropped by Julie's office to suggest that Julie, as the society's director, should also heft a shovel. Julie had expressed her humble thanks for the honor and tried to change the subject.

"So we'll require two shovels," Mary Ellen had then said. "I'll take mine home as a memento of the occasion, and you can keep yours here in your office." Eager not to prolong discussion of a point of such little significance, Julie had promptly agreed.

But this morning Mary Ellen had returned—this time to propose that there be *four* shovels—"one for each of us," she had said. Responding to Julie's quizzical look, Mary Ellen had explained: "You, me, and Steven and Elizabeth. I think they should each take a scoop, too. I'm sure Clif Holdsworth would be happy to provide the extra shovels. He should do *something* for this project."

Julie couldn't miss Mary Ellen's dig at Clif Holdsworth. Trustee and treasurer of the Ryland Historical Society, Clif owned the local hardware and lumber store and so could readily provide shovels. He was quite well off, but had contributed only $1,000 to the construction project, a fact that rankled Julie almost as much as it obviously did Mary Ellen.

As for the addition of Mary Ellen's son and daughter-in-law to the ceremony, Julie would be happy to comply, even though Steven—Julie thought of him as Always-Steven-Never-Steve—and his wife hadn't been involved in the planning of the Swanson Center and were, as far as Julie could tell from brief conversations with them, uninterested in the whole idea. Steven had at least been polite, but Elizabeth was simply cold about the project—and about pretty much everything else, really.

After Mary Ellen left, Julie had reluctantly called Clif Holdsworth to ask for the extra shovels. With equal reluctance, he had agreed. But fifteen minutes after that, Mary Ellen had called Julie to say she thought Steven and Elizabeth should share a shovel. "Elizabeth isn't really a Swanson, of course. She still uses her maiden name, you know," Mary Ellen had explained with no small amount of distaste in her tone, "so I don't think she needs a separate shovel. Wouldn't it be better, symbolically, if the married couple used the same one?"

Julie agreed—and decided not to mention that she had already called Clif to ask for four shovels. She also decided not to call him back to reduce the order, guessing that before tomorrow morning Mary Ellen was likely to think of someone else who needed a shovel. Actually, Julie wondered if Mary Ellen was physically capable of lifting one herself. She was very tall and achingly thin. Julie couldn't quite put a finger on Mary Ellen's age, but she was aware that the gray-haired, patrician-looking elderly woman had grown more angular and grayer over the past year.

Anyway, the main thing was to get the ceremony over with and the construction under way, Julie thought. No, the main thing, she reminded herself, was to keep Mary Ellen from driving her crazy and stretching out the project to the point where the new building wouldn't be completed until Julie retired! And since she was only thirty-five and had been in the job for just a year, her retirement wasn't exactly on the horizon.

The new building had been one of the reasons Julie had accepted the job as director of the Ryland Historical Society. It would expand the society's three-building campus and provide secure, climate-controlled space for the papers and artifacts currently crammed into the archives/library and attic of the building where Julie's office was located. That building, Swanson House, was also named for the family, which had roots so far back in

Ryland that even Julie hadn't sorted them out yet. Mary Ellen took particular delight in the fact that with the new center named in her husband's honor, the Swansons would have an even bigger presence at the society. The new Swanson Center would support better public programming and attract more scholars and genealogists to use the rich collections. It would, in other words, improve the image and reputation of the Ryland Historical Society—and of its new director. Julie wasn't at all ashamed of her ambition. If she helped her career by helping the Ryland Historical Society, wasn't everyone a winner?

Besides giving her career a boost, the job had appealed to Julie for another reason: Ryland, Maine, was a two-hour drive from Orono, where her boyfriend taught American history at the University of Maine. She and Rich O'Brian had met in graduate school at the University of Delaware. He finished his doctorate a year before her and took the Maine job, and during that year they kept the relationship going by commuting by plane as their finances allowed. So when the Ryland job became available, Julie pursued it enthusiastically, and when she got the offer Rich was as happy as she was.

Their relationship was evolving. During the past year they had settled into an easy pattern for their visits. They'd enjoy one of Rich's gourmet meals, run and hike, or just sit reading or working. Julie kept trying to engage Rich in the board games and jigsaw puzzles she was drawn to, but he usually begged off on the grounds of having to read student papers or prepare lectures. Rich was quiet, steady, supportive, and loving. He was easy to be around, comfortable enough in his own skin to let Julie relax in hers. While she was ambitious and outgoing, he was self-contained and quiet. Julie liked to take hold of problems and solve them, and Rich enjoyed contemplating the bigger picture. She was a doer and Rich a thinker. As much as she hated the cliché, she had to admit that the old saw about opposites attracting applied to them. But she just wasn't sure what the long-term held—or even what she wanted. Marriage? After so much time together, neither could help talking about it, but the conversations had been casual and indirect, and Julie sometimes did wonder what life would be like if they were together all the time. Would her frenetic pace wear him out? Would his constantly calm manner drive her mad? Well, she was prepared to see how things developed; and since Rich wasn't pushing for more, that part of her life was fine.

As for work, after a year in the job she had no regrets, despite her tumultuous start that involved discovering that a number of precious artifacts were missing from the historical society and then, soon after, finding the murdered body of the former director. She was working to put all that behind her, however, and truly was enjoying the job. The position was a great fit with her doctorate in museum studies, and she felt she was mastering the job and learning the ways of small-town New England life. Julie would have been happier if Mary Ellen hadn't been so difficult, but she knew she'd meet Mary Ellens everywhere she went in her line of work. So she remained calm and suffered in silence at the endless meetings in which the benefactor bobbed and weaved and kept plans up in the air. But now it looked like actual work would begin. The ceremonial groundbreaking tomorrow would signal the start. Julie was more than ready. She just wasn't sure how many shovels they would end up needing.

Chapter 2

It could have been the sunrise, dazzling already at just a little after five o'clock. Or it could have been the plaintive moaning of the doves that, like a search party in pursuit of a body, fanned out across Julie's new backyard to see what seeds or bugs the grass would yield. Or it could have been the excitement the day promised: July third at last, and groundbreaking for the Swanson Center.

Whatever the reason, Julie was awake and ready to go. But Rich was still sleeping. She turned to face him, partly hoping her gaze would stir him, partly just happy to look at his handsome face and hairless but muscular chest exposed above the sheet. He extracted his arm and reached down to pull the sheet higher.

"Awake?" Julie asked.

"I guess I am now. What time is it?"

"Five-fifteen. But the sun's been up for a while."

"God."

"I just don't want to miss such a beautiful time of day. Want to take a run before breakfast?"

Rich was by far the faster one, and Julie liked to run with him because his pace made her push herself. They left the house through the back door and after stretching headed across the garden and out to the street toward the historical society, passing her office in Swanson House, a straightforward three-story structure built in 1865. Below it were Ting House and then Holder House, both Greek Revival structures painted pale yellow. Ting was maintained as a period house, its rooms furnished in the style of the 1840s and open for guided tours. Holder was the society's welcome center and museum, with galleries for rotating exhibits and the gift shop. Behind them was a long shed, covered with rough siding boards, divided into rooms where volunteers gave demonstrations of nineteenth-century crafts—spinning, weaving, blacksmithing, cooking. The new Swanson Center would stand at the end of the crafts shed and directly behind Swanson House. She gestured for Rich to turn right, and they cut through the parking area and toward the open space where the new building would be. A yellow backhoe was waiting, as was the dark green tent erected yesterday at the site of the groundbreaking.

"Through the woods," she shouted to him, and he led them toward an opening in the trees at the back of the construction site and into the wooded area that separated the historical society's campus from the street behind it. They followed the street down to the bottom of the hill and cut across the park and onto the paved walk beside the river. The view of the water was dazzling, with the early sun glancing off it and illuminating the birches on the opposite bank. At the end of the pavement they turned left and headed back up Main Street toward the Town Common. The town's shops were grouped on lower Main, but as the street rose to the Common they gave way to well-kept residences: Victorian and classic-revival houses mixing in a pattern produced by changing tastes and the vagaries of land ownership. The lack of uniformity in styles created the overall impression of a very dense, rich architectural treasure trove. It was not for nothing that Ryland was called "Maine's loveliest mountain village."

At the entrance to the Common, Rich paused. "Enough?" he asked.

"Maybe ten minutes more," Julie replied. "Let's go up past the inn."

Beyond the Ryland Inn—a stately structure in white—lay its golf course and along its eastern side several dozen townhouse condominiums. They jogged along the edge of the golf course and into another wood above the townhouses. Rich jogged in place till Julie caught up.

"Where to?" he asked.

"Home. Keep to the left, back toward the street."

When they were a few blocks above her house, Rich cut back onto the Common and came to a stop by the gazebo. "Walk now," he said and put his left hand on his right to check his pulse. "Let's get the old heart rate back to normal."

"God, it's a beautiful town," he said as they walked down the Common and then turned back toward her house.

"It is, isn't it? I feel so at home here now. It really is a great place."

"And this?" he asked, pointing to the three buildings of the Ryland Historical Society.

"The job? Yeah, I love that, too, even though there have been times this past year when I wondered if we'd ever be able to build the new center."

"Because of Mary Ellen Swanson?"

"Of course! She can be such a pain in the butt. But when the groundbreaking is over today, she won't be able to keep second-guessing everything. And I shouldn't complain: Mary Ellen's been good to me—and to the society."

"Must be nice to be rich."

"And generous. You have to say that for her. Anyway, to answer your question: Yes, I love my job. It's taken a little longer than I thought to feel at home here because, well, you know, and everyone knows everyone else and knows what's going on, but I've really gotten to like that. Maybe someday I'll even be accepted."

"Don't count on it. You'll always be 'from away.' This is Maine."

"But that's part of its charm!"

They were standing in front of her house now, and Julie was almost tempted to stride up the walk, take the four steps up to the long porch, and enter through the front door. If she had, it would have been the first time. But she headed for the side. "Still not ready?" Rich asked.

"Getting there. Maybe in a day or so. Before you have to leave." Julie led the way around to the garden, and they entered via the back door.

Julie had only lived in the house for a month. The Ryland Historical Society owned it, and Julie got free use of it as part of her job. For the last year, however, she had been living in a condo at Ryland Skiway, the resort just north of town, because when she had started work the house's former owner, Worth Harding, was still in it. Founder of the historical society and its director until he retired and Julie was hired, Harding intended to donate the house as a director's residence and to extend the society's land holdings farther up Main Street. But before he moved out, he was murdered—in the house. Julie had been the one to find his body in the front parlor, and she had helped identify the murderer and solve the series of thefts at the historical society that she had uncovered right after she arrived. That was just a little over a year ago, but Julie couldn't shake the memory of finding the elderly Harding, his head smashed by an iron skillet, lying on the floor by the sofa in the front room. It turned out that another historical society trustee, Martha Preston, had been the murderer.

For a time Julie had doubted whether she could ever take up residence in Worth's house, but the appeal of it was too powerful. She loved Victorian architecture, and Harding House, as it was now called, was a classic. Since finally moving in, she avoided the front parlor as much as possible, and hadn't entered from the front door because that had been the route she had taken when she had discovered Harding's body.

While Rich fixed breakfast, Julie showered and then dressed in the outfit she had laid out earlier. She didn't usually dress with such care. After hearing that Julie wanted to do graduate work in museum studies, her mother had said she'd have to stock up on twin sets and pearls. Julie laughed at the time, not fully understanding; but she subsequently came to appreciate her mother's comment after seeing so many women in museum jobs wearing an unbuttoned sweater over a jumper, topped off with a string of pearls. Julie didn't own pearls; indeed, she had few pieces of jewelry. And though she owned plenty of sweaters and turtlenecks that could have been combined into a respectable twin set, that was not her style. Her style, she realized, was almost no style: slacks or skirt and a turtleneck, or sometimes a cotton blouse, plain or at most striped, never patterned. She kept her light-red hair carefully clipped and groomed to mid-ear length, complementing her pale, oval face and blue eyes.

She checked herself in the mirror. At five-foot-six, she was tall enough to command attention but not tall enough to be regarded as looming. She was slender and well-proportioned, attractive, but not so much that men other than Rich would do a double-take on the street. She looked professional and pleasant in her tan skirt and blue blazer over a pink silk blouse. Not quite a twin set, she told herself, smiling, but a little different from her usual uniform. When she entered the kitchen, Rich, handing her a cup of coffee, noticed her attire and said, "Very nice. Big day."

"Two days, actually," she said. "Don't forget about the Fourth of July concert on the Town Common tomorrow. We sponsor it, and it's a big deal for the society."

"Right. What time should I show up today?"

"The ceremony is at eleven-thirty. Are you sure you want to come?"

"I wouldn't miss it for anything. Like I said, it's going to be a big day!"

Chapter 3

"They want a check today," Mrs. Detweiller said in the general direction of Julie's office.

Working at her desk for more than an hour, Julie hadn't heard her secretary enter Swanson House, but now that she was here Julie knew without looking at her watch that it was nine o'clock. Not 8:55 or 9:08. What Mrs. Detweiller lacked in interpersonal skills—like plain old friendliness—she made up for in punctuality and every other secretarial competency. So she endured Mrs. Detweiller—and after a year of working with her still called her *Mrs.* Detweiller, since she insisted on referring to Julie as *Dr.* Williamson. In her early days on the job, Julie had more than once implored the woman to call her Julie, but the secretary's response was always the same: "Oh, I couldn't do *that,*" suggesting by the emphasis that Julie might be suborning her to, at the very least, a criminal misdemeanor. The "doctor" title Mrs. Detweiller insisted on, Julie had come to understand, was less a term of respect than one of distancing. She had earned her doctorate, but included in the local use of the title was, Julie felt, an implicit "but not a *real* one."

"What check, Mrs. Detweiller? And who's *they?*" Julie answered as she walked out to where her secretary stood in the main office.

"For the tent. They want the check today. It certainly seems like a lot of money for nothing—we haven't had rain for weeks."

"Here," Julie said, reaching for the paper Mrs. Detweiller was waving in front of her. "I'll sign that and you can write the check for them right away. Are they still here?"

"On their way. They called and asked if they could pick up the check when they remove the tent, after the ceremony. Such a short time for so much money."

"Well, it was good insurance, though. If we hadn't had it, it might have rained and spoiled things. And, the way the sun is shining out there, we might be glad we have it for the shade, don't you think?"

"I suppose it is a special day." And then from the door as she was withdrawing, Mrs. Detweiller added, "And you're dressed for it, Dr. Williamson. Very nice."

Was it possible, Julie wondered, that Mrs. Detweiller had actually complimented her? Or was she being sarcastic? And was it so obvious that Julie's style of dress today was so different from her everyday? She sat down at the table she used as a desk and smiled, not at the comment about how she looked but at the remark about the tent. Mrs. Detweiller hadn't been alone in criticizing Julie for renting the fifteen-by-thirty-two-foot tent. Several trustees had questioned her decision, too, but she was determined that nothing would spoil—or delay—the ceremony.

She jotted some notes for the toast she planned to make to the Swanson family at the luncheon. Then, glancing up, she noticed the four gleaming shovels leaning against her bookcase by the window. She decided to take them over to the tent. It was still two hours until the ceremony, but she was antsy. She tied a bright red ribbon on each shovel and then, with some degree of difficulty because it was a clumsy load, walked over to the site. She lined the shovels up on the table at the end of the tent, wondering if Mary Ellen would decide to use all four after all.

"I can't see the harm in chicken," Mrs. Detweiller said to Julie when she returned to the office from the construction site.

"Well, I can't either, but what's the problem?"

"Elizabeth Swanson! She called the inn this morning to request a vegetarian meal. They phoned to see if anyone else wanted something other than chicken. I told them no. At least no one said anything to me. That Elizabeth—just like her to call the inn directly instead of going through me."

"Oh, well. We certainly don't want to make Mary Ellen's daughter-in-law unhappy."

"There's not much you or I can do to prevent *that*, Dr. Williamson. Mrs. Swanson—the younger Mrs. Swanson—wouldn't be happy if she weren't unhappy. It's easy to see why our Mrs. Swanson doesn't care for her son's wife."

"Lots of people prefer vegetarian food, Mrs. Detweiller," Julie said in an attempt to distract the woman from further comments on the topic of Mary Ellen Swanson's family relations. "I'm just glad she called ahead of time instead of waiting until we got there. Is everything else okay at the inn?"

"As far as I know. But it might be a good idea for you to go over and check things out. They use so many young people now and you can't really depend on them to do things right. If you know what I mean."

While Julie wasn't sure she *did* know what Mrs. Detweiller meant, the opportunity to walk across the Common and inspect the room where the lunch would be held represented another way to use some of her nervous energy. "That's an excellent idea, Mrs. Detweiller. I'll walk over there now. I should be back in half an hour and still have some time before the groundbreaking in case anything comes up."

As it turned out, checking the room had been a good idea, because the staff at the Ryland Inn had ignored the plan for placing the tables that Julie had provided last week. Instead of setting a head table—for the Swanson family, Julie and Rich, and trustee chair Howard Townsend and his wife—and other tables of seven and eight for the rest, the staff had put a long table for twelve at the front of the room facing tables for four. The catering manager assured Julie he would correct the problem, but she lingered to make sure, and it was ten-thirty before she returned to her office. Without providing all the details that she knew Mrs. Detweiller would have welcomed, Julie thanked her secretary again for the suggestion and said the inn had, indeed, made a mistake.

"Always good to keep an eye on them," Mrs. Detweiller said with deep satisfaction.

"I'll just finish up in my office," Julie said. "If I lose track of time, could you call me at eleven? I'd like to be sure I'm over at the site in case anyone comes early."

But it was not Mrs. Detweiller who interrupted Julie at work, and it wasn't at eleven. Ten minutes after she entered her office, Julie heard Howard Townsend in the outer office. If she didn't know Howard as a quiet, dignified, and entirely self-composed man, she would have sworn he was shouting. And when she walked out to see what was happening, she realized he was.

"Horrible, just horrible," he was saying, as much to the air as to Mrs. Detweiller. "We have to call the police. Oh, Julie," Townsend continued when he saw her, "Mary Ellen is dead."

CHAPTER 4

"Howard, what do you mean—when did Mary Ellen die? Are you okay?" Julie added when she saw his ashen face. "Maybe you should sit down."

Howard Townsend didn't so much sit down as melt down, letting his old, lanky body slip onto the small couch directly across from Mrs. Detweiller's desk. "Do you need water?" she asked.

"Please," Townsend said. "But first we have to call the police."

"Mrs. Detweiller, would you get some water," Julie asked as crisply as she could, presenting an artificial calmness. "Now, tell me, what's happened?"

"Mary Ellen's dead," Townsend said in such a low voice Julie found herself bending to hear him. "I found her . . . her body. At the construction site."

Now Julie felt the need to sit; before responding she lowered herself to the couch. "I don't understand," she said.

"At the groundbreaking site," he continued. "I came early. Just to be sure things were in order. And I found her there. Dead. Oh, thank you, Mrs. Detweiller," he said as he reached for the paper cup of water. "We should call the police, the ambulance, but I think it's too late. I'm sure she's dead. She couldn't have lost all that blood and survived."

"Blood?" Julie practically screamed. "What did you see?"

"First the police and the ambulance. Mrs. Detweiller, please ring them."

Julie felt slightly relieved to hear Howard's naturally authoritative tone returning. "Now tell me what happened," she said.

"What happened? I don't know. All I know is that Mary Ellen was lying beside the table, under that tent, facedown, and the blood was everywhere. It was terrible!" Howard rose from the couch, but Julie put her arm on his shoulder and gently pushed him back. Except for crisp handshakes, this was the first time she had ever touched him.

"They're all on their way," Mrs. Detweiller said as she put the phone down. "Then I'll go meet them," Howard said, and again stood, but this time steadily enough that Julie didn't feel the need to restrain him.

"I'll go with you, Howard."

"You shouldn't see Mary Ellen like that. You stay here."

"Of course I'll come," she said. "You can explain on the way."

"There's not much more to explain," Howard said as they walked from her office and turned toward the construction site. A man in a khaki uniform, in his mid-thirties and fit enough to run but panting as he reached them, sprinted from the street.

"Thank you for responding so quickly," Howard said to Ryland's police chief, Mike Barlow. "I told Julie not to come, but she insisted."

The three of them picked up their pace. There was the backhoe, and there was the tent. And there was Mary Ellen Swanson's body, lying just as Howard had described. Mike gestured to the other two to stay back and bent down. He reached for Mary Ellen's right arm. Julie could see him searching her wrist to check for a pulse. How gentle he is, Julie thought, like he's comforting a child who fell off her bike. Then she saw the blood that covered Mary Ellen's body, beginning at her neck and continuing down both legs.

"Are you okay, Julie?" Howard asked, right before Julie abruptly turned away and began to heave. She was sure she was going to vomit, but all she could manage were dry heaves, accompanied now by tears, hot, salty tears pouring down her face and onto her blouse.

"No," she answered between heaves. "I mean, yes, I'll be all right in a minute. It's just . . ." Another heave came, and then another, and then Julie knew she *was* going to vomit, and up came her breakfast, shooting out of her and onto the grassy area beside the tent. "I'm sorry, Howard," she said as he put his arm around her shoulder.

Mike stood and walked backwards from Mary Ellen. He pulled the portable radio from his belt and spoke rapidly into it. "No sirens, Jerry" were the only words Julie caught. Barlow reattached the radio and came over to where Howard and Julie were standing.

"Okay, Julie?" he asked.

"I'll be fine in a minute. Don't step there."

Mike pulled himself back from the pool of vomit. "You should sit down, but not here; you can't disturb the scene." He gestured toward the rows of chairs at the back of the tent, chairs for the celebrants who would be coming shortly for the groundbreaking. That got Julie's attention.

"We've got fifty or sixty people coming here for the ceremony in about a half-hour," she said. "We've got to stop them."

"Yeah, I don't want anyone around here," Mike said. "Can you get some of your folks to stand over there by the parking area and keep the guests out?"

"I'll see who's around to help—some volunteers should be here by now."

"If I can help, Julie," Howard offered in a tone that made her think he wasn't really prepared to take on such lowly work.

"Maybe you should just go back to my office and wait, Howard," she replied, and he assented quickly and began to walk toward Swanson House.

Julie turned back to speak to the policeman again and then glanced at the table. "The shovels," she said.

"What?"

"The shovels. I put four of them here earlier, but there are only three now." She pointed to them, each still wearing its red bow. "One's missing."

"You're thinking someone used a shovel to hit Mrs. Swanson?" Mike asked.

"I don't know, but just look at her." Julie took one quick glance at the bloody body and quickly turned back to the policeman. "Something caused all that blood, and one of the shovels is missing."

"I'll check around here as soon as I get some backup. Was it like these?"

"Exactly the same. Clif Holdsworth supplied them, and I tied the ribbons on them and brought them all over here this morning."

"What time was that?"

Julie consulted her watch again. "It must have been around nine-fifteen or nine-thirty. Mrs. Detweiller came in at nine, and we talked a bit, and then I came over here."

"And Mrs. Swanson wasn't here?"

"No. Well, at least I didn't see her, and if she was around you can be sure she would have made herself known." Julie began to cry again.

"Hey, it's okay," Mike said.

"Mary Ellen was so excited about this groundbreaking, and about the project. It's just so awful!"

"We're not used to violent deaths in Ryland," Mike said. "But this is our second in a year."

"Don't remind me," she said as the memory of Worth Harding's body rose before her. Just when she thought she was getting free of it so she could live in his house.

"Damn, Jerry!" Mike said as the siren wailed behind them. The black-and-white Ryland Town Rescue vehicle stopped in the parking area beside Holder House, its blue lights flashing. "I *told* Jerry not to use the siren," he added.

"Over here," Mike shouted as he waved to Jerry and the second medic. "You better go organize your troops," he added to Julie. "Don't explain anything; just tell them to keep folks away and say the ceremony is off."

Julie nodded and walked past the arriving pair from Town Rescue, nodding but not speaking to them. She went into Holder House first and rounded up three volunteer guides. With the town rescue vehicle right outside the window and the police chief clearly visible by the tent, Julie found it impossible to pretend nothing significant had happened. "There's been an accident at the groundbreaking site," she said, "and we have to postpone the ceremony. People will be coming soon, and we need to stop them from gathering there and explain."

Julie wasn't sure what to make of the fact that no one asked for details. Maybe they already knew what happened. Or maybe, good Mainers that they were, they were just practicing avoidance, a trait Julie had noticed more than once in her time in Maine. Among themselves, they might gossip and speculate, but, around an outsider like her, they went on about their business. So they left the building and took up the places Julie had suggested, two by the parking area and the third at the corner of Ting House, to intercept those who would arrive on foot and go between the buildings toward the site. Realizing that others might come down Main Street and enter behind Swanson House, she decided to go there herself. The first person she encountered was Rich.

"God, I'm so glad to see you!" she said as she grabbed hold of him. "Mary Ellen Swanson was killed—at the construction site. We're stopping people from going back there. Can you help?"

"Jesus! What happened?"

"I don't know. Howard Townsend found her, and came to tell me, and Mike Barlow's there, and Town Rescue. I can't believe this is happening. Not after Worth. What is it with me? I come to town and Worth is killed. Now poor Mary Ellen. Am I a jinx or something?"

Chapter 5

"I canceled the lunch," Mrs. Detweiller informed her as Julie returned to her office.

"Oh, thank you, Mrs. Detweiller. I didn't even think of that."

"We'll have to pay for it because we canceled so late."

"We'll work it out," Julie said. "I'll be in my office for a while."

Crying, she added to herself as she closed the door behind her. Julie wasn't a natural crier; she tended to keep her emotions both under control and to herself. But the enormity of Mary Ellen's brutal death simply had to be recognized. Her tears flowed.

"Anyone here?" Mike asked from the outer office several minutes into Julie's crying session.

"Yes, come in," answered Julie, wiping her eyes.

Although Julie didn't consider Mike exactly a friend, she liked and respected him. Last year when items went missing from the historical society and then Worth had been murdered, Mike had discouraged Julie from trying to solve the cases. But when she persisted, he accepted the futility of his position, and Julie really considered that they had been partners. Not that she expected Mike to feel the same. Still, they had a good relationship, and Julie regarded him the way everyone else in Ryland seemed to: as a neighbor who wore a badge because he genuinely wanted to help.

"Just a few things I need to talk to you about," Mike said when he was seated across from her. She nodded. "I just got back from telling Steven."

"That must have been hard."

"Always is, but telling someone his mother was a homicide victim sort of raises the ante. Anyway, he said he and his wife and mother had breakfast and then Mary Ellen said she had to meet you at the tent at ten o'clock."

"Me?"

"That's what he said. I didn't remember you saying anything about that, but maybe you forgot."

"No, we didn't have plans to meet. I mean, I figured Mary Ellen would be around this morning, to make changes in the ceremony or something. But we didn't have an appointment. I told you that I took the shovels over around nine-fifteen or nine-thirty, and Mary Ellen wasn't around."

"What did you do then?"

"I came back here, and Mrs. Detweiller suggested I go to the inn to check on the arrangements for lunch. So I was over there until about ten-thirty, and when I got back here, that's when Howard came in to tell me about Mary Ellen. You know the rest from there."

Mike wrote some more notes on his pad. "Okay, between say nine-thirty and ten-thirty you were at the Ryland Inn. Who did you talk to?"

"You're checking my alibi!"

"I am, sorry, but Steven said his mother was meeting you at the tent, and I have to know where you were since you say you weren't there."

"Brian is the catering manager," Julie said. "I can't remember his last name."

"Handley," Mike offered.

"I think so. Anyway, he can tell you I was there—I'm sure he wasn't happy about it. But, I can't be absolutely sure of the time—I mean 'from nine-thirty to ten-thirty,' like you said, doesn't sound right. I don't think I spent an hour with him, but I'm not sure of the exact time I got back here from the tent, or the exact time I left for the inn, or how long it took me to get there and back. Is it so important?"

Mike looked at her for a few seconds before responding gently. "Take it easy, Julie. I know you're upset. Just bear with me. I wouldn't be doing my job if I didn't ask these questions. You understand how these things go. Frankly, I wish the State Police detective would get here and take over, but until he does I have to get this investigation going."

"Fine," Julie said. "Do what you need to do. Is there anything else Steven Swanson said about me?"

"Not a thing. And understand that he wasn't accusing you. He was just answering my question about where his mother was this morning."

"I'm sorry. I'm just so upset. I can't believe someone would do something like that to Mary Ellen. But it's more than that, I guess."

She continued, "I know this is crazy, but I keep thinking of Worth Harding. Finding him on the floor. Seeing Mary Ellen, and all that blood, just brought everything back from last year. Just when I've finally moved into Worth's house . . ."

"You'll be fine there. Remember the police station is just a block down Main Street. You can call anytime if you're nervous."

"Thanks. And I'm sorry about jumping all over you. It just threw me—what Steven said, which isn't true, and then you asking me about where I was and when."

"I understand. Is this going to delay things?" The sudden change in topic brought a blank look to Julie's face. "Mrs. Swanson's death," he said. "I mean, can you still go ahead with your new building?"

"Oh, I guess we'll be delayed—that depends on how long before the digging can start."

"Which is up to the staties. Depends on how long they need to cover the crime scene. But I meant about the project itself."

Julie went blank again.

"Sorry," the chief said. "I don't mean to be talking in riddles. Everyone knows Mrs. Swanson was the sponsor of the project, or at least the biggest donor since it's going to be named for her husband. I was just wondering if her death affects that."

"I'd assume Mary Ellen's pledge would be paid by her estate."

"That's good then. And I guess it means no one killed her to keep her from giving away the money. Well, I need to go."

What a strange idea, Julie said to herself after Mike left. Why would he even think someone would kill Mary Ellen to keep her from giving money to the Ryland Historical Society?

Mrs. Detweiller came in with a phone message. Howard Townsend had called an emergency meeting with the trustees for that evening.

Chapter 6

Rich stopped by Julie's office after helping usher arriving guests away from the site.

"Are you going to be tied up all day here?" he asked.

"Howard just called a special board meeting for six tonight, so I have to be there. And, I guess I should call the contractor and let him know what happened, and that they can't start work until the police say they can. But other than that, it's hard to know what to focus on. I'll try to stop home before the meeting."

Julie was happy Dyer Construction's phone was answered by a real person, and even happier when that person put her through immediately to Luke Dyer. "I know all about it," he interrupted as Julie started to explain the situation. "Word travels fast. Talked to Barlow. Terrible shame about Mrs. Swanson. I liked her. Known the family for a long time," he continued. "My dad and her husband were friends—well, acquaintances, anyway. And she was pleasant enough to deal with about the land we're buying off her for the condos. Sad. How long do you think it'll be before we can get started?"

Julie marveled at how quickly people seemed to dismiss the hours-old tragedy and move on from it, but she concentrated on the practical. "It's up to the State Police," she replied. "I'll check with Chief Barlow and keep you informed."

"I guess that's okay," Dyer said, "but I've got the condos to get to, and I can't let that backhoe sit around down there for too long. If you don't get a go-ahead by the weekend, I may have to pull it for a few weeks. We only need a couple of days to dig your foundation. Just keep me informed, okay?"

Dalton Scott, the architect and board member who chaired the trustees' building committee, had been enthusiastic about letting the construction contract go to Luke Dyer, but Julie had never been totally convinced. She accepted Dalton's opinion that Luke did good work, efficiently and at a reasonable price. She just didn't warm to Luke. He always seemed in a rush and was rarely more than polite. But then she had never been responsible for overseeing a construction project before, and that was another reason she was glad Dalton was the chair of the committee. Dalton had given up his architectural practice near Boston and moved to Ryland six or seven years before Julie had. He was now the proprietor of the Black Crow Inn, and Worth Harding had wisely invited him to join the board of the Ryland Historical Society in anticipation of building the Swanson Center. She liked Dalton a lot, and she and Rich had quickly become friends with him and his girlfriend, Nickie Bennett. Dalton, in fact, had helped Julie solve the previous year's apparent thefts at the society, and she valued his intelligence and good humor at board meetings, and especially in dealing with Mary Ellen over the project. So if Dalton recommended Luke Dyer, that was enough for Julie, even though she still was uncomfortable with him.

Howard phoned to see if she had gotten his earlier message about the six o'clock meeting, but Julie knew he was mainly curious about any new events. Julie reported on her conversation with Luke and how he might be taking the backhoe for another job.

"Yes," the board chair said, "Luke and Frank Nilsson are doing that big condo development out at Birch Brook. You must have heard about it. Mary Ellen sold Frank the land, in fact. Sort of surprised me because I always thought Luke's family owned it, but it turned out Dan Swanson had bought it just before he died. Imagine Mary Ellen made a pile on that—it's a big plot, beautiful site just above the river. Anyway, Luke won't stiff us—old Ryland family, after all, very community-minded. If he said he could handle both projects, he will."

Looking out her window after the phone call ended, Julie saw Mike talking to a sheriff's deputy and went out to meet him.

"Any luck?" Julie asked when the deputy had headed off to the crime scene.

"With?"

"The shovel. It just has to be—"

"We don't know that, Julie, and even if it is, whoever killed Mrs. Swanson wouldn't be dumb enough to throw the murder weapon into the woods so close."

"Then you think it was the shovel?"

"A working hypothesis, Julie, but let's drop that."

"How about my alibi?"

"Haven't had time to check. Was that what you wanted?"

Julie didn't like Mike's abruptness but understood it. "No, I'll let you go now. Sorry to interrupt your work."

She decided she was exhausted—physically and, especially, emotionally. It was time to go home for a break—and a nice glass of wine—before the meeting.

Chapter 7

The members of the board of trustees of the Ryland Historical Society were assembled. Julie was relieved to see them—or most of them. There was Dalton, of course, and Loretta Cummings, also a favorite of hers. Julie couldn't fathom Loretta's perennial cheerfulness, but it was a canny, practical cheerfulness that Julie attributed to Loretta's role as principal of the local high school, popular with parents, teachers, and even students. Henry LaBelle, an attorney, was equally canny and practical, but in a more sardonic, world-weary way. Then there was Clif Holdsworth, nearly as old as Howard and as well established in the community. Clif was normally polite with Julie, if slightly condescending. She knew he'd never fully accept her since, unlike him, she wasn't a fourth-generation Rylander.

"This is a tragic day," Howard said to the small group after they had settled into their seats. "We've lost a very valuable trustee and friend," the chair continued. "I can't tell you much, but this is what I know at this point in time." After Howard briefly described what he knew, he paused to ask if there were questions.

"We're sure Mary Ellen was killed?" Dalton began. "No chance of a natural death?"

"So it seemed to me, Dalton," Townsend answered, "and my sense is that Chief Barlow considers it murder. Do you agree, Julie?" She did. "And perhaps you'd like to add to my report," he continued.

Julie said she couldn't improve on the chair's report except to add that the chief had asked her not to discuss with anyone else what she had seen.

"That's quite correct," Howard said, "and I was told the same. I trust I haven't said anything I shouldn't have, but I believe the trustees are entitled to some explanation. Are there any other questions?"

"Is there anything we can do as trustees to help you, Julie?" Henry asked.

"I can't think of anything now, Henry. We just have to wait till we hear from Mike Barlow, I guess."

"I know this sounds harsh, but it needs to be asked for practical reasons: What about the construction?" Dalton asked. "Luke Dyer was all set to start the excavation today as soon as the ceremony ended."

"I'm sure Barlow will keep the site protected for a bit," Henry said.

"He called for the Maine State Police and the Sheriff's Office to do that," Julie said. "So I think we'll have to wait."

"I understand," Dalton said, "and, again, I know this sounds awful, but I hate to lose good weather. We really need to get the site work done so we can get a shell up before winter."

"I'm sure Mary Ellen would agree with you about proceeding, Dalton," Howard said, "but we'll just have to see what the police tell us. Perhaps you could be in charge of that, Julie—checking with Barlow, and then letting Luke Dyer know?"

"Of course," Julie said.

"There won't be any other problems about the project, will there?" Clif asked. Julie and Howard exchanged glances, neither sure how to respond. "About the money," Clif said. "I *am* the treasurer, after all, so I suppose I'm the one who has to ask. Do we still get Mary Ellen's money for the building?"

"I wouldn't see why not," the chairman answered. "Julie?"

"I agree. Mary Ellen pledged $1 million, as you know, and then she added that $100,000 challenge last year so we could finish the fund-raising, and at least half of that is in, isn't it, Clif?"

Julie knew very well that $600,000 of the pledge was already in the society's construction fund. She also knew that Mary Ellen had told her she wanted to complete the pledge with a $500,000 gift over the summer. But Julie had learned to defer to Clif on financial matters. Doing that was easy, but what wasn't easy for Julie was participating in this conversation about the project and its funding so soon after Mary Ellen's death. She couldn't quite believe her ears.

"I believe we have at least half, yes," Clif replied. "But I'm thinking about the rest of it—is that pledge binding on the estate, Henry?"

Henry paused before answering. "Let me make my situation clear," he began. "I can speak as our solicitor, but most of you know that I'm also Mary Ellen's attorney. So I have a conflict of interest here. As your solicitor, I can advise you that Mary Ellen's written pledge clearly protects the society by indicating that in the event of her death, her estate will honor it. It's quite specific, and frankly, I made sure of that, to protect the society, but I also made it clear to Mary Ellen that she had every right to have another attorney draw it up for her or to ask me to withdraw as the society's solicitor in that instance. But she was content, and I feel confident of my ethical conduct."

"Of course, of course," Howard said. "No one here doubts your ethics, Henry."

"Thanks, but I just want to be sure everyone here understands how the pledge was written—and that the society will get the rest of the gift. I'm sure of that."

"Enough money in the estate to cover that?" Clif asked suspiciously.

"That's not for me to say under the circumstances," Henry answered, "but if I were the treasurer I would sleep soundly."

"I assumed Steven Swanson would get it all," Clif continued, undeterred by Henry's tact. "I'd say he needs it, to keep that wife of his. Not that Mary Ellen would be happy about *that*. But I suppose Steven can't stop the rest of it, can he?"

"No, but I wouldn't think that would be an issue."

"So there's a lot of money, enough for us and Steven, too?"

"Clif, you know I can't really say any more about that."

"Fine, fine. I'll take your word for it."

"Any other questions?" Howard asked, clearly eager to put an end to the exchange between Henry and Clif, questions of money and estates not being matters the chair considered fit for public airing.

Loretta said, "I'm wondering about tomorrow's concert. It's such an important community function, I hope we can go ahead with it."

Julie hadn't thought that far ahead—tomorrow, the Fourth of July, seemed years away. When she admitted that, Loretta was quick to support her. "Oh, of course you haven't; I don't know how you keep on top of everything so well. I just thought while we're together we should discuss it and make sure the board is in agreement. For my part, I'll repeat that I hope we have it."

"What would it cost if we canceled?" Clif asked.

"Cost?" Julie said.

"Isn't there a cancellation fee or something for the band?"

"Yes, I think there is, but I'm honestly not sure. I could go check the contract."

"I don't see any need to do that," Howard said. "I agree with Loretta—the concert's an important event for us, good community relations. I certainly think Mary Ellen would agree."

It amused Julie to hear Howard for the second time invoking Mary Ellen's postmortem support, but she was glad he did, and the other trustees seemed equally happy for the chair's decisiveness and greeted it with vigorous head nodding.

"So if there's no objection," Howard continued, "we'll proceed with the concert."

"How about if we dedicated the concert to Mary Ellen," Loretta asked. "Maybe Julie could announce that at the beginning? I think it would be well received."

"An excellent point," Howard said. "If there's no objection . . ."

"This isn't a formal meeting, Howard," Clif pointed out. "Unless our solicitor says we should go into formal session here."

"I don't think that's necessary, Clif," Henry said. "I'd be hard-pressed to imagine why we need a formal meeting and resolution to accomplish a simple act of humaneness like dedicating tomorrow's concert to Mary Ellen. It doesn't carry any legal obligations, for goodness' sake."

"Maybe Steven thinks it would," Clif said. "Maybe he'd hold us to naming the concert for her in the future. Perhaps we should ask him."

Clif's suggestion, though in keeping with his usual behavior at trustee meetings, seemed so bizarre to the others that for a few moments no one spoke. Julie finally did.

"Maybe I'll just *tell* Steven Swanson what we're going to do, so he'll be aware. It would be a courtesy to let him know, and maybe a nice idea at a difficult time."

"Excellent," Howard pronounced. "Tell him how much we valued his mother, want to honor her, know she would agree, et cetera. Very nice. Anything else?"

Clif moved forward in his chair, a sign to Howard that he had something further to ask—or say. But then he shifted back.

"Clif?" Howard asked. "You look like there's something else on your mind."

"Nothing the board needs to be concerned with."

"Fine, then. Now there is a matter we need to consider, but this isn't the right time to discuss it in detail. Let me just mention it briefly so you can all think about it, and then we can talk about it at a formal meeting later. Mary Ellen's death leaves us diminished in many ways. When we lost Worth Harding and Martha Preston as trustees, we agreed to spend some time seeking new members. I just want to remind you that we now have three vacancies on the board of trustees. Thank you all for assembling so quickly for this little session. I look forward to seeing you at the concert tomorrow."

As the rest of the trustees filed out, Dalton offered to help Julie return the chairs, but before she could decline she noticed Clif standing awkwardly by the door. She was sure she knew what he wanted. So she accepted Dalton's offer to handle the chairs and walked over to the treasurer. She debated making it easier for him by bringing up the topic herself but, impishly, decided to make him do it.

"The shovels," Clif said as soon as he and Julie were alone in her office. "Since we're not having the groundbreaking, I thought I'd collect the shovels and take them back to the store."

"You'd have to check with the police chief about that," she said. "I think he plans to keep the whole site taped off."

"Oh. Well, maybe you could get them tomorrow or whenever he says it's okay."

"I'll do that," Julie said.

When Clif left without another word, Julie wondered how he would take the news that only three of the four shovels he had provided were left at the construction site. She couldn't even contemplate what he would make of the likelihood—a likelihood that grew stronger as Julie thought about it—that the fourth of his shovels had been the murder weapon.

Julie went to her office to phone Steven Swanson at his mother's house. She dialed the familiar number. Hearing Mary Ellen's voice on the answering machine brought tears to her. The voice gave the phone number rather than the name and invited the leaving of a message. It was all too weird—hearing Mary Ellen's voice and then leaving the message for Steven about his mother. His *dead* mother.

After leaving word about the concert dedication, she recited both her home and office phone numbers and then hung up. She was glad to be able to communicate with Steven Swanson so indirectly. She didn't feel awkward about the message itself, but if he had answered she might have asked Steven why he had said his mother was meeting her.

Maybe Mary Ellen had gotten it into her head that she had a meeting scheduled with Julie. This was not beyond the realm of the possible—Mary Ellen had scheduled dozens and dozens of meetings with Julie, and many times had changed or canceled the appointments. The other explanation was that Steven had made up the story. Why, though? To cast suspicion on Julie? If so, did that mean *he* had something to hide? Having seen the bloody body, Julie doubted any child could have done such a thing to a parent. But then she reminded herself she really didn't know Steven Swanson.

Chapter 8

Rich set chicken out to cook on the new barbecue grill he had brought for Julie as a housewarming gift, half apologizing when he presented it to her because he admitted he'd be using it more than she would. They sat in the back garden sipping wine in the long light of midsummer.

"How are you doing?" Rich asked her. "I think you should talk about it. It's either that or a game of Scrabble."

Julie laughed. "I could be bought off," she said.

"Doubtful. Go ahead."

And so she talked, and Rich was right that discussing the murder helped calm her. The half bottle of sauvignon blanc she had drunk over dinner didn't hurt, either. "Maybe just one more glass," she responded when Rich offered to open another bottle after dinner. "The first question I have—" She stopped abruptly.

"Do you think I'm wrong here?" she asked Rich. "I mean, Mary Ellen was killed today, and Howard held a trustee meeting as if we had to deal with a leaking roof or a power outage or something. I was in such a daze through it all that I just went along, but it hit me afterwards how absolutely nuts the whole thing was." Rich laughed. "But now I'm just as bad, aren't I? Talking about the murder like some abstract thing, something I read about."

"I think it's good for you to talk about it, just as long as you don't think of playing detective again like you did last year with Worth's murder. You know how I feel about that. So what's your 'first question?' "

"Well, obviously, it's why was she killed? Who would want to kill Mary Ellen?"

"You, at least on a couple of days. You found her pretty hard to deal with on the project."

"Oh, stop," Julie said, pouring herself another glass of wine. "True. There were several times I wanted to strangle her. In fact, Dalton once said he was prepared to do it with his bare hands if she kept messing up the planning."

"You don't think Dalton did it?" Rich asked, giving her a wink.

She giggled. "No, of course not! But the fact is, she could be damned annoying. If we're going to figure out who killed her, we need to think about why."

"Julie *we* are *not* going to figure out who killed her. Get that out of your head!"

"We can still speculate, can't we? Now, if she could be so annoying to people who liked her, like Dalton and me, imagine what someone who didn't like her might feel like doing."

"Were there others you know who didn't like her?"

"I can't say I really knew her that well. We played our roles—she was the generous benefactor and trustee, and I was the grateful director of the Ryland Historical Society. But as to her friends . . ."

"Or enemies?"

"Right. Well, I just don't know. Apparently she has lots of money. I mean, I knew she could afford to give us a million, but she paid that out over time in small amounts."

"But not all of it?"

"No, but that's interesting, too. She told me she was going to pay the final half-million this summer. And Henry LaBelle—he was her attorney—said that that wouldn't be a problem now, and that her son would still inherit quite a bit. Henry was discreet, but that's how I read what he said. Oh, and speaking of her son, did he call here? I forgot to ask."

"And I forgot to tell you. Sorry. Yeah, he left a message while I was in the shower just before you got home. He sounded nice—a little tired, but pleasant. Thanked you for calling, said his mother would have been honored to have the concert dedicated to her.

He said he didn't know if he'd be there, but that he'd like to get together with you later to talk about the building project."

"I wonder what about. Maybe he's just like his mother and will want to make changes in everything."

"Well, if he's going to inherit a lot of money, maybe he's going to add to her gift or something."

"Hmm, that'd be nice. Anyway, Howard said the contractor, Luke Dyer, is the one building that big condo development just outside of town, and it was Mary Ellen who sold the land to him and some other guy—Nelson. No—Nilsson. Frank Nilsson. I think I've actually met him once or twice around town. Howard said Mary Ellen must have made a lot of money on the sale. Maybe that's where she was going to get the half-million."

"So what if it is? That doesn't have anything to do with you or the historical society. You don't need to get involved in this."

"I know I don't *have* to get involved, but I *am* involved—it happened at the historical society, and Mary Ellen played a big role there. And, it's the second murder since I've been here, and . . ."

"And you feel responsible?"

"Not responsible. But already involved—because of the society, because of Mary Ellen, because Steven told Mike that Mary Ellen was meeting me."

"But your alibi will check out."

"Of course! It's just that I'm in the middle of all this."

"I guess so. And you can't help yourself because you're a trained historian and you like to solve puzzles?"

"Maybe that, too."

Chapter 9

Every Fourth of July Julie could remember from her childhood had been humid and blisteringly hot. The Ohio River town where she grew up might as well have been deep in the heart of Dixie because no matter what the weather was like at the end of June, you could be sure early July would be scorching, and heat and muggy skies always accompanied the parade and fireworks in Julie's remembered Fourth of July celebrations.

Maine is so different, Julie thought as she woke briefly at five o'clock on the morning of the Fourth and reached to pull the blanket over her. She slipped back to sleep, pleased that the holiday would actually offer pleasant weather.

An hour later she sensed Rich's presence by the side of the bed. Why was he wearing shorts and a sweatshirt?

"Ready for a run?"

"Huh?"

"Oh, don't be so eloquent at this early hour. I just thought after last night's wine consumption you'd benefit from a good workout—say five miles before breakfast?"

In ten minutes she was dressed and ready to join Rich in the garden where he was stretching. As they had the day before, they cut through the garden to the small side street and headed toward the back of the historical society's campus. And just as it had been yesterday, the bright yellow backhoe with its Dyer Construction lettering was sitting patiently. But the rest of the scene was different: a blue State Police car sat on the curb by the street, and a uniformed trooper stood beside it, lazily surveying the site. When his head turned to Julie and Rich, he yelled at them: "Stay back from there! This is a crime scene!" Rich gestured in a half-wave, half-salute and cut to his right, along the side street. Julie followed. Rich led them through the residential section that ended in a small bluff, then he turned westward, and they entered the wooded area directly behind the construction site.

"Think it's okay?" Julie asked between breaths. "Mike was going to search here for the shovel."

"It's not taped off," Rich said.

As they jogged through the woods, Julie swerved her head from side to side, hoping to catch sight of a discarded red ribbon, but they reached the end of the wood and came onto the historical society's parking lot without her seeing anything more interesting than a few empty beer cans. They paralleled yesterday's route, down Main Street and toward the river. When they cut back up toward the Common Julie realized she was tired and signaled to Rich to slow down.

"Think I'm feeling the effects of last night," she said. "I'm going to just walk in from here, but go ahead and run if you like." He did, while Julie, falling farther behind, slowed to a brisk walk. It was unusual to see so much activity this early in the morning on the Common: two town trucks stopped by the gazebo, and a handful of workers stringing bunting. The concert and picnic began at eleven o'clock, but the Common would be well decorated before then because the parade started at ten. She stopped to survey the scene but found she was shivering. It must be 50 degrees, she thought, and decided to resume her running pace. At the top of the Common she met Rich coming back toward her.

"I went up to the golf course," he said. "You okay?"

"Fine—but cold. I can't believe it's the Fourth of July."

"Perfect running temperature."

"Feels more like March," Julie said. "But that's fine with me—I was dreading boiling in the sun at the concert."

"So what's the drill today?" Rich asked when they were back in the kitchen and he was starting the coffee.

"First I warm up with some of that coffee," Julie said. "Then breakfast, and a hot shower."

"And off to work?"

"I'll stop by the office, but we don't open till noon. Parade's at ten, concert and picnic at eleven. I'll have to check on the band and make sure everything's set at the gazebo, but after that I hope we can just spend some time together."

"That sounds good. Hope you didn't stay awake last night thinking about Mary Ellen or about solving her murder," Rich said as he poured orange juice and toasted bread for them.

"I slept fine—better than I expected—but talking to you about it last night was helpful. Thanks."

"My pleasure. I just hope you'll stop thinking about this thing."

"I can't help thinking about Mary Ellen, if that's what you mean, but I'll try to stop playing detective. It's just—well, what you said last night: I like to solve puzzles."

"But her death isn't your problem."

"Well, it's *sort* of my problem, but I'll try."

Stopping at her office before heading to check on preparations for the concert, Julie saw the blinking light that signaled a message. She punched PLAY and sat down to listen.

"I left a message at the other number, but I thought I better leave it here, too. This is Steven Swanson. I'm sure my mother would have been pleased that you're going to dedicate the concert to her. Under the circumstances, I'm not sure if I'll be there, but if I do go I'd like to get together to talk. If not, maybe I can see you later. My wife has to go back to New Hampshire, but I'll be around Ryland for the next few days to make arrangements . . . for my mother. Good-bye."

Rich was right that the tone of the message was quite pleasant, and the fact that he had left the message at both numbers made

Julie think he was a careful person. She wondered what he wanted to talk to her about, but he must have a hundred issues to deal with, and some of them might well concern the Ryland Historical Society.

The red light continued to blink, alerting Julie to another message.

"Hi, Julie. Henry LaBelle calling Tuesday evening. Didn't want to bother you at home, but I need to follow up with you on what came up at Howard's little meeting. Give me a ring, but if I don't hear from you before, I'll look for you at the concert. Take care now."

Because it was a holiday, she decided to call his house, apologizing for doing so when Henry answered.

"No problem," he replied. "Glad you called. Look, I wanted to say that I thought Howard's having that board meeting last night was a terrible idea. It just felt awful, sitting there talking about whether Mary Ellen's pledge would come through when the poor woman had just been killed a couple of hundred yards away."

"I felt that way, too, Henry. Howard didn't ask me . . ."

"Of course not. Howard never asks. I guess we have to be grateful that he's so dedicated, but it just seemed so cold. And then Clif probing about the estate . . . well, that got to me."

"You handled it very well."

"Thanks. I came close to saying what was really on my mind, but then I'm a lawyer after all!"

Julie joined Henry's laugh. "I guess we were all in shock," she said.

"That's putting a nice spin on it, so let's leave it at that. The other thing I wanted to say is that I felt bad that maybe you were left in doubt about the rest of Mary Ellen's gift."

"You said it would come, and she told me she planned to give all the rest this summer, so I'm not too worried."

"Well, you shouldn't be worried at all. I called because I wanted you to understand that the full half-million will be available in cash after the closing. It will take a little time to probate this, of course, but I think under the circumstances I can persuade the court to release the money to the society. I know Clif well enough to realize that unless the money is forthcoming, he'll want to put a hold on the project so the society doesn't have to borrow too much. I didn't want you to be worried about that. Now, like I said, it'll take time to distribute the whole estate, but I think we can make a good case that the $500,000 should come right away. The only problem would be Steven, and I wanted to mention that to you, too."

"He's happy with the dedication of the concert, by the way," Julie interrupted. "I haven't talked to him, but he left a couple of messages for me saying that, and that he wants to get together. I'm hoping to see him at the concert."

"Steven may just want to be sure everything's in place on the project. But when you talk to him, maybe not today because it's so soon after, I think it would be sensible to mention that Mary Ellen told you she was going to give the final installment of the gift this summer, and that you'd be grateful if he agreed so we can cut through the paperwork. He may even bring it up himself. You can tell him I'll be happy to discuss it with him. I'm going to try to see him today, too. But my point, Julie, is that I don't see any trouble about getting the half-million soon."

Before the call, Julie had been wondering if she was the only person in Ryland who wasn't thinking about Mary Ellen's money. Now she was glad to know that Henry shared her view of yesterday's trustee gathering—and also glad, she had to admit to herself, that the rest of the gift would soon be available.

Chapter 10

When Mike hit the siren of the Ryland police cruiser to signal the start of the parade, Julie and Rich were standing at the top of Main Street where it curved to go around the Common. Both sides of the street were lined with families.

After the police cruiser passed by, the heart of the parade came up the hill: decorated hay wagons and other floats from local businesses; marching Boy and Girl Scouts; clowns tossing candy that little kids ran into the street to retrieve; the high school marching band; a contingent of American Legion old-timers in military uniforms gasping to keep pace; and finally the flotilla of fire trucks, a pumper and ladder truck from Ryland and pumpers from a half-dozen outlying communities. Julie remembered from last year that the trucks, their sirens on and lights flashing, to the delight of the children, signaled the parade's end—or at least the end of its first phase, since all the vehicles and marching groups except the fire trucks took a turn around the Common and came back down Main.

"I better go check on the band," Julie said as the last of the fire trucks passed.

"I'll stake out a spot by the gazebo for us," Rich said.

At exactly eleven, the American Legion group that had shuffled through the parade marched with greater confidence onto the Common and presented the colors as the people rose from their blankets to sing "The Star-Spangled Banner." When they finished and the honor guard marched out, Julie walked to the microphone and gave her welcome, including the dedication of the concert to Mary Ellen Swanson. Then she found Rich on a blanket by the gazebo and sat down to enjoy the concert.

As the band launched into a medley of patriotic songs, Julie surveyed the scene. After only a year in Ryland, she was pleased at how many faces were familiar. All the trustees were there: Dalton with Nickie Bennett, Howard and his wife, Loretta and her husband, Henry and his family, Clif with several children and grandchildren, many of the volunteer guides, Tabby Preston from the library, and even Mrs. Detweiller with a man Julie supposed was Mr. Detweiller, though Julie had never met him.

When the band took a brief break, the crowd rose nearly as one and stretched by their blankets or walked lazily around to greet neighbors. At the edge of the crowd Julie was surprised to see Steven Swanson talking with a man she at first didn't recognize, and then recalled as Frank Nilsson, the developer Luke Dyer was working with on the Birch Brook condos. Julie considered walking over to talk with him since she still hadn't expressed her condolences in person, but before she could decide, the bandleader waved to her to indicate they were ready to resume. That was also Julie's signal to remount the gazebo and remind the crowd of the cookies and lemonade awaiting them afterwards.

As the band broke into the collection of Sousa marches to end the concert, Julie leaned over to Rich and told him she needed to head to the society to be sure everything was ready. She slipped away as unobtrusively as she could and sprinted across the street. Standing by the first table by himself, with a glass of lemonade in his hand, was Steven Swanson.

"Mr. Swanson," Julie said formally and reintroduced herself. "I'm so very sorry about your loss. It's a loss for all of us who knew your mother. Please accept my condolences."

"I remember you, Julie," Swanson said. "And please call me Steven. Thanks for your sympathy—and for dedicating the concert to Mom. I'm sure she would have been very pleased. Hope you got my messages, by the way."

"I did. Thanks. I hated to bother you at such a time."

"It's all so complicated and strange," he said. "I realized Mom was getting along and that eventually she'd, well, obviously we all will. But not like that. God, it's just so hard to think about." He rubbed his hand across his eyes and then stood silently again.

"I'm sure it is. I talked to your mother just the day before, and I know how much she was looking forward to the groundbreaking. It's so hard to accept she's gone. She was so . . ."

"Lively?" he suggested. "That's just what I was thinking. I mean, she was seventy-four, and I know that's not old today, but she acted more like she was in her fifties. Dad was almost ten years older, and so when he died it didn't seem so strange. That was almost five years ago. And then he went . . . well, he died at home." Not murdered, Julie thought, and had to stop herself from saying it aloud. "Not like Mom," he concluded. "Anyway, you said you saw Mom the day before, but I thought she was going to see you yesterday morning—at the tent, before the groundbreaking."

"Really?" she said, feigning surprise. "Your mother didn't say anything to me about getting together then, but of course she might have decided to come by. Was there something she wanted to talk to me about?"

"My mother *always* had something to talk to someone about, didn't she?" Steven smiled and laughed slightly. "But she did say, at breakfast, that she couldn't dawdle because she had to meet you at the tent. Maybe she hadn't told you. That would be typical of Mom, just assuming what was in her head was in yours."

Julie laughed and asked again if his mother had mentioned if she had something specific to meet about.

"About her contribution to the historical society," he said.

Julie waited for more, but Steven turned silent again. Julie felt time slipping away—the concert would be over in a few minutes, the crowds would descend on the historical society's grounds, and Julie would lose the chance to talk with Steven. "What about that?" she asked more abruptly than she knew she should.

"Well, she had some ideas, and I guess she wanted to talk to you about them. But you didn't see her?"

"No."

"Well, we'll have to work this out. I need to talk to her attorney. Anyway, I've got to go now. I'll be seeing you, I'm sure."

Steven turned and walked away before Julie could say more. Howard Townsend was coming toward her. "You remember Mrs. Townsend," the board chair said to her, and the two women shook hands. "Lovely concert, Dr. Williamson," Mrs. Townsend said. "A little chilly, though," she added, and Julie felt the need to apologize for the weather, in addition to asking Mrs. Townsend to call her Julie. "Well, it beats heat, doesn't it?" Mrs. Townsend said, and hugged herself through the winter parka she was wearing. "Hot tea might be better than lemonade, don't you think, Howard?" she said to her husband.

Not a word about Mary Ellen, Julie thought as the Townsends retreated in search of warmth. Unbelievable. You would assume, Julie thought, that at least Mrs. Townsend, seeing Julie for the first time since the murder, would say something—anything. She had known Mary Ellen for years, but she was as cold as her husband. Did anyone care? she wondered.

"Dr. Williamson," a man's voice said politely behind her. She turned to face Ben Marston, a longtime volunteer guide at Ryland Historical Society. Julie had been grateful to him last year when on one of his tours he had discovered a painting everyone thought had been stolen. She had seen him only a few times since. "I'm sorry to interrupt you," Ben continued, "but I just wanted to say how terribly sorry I am about Mrs. Swanson. She was such a wonderful lady. Ben Marston, by the way," he added.

"Of course, Ben. It's so good to see you again. And please, call me Julie. We've missed you over the winter!"

"And spring, too," he said. "We decided to stay down in South Carolina a little longer this year, but I'm back and ready to give tours."

"Thank you for that. And for your nice words about Mrs. Swanson."

"Oh, she could be a handful, couldn't she? Had a few run-ins with her myself, but still and all, she was certainly generous to the society."

"You can say that again!"

"It must have been terrible for you . . ."

"Howard Townsend is the one who found her, but, yes . . . well . . ." A vivid, complete image of the murder scene came so suddenly into Julie's mind that she couldn't finish her sentence.

Marston put his arm around her shoulder, lightly, and with a fatherly touch patted her once and then withdrew his arm. "I shouldn't keep you," he said. "You've got a lot to do here today. I didn't mean to upset you."

"Oh, no! I'm glad you brought it up. In fact, I've been so surprised at how little people say. It makes me think they just don't care."

"You're not a Mainer, Dr. Williamson. It's just how we are. My wife's the same. She moved here from New Jersey when we got married, and that was almost forty years ago, and she says she still can't believe how reserved we are—'frosty' is what she calls it. But I tell her it's not how we *are*, just how we *act*. We're afraid that if we showed our feelings, well, they'd get out of hand and sort of take over and run us. But people do care."

"Thank you, Ben. That makes me feel better."

"Better not show it, though," he said and winked, and they both laughed. "Well, I've got to go find my New Jersey bride now. Take care of yourself; see you around."

Marston's comments made Julie feel so good that she found herself eager to talk to others, but, as she was moving toward the table with the treats, she was stopped by a burly man wearing a red flannel shirt and rough corduroy jeans. "We need to talk," he said brusquely.

"Oh, Mr. Dyer," Julie said. "Did you enjoy the concert?"

"Sure. Look, I've got to get my crew to Birch Brook. You find out from the cops if we can do the excavation by the weekend?"

"I talked to Chief Barlow, but he says it's up to the State Police. I'll check again today."

"If we can't do it tomorrow, I've got to pull that backhoe out. You let me know."

Luke walked away. Julie wanted to find Mike but knew she should work the crowd first. She passed among the people lining up for lemonade and cookies and introduced herself and welcomed them to the Ryland Historical Society. It was the kind of work she enjoyed, putting a public face on the society, but she cut it short when out of the corner of her eye she saw Mike and Henry talking.

"Nice concert, Julie," the attorney said when she approached them.

"Thanks."

Mike nodded but didn't speak. Julie realized she had interrupted them, but Luke's threat to abandon the site excavation troubled her, and she asked again when the site would be available. Mike said he'd check with the State Police that afternoon and let her know. Julie sensed the two men would prefer her to leave them to their conversation, but she decided to wait them out. Finally Mike said to the attorney: "I'll get back to you about that, Henry. You home later today?"

Henry said he would be. He looked over to the refreshment table. "Better go keep a closer eye on my kids," he added. "They'll wipe out those cookies if I don't."

When Henry left, Mike said to Julie: "I see you were talking to Steven Swanson."

"I hadn't seen him to express my sympathy before," Julie said.

"He say any more about that meeting you and his mother were supposed to have?"

"He brought it up. He admitted that Mary Ellen sometimes didn't bother to tell people that she had an appointment with them. That's just the way she was."

"Did he tell you what his mother wanted to talk to you about?"

"Her 'contribution to the society.' I don't exactly know what that means—if she meant in general or something in particular."

"That's what he told me, too. Henry's the one who knows about all this, but I wasn't able to finish my talk with him just now."

"Sorry. I didn't mean to interrupt. Don't let me keep you if you want to talk to him now."

"Better to see him in private anyway."

As the police chief turned and walked off, Julie was tempted to yell out again that she was sorry about the interruption. She *was* sorry she had annoyed Mike, whom she both trusted and liked. At least he didn't seem to be making so much of Steven's statement that his mother had planned to meet Julie at the tent before the groundbreaking. But then he didn't say anything about checking her alibi.

"We've met, Dr. Williamson," the man who interrupted her thoughts said as he extended his hand. "Frank Nilsson," he added.

"Yes, of course, Mr. Nilsson. Good to see you again. Hope you enjoyed the concert."

"Always do. Glad you folks decided to dedicate it to Mary Ellen. God, what a tragedy! She was quite a woman."

"Yes, we'll miss her, and we're all so grateful to her."

"Very community-spirited. Generous. Especially to the historical society. I was just saying to her son this morning that we should try to wrap things up fast so you'll get Mary Ellen's gift as soon as possible. Don't know how Steven's going to handle it, but then I imagine his wife will have something to say about that."

Julie looked at him blankly.

"Mary Ellen's half-million, I mean. She really wanted to give it to you this summer, as soon as we closed. Fine with me. I'm eager to get it done, and I don't see any problems now."

"Sorry. I'm still a little confused."

"The land deal. Thought everyone knew. Mary Ellen was selling me the land Dan owned out at Birch Brook. For a condo development."

"I did hear something about that," Julie said.

"She wanted to give the rest of her contribution as soon as possible, so you could get the new building up. So she was going to use the proceeds from the sale to do that. But then, well, you know Mary Ellen, always changing her mind, back and forth and back again. But the deal should go through now, if Steven cooperates, don't know why he wouldn't, and the money will be available right away. Might be a good idea if you let Steven know how important this is to the society, how much his mother wanted it. A word from you might help," he said, and then excused himself.

The rest of the day was such a blur that Julie didn't have time to consider Frank Nilsson's comments. Although the tours for the day had been assigned to volunteers, Julie was busy right up to closing time at four o'clock, strolling around to chat with visitors, answering questions, and encouraging the volunteer guides. When the crowds dispersed she pitched in with the volunteers to clear the tables and restore order to the historical society's grounds.

After dinner with Rich they talked about the day's events, and Julie told him what Ben Marston had said. "It was so sweet of him, Rich. I was beginning to think no one really cared about Mary Ellen—for herself, I mean; they certainly care about her money. But I'm sure what Ben said is true—they're just keeping their emotions in control, just being New Englanders."

"Could be," Rich replied. "I wouldn't know."

"But *you're* a New Englander."

"You think so because I'm so cold, but remember I'm from Boston."

"That's what I meant."

"You haven't figured it out yet, have you? I wonder how long you'll have to live in Maine before you understand New England starts at the Portsmouth-Kittery Bridge? Anyway, I think you've had enough emotion—for a non–New Englander—to last you a few days. How about bed?"

"You'll check the locks, won't you?" were her last words as she climbed the stairs, and Rich wasn't certain she even heard his answer. But he was careful to see the house was safely locked—as safely, he said to himself as he made his way upward to the bedroom, as an old house can be.

Chapter 11

Tours! When Julie took the job of director of the Ryland Historical Society, she thought she knew how demanding the work of a small museum would be. For the most part she had been right, but she hadn't known just how much of her time would be taken up by giving guided tours. To be fair to herself, that part of the job had grown in the past year, following the resignation of the assistant director, whose main responsibility had been to organize and conduct tours of the buildings for school groups, senior citizens on bus tours, and the other visitors who showed up to see the period rooms, costumes, displays of artifacts, and crafts shed. She had decided not to hire a new assistant immediately, waiting instead to complete the planning for the new Swanson Center so she could evaluate what kind of work the expanded facilities would require. In the meantime, she had taken upon herself most of the work, and she had to admit that she was beginning to tire of the relentless pace of tour-giving.

Especially today. With the emotions of Mary Ellen's violent death so raw, the hard work of organizing and carrying off yesterday's successful Fourth of July concert behind her, and the need to follow up on so many details, this was a day Julie would have preferred to spend quietly at work in her office. She was still amazed at how much paperwork the job required: correspondence, budgets, bill paying, volunteer scheduling. But she had a tour organized for ten o'clock and another at one, and if the enthusiasm of the summer crowds following yesterday's concert was meaningful, she would probably have to slip in at least one more to accommodate people staying on in Ryland for the long holiday.

A little before ten she took a call from Mike. "The state guys say they've done what they can to the site," he told her. "They'll remove the tapes this morning, so you can tell Luke Dyer it's okay to start digging."

"That's great! Did they find . . . ?"

"The missing shovel? No. And I've been through the woods with a fine-tooth comb, but then I never expected it to be there anyway. It'll turn up."

"So you think it was the murder weapon?"

"Did I say I thought so?"

"No, but you're looking for it."

"Let's just say I'd be happy to find the shovel. Meantime, you can tell Luke to get started."

"Thanks, Mike. And I'm not pushing or anything, but did you have a chance to check at the inn?"

"At the inn? Oh, your alibi. Sorry. Yeah, Brian Handley says you were there giving him a hard time. So I'm satisfied."

"I'm not a suspect?"

"Never said you were, but you know I have to tie up all the loose ends."

Of course she knew he hadn't suspected her, but Julie was relieved to hear that her alibi was confirmed. And relieved to hear him joke about her giving Brian Handley a hard time. She called Luke Dyer's office and left a message. Mrs. Detweiller came to the office door to remind Julie that it was time for her tour. She headed to Holder House, the building farthest down Main Street and the one containing the gift shop, as well as the historical displays in the large room where she did the welcome and orientation.

Over the past year, Julie had developed labels to describe tour groups. "Polyester" meant senior citizens, the women in pantsuits and the men in golf shirts, almost always on bus tours of northern New England and looking for a rest stop where the bathrooms were clean and the tour content inoffensive. "Backward caps" were the teenagers herded by middle- and high-school teachers, happy to be out of class but rarely interested in the history of Ryland. "Cuties" referred to the elementary students who, though as much prisoners as the teenagers, showed genuine excitement in how people lived in older times. "Buffs" were the self-styled experts on local history, those who couldn't resist correcting or amplifying Julie's comments. The "Triple A" crowd consisted of travelers—retirees during the fall, families in the summer—who were passing through Ryland or spending a weekend there and had read the description of the museum in the Maine edition of the AAA guide. They were the most mixed: gangling teenagers clearly embarrassed to be with their parents or grandparents, little children entranced by history, bored husbands accompanying their wives with a passionate interest in painted furniture, slow-moving seniors with time on their hands, the occasional buff who used to live in town before retiring to Florida and eager to point out that the old pair of ice skates on display looked exactly like the ones he had lost at the pond thirty years ago. Because of the challenge they represented—the need they created for Julie to range widely and find interesting things to say to people with such varied interests, or lack of interests—she actually liked them best.

Today's ten o'clock group was definitely "Triple A" material: several grandmothers, two middle-aged couples, one young couple with an unruly four-year-old, and two boys with their caps reversed whose age Julie placed at thirteen or fourteen. Tickets for the tours were sold in the society's gift shop at the front of Holder House, an example of shameless commerce Julie strongly supported since it meant the gathering group had time to examine possible purchases in the shop while they waited for the tour to begin. She assembled them there and led them to the orientation room, where glass displays and wall hangings illustrated periods of Ryland's past. After welcoming them, Julie followed her custom of asking where they were from—all, in this case, were what Julie, adopting local custom, had already come to label "from away"—not from Maine. She gave an overview of the society, previewed what they would see in each building, and did an abbreviated town history. She liked to conclude the orientation by asking if anyone had a special interest so she could make a point of satisfying it as they proceeded through the buildings. One of the grandmothers, not unexpectedly, mentioned quilts, and one of the middle-aged men, also not unexpectedly, said "guns." Julie knew exactly how she would address their interests. But when one of the adolescents asked to see the murder site, Julie was momentarily flustered.

"You know," he prodded, "where the lady was killed. Can we see that?" The boy was quickly muffled by his embarrassed father, but Julie realized she was going to have to have a line of patter to address the issue.

"We did have a very unfortunate accident here on Tuesday," she said, "but the area is being excavated this morning to begin the construction of our new building. I'll point it out when we go over to the crafts shed."

"Accident?" she heard the boy say to his peer. "They chopped her up, that's what I heard." Julie was happy to see the father step forward again and place a strong arm around the two boys and speak sternly to them.

Despite the inauspicious beginning, the tour was a success, something Julie gauged by the way she held people's attention during the tour and by the number and quality of questions both during and afterwards. In this case, what was planned as a fifty-minute tour extended to over an hour and a quarter, and at the end the group was generous in its thanks. The two adolescents had been held in check by the father; the middle-aged man's interest in guns and the grandmother's in quilts had been satisfied; and the four-year-old had actually stopped running and babbling when Julie had shown him the collection of antique toys—his surprise that there were no Tonkas amused her.

Back in her office, Julie learned from Mrs. Detweiller that Luke Dyer had stopped by to say the work was under way and that Henry had called. She phoned Henry at once.

"I figured I should get ahold of you since you know I was talking to Mike Barlow at the picnic yesterday," the attorney said.

"Sorry I interrupted."

"No problem. Mike and I talked last night. Some interesting things have developed. You have time to talk now?"

"Sure."

"Maybe you've heard some of this already, but I had a long talk with Steven Swanson yesterday and got some things clarified. So let me try to sort this out. Two parts: one, the half-million of Mary Ellen's pledge; two, Mary Ellen's will. On the first, like I said a couple of times, there's no question about the funds being available. The question is getting the probate judge to release them prior to settlement of the estate. It's not a slam-dunk, but with Steven's cooperation I'm pretty sure we can persuade the court that Mary Ellen intended to give the historical society the money right away, and that the society relied on that expectation in breaking ground, et cetera, et cetera. The point is the money will be there, and I don't want you to be concerned about that."

"I'm not. I know you can't talk about her estate, but I trust you that there's enough."

"I'm not talking about the estate now—just the cash. That's what the society needs, and it'll be there. See, Mary Ellen agreed to sell the land out at Birch Brook to Frank Nilsson and Luke Dyer—mostly Frank, but Luke's got a piece of it, in addition to doing the construction. Mary Ellen signed the P and S in early June."

"P and S?"

"Sorry. Purchase and sale agreement. Anyway, she was never really comfortable about it."

"About selling the land, or about the price?"

"Both. Dan, Mary Ellen's husband, bought that land from Paul Dyer, Luke's dad, just a couple of years before he died."

"Who—Swanson or Dyer?" Julie interrupted.

"Both, as a matter of fact. Paul Dyer died about a year after he sold, and Dan Swanson died maybe a year after that. Anyway, Dan really loved that piece of land—great views, river access. I think Mary Ellen got to feeling guilty about selling it, or maybe she figured she could do better, but she asked me to put a clause in the P and S that gave her some time to think it over. Frank was naturally eager to get it settled since he and Luke had to line up financing for the construction. I think he recognized that if he didn't allow the back-out clause Mary Ellen wouldn't sign, and he'd have to delay. He probably figured she'd just let the date ride and the deal would go through. Which is just what happened. And so the money will be available very shortly. We'll go to closing next Monday."

"But who sells? Steven, I guess."

"No, I'm the executor of the estate, and I have full power to close the deal since the back-out date passed."

"When was that?" Julie asked.

"Today, as a matter of fact. The clause gave Mary Ellen thirty calendar days to withdraw without penalty, and that's July fifth."

Julie was idly doodling on the yellow pad in front of her as the attorney talked, but when she looked down she saw she had written "July 5th" and underlined it. "Hold on a second, Henry. You mean that if Mary Ellen hadn't been killed on Tuesday she could have backed out of the land deal?"

"Had until today to do so, like I said."

Julie couldn't believe that Henry wouldn't see the significance of this fact, but she decided to let him continue, assuming that his part-two item would cover it. "Okay. Go ahead—you said the second thing was the will."

"Right. I need to ask you a question about that. Frankly, I've been sort of putting this off because I wasn't sure about what my duty was—I have a dual duty on this, to the estate and to the historical society. But I talked to Steven about it, and he agrees I need to ask you just to be sure." Henry hesitated, and Julie heard him take and swallow a sip of something. "Julie," he resumed, "did Mary Ellen mention anything to you about changing her will to benefit the Ryland Historical Society?"

"I never talked to her about her will, just about the gift, and the fact that she wanted me to know she would pay it off this summer."

"Which makes it sound to me like she intended to go through with the land sale," Henry said.

"You mean she didn't have enough money otherwise?"

Henry laughed heartily. "Don't mean that at all. Mary Ellen had huge assets, but like most good Yankees she kept them in stocks and bonds and land. Not exactly liquid, especially with the market the way it is. She could have raised the half-million in cash easily, but she wasn't the type to sell into a bad market if she could hold on to get more gains. The thing is that the land deal provided cash so she wouldn't have to liquidate anything. That definitely appealed to Mary Ellen. But like I was saying, if she told you she was going to have the money shortly, then I'm sure she wasn't going to opt out of the sale. And that's what Steven thinks, too. But back to the will. The reason I asked you if Mary Ellen had talked to you about it is that Steven told me she had mentioned it to him."

"When?" Julie asked.

"Interesting timing. Over breakfast Tuesday morning, apparently for the first time. She told him she was thinking of changing her will to leave one-third of the estate to the historical society."

"Wow!" was all Julie could say.

"If you knew the size of the estate, Julie, you'd be saying double wow. But let me be clear about this—she didn't change the will, and didn't even mention the idea to me, so I don't think the society can pursue this."

"What do you mean by that, Henry?"

"Just that if she had told you she was going to make the change and then didn't, because she didn't have time, the society might have grounds for contesting the will."

"We wouldn't do *that!*"

"Well, not with me as solicitor! That's when I'd have a plain and visible conflict. But I had to advise Steven of the possibility, and that's why I needed to know if Mary Ellen had talked to you."

"Maybe that's what Steven thought she was going to do on Tuesday morning. He told Mike Barlow his mother was planning to see me before the groundbreaking, but she hadn't mentioned that to me. But Steven might have thought so, especially if Mary Ellen just brought up the idea of a change over breakfast that morning."

"I suppose. Anyway, it's obvious Steven would not have been happy if she had."

"No, I guess not," Julie said slowly, pondering the implications. "But did she tell Steven why she was going to do that? Could she have decided to back out of the land deal and then change her will so we got the money that way?"

"That's certainly a reasonable inference," LaBelle said.

"But because she was killed she couldn't back out?" Julie practically yelled over the phone.

"Well, obviously. But I doubt we can conclude she knew she was going to die and therefore couldn't exercise the cancellation option."

"No, but she had Tuesday and Wednesday and today to cancel. Or so she thought."

"Sure. I see what you mean. But I don't think that's the issue here. The idea of changing the will had more to do with Steven."

"How so?"

There was a long pause, and Julie heard the sip and swallow again at Henry's end. Finally he continued. "Look, this is where my legal duty gets blurry, but I talked to Steven about this, and he said I should go ahead and tell you. He wants everything out front."

"Okay, but I'll keep it to myself if you want me to."

"That would be best. Here's the thing: Mary Ellen told Steven and Elizabeth—or Steven says she did; I can only repeat what he told me—that she was going to change her will to leave one-third of the estate to the historical society if at the time of her death Steven had no heir."

"No heir?" Julie repeated. "What century is this?"

"Means what it says: Steven and Elizabeth have no children, and Mary Ellen never missed a chance to criticize them for that. God, Julie, I've got a pack of kids, and on lots of days I'd be happy to loan or sell a couple to Mary Ellen or anyone else who was interested, but obviously Mary Ellen wanted grandchildren."

"And Steven?"

"Who knows? Didn't want to, couldn't, whatever. And, from what I know of Elizabeth, she's not exactly maternal. But look, this isn't for me to say, and it's not the point. The point is that to act properly here, I needed to know that Mary Ellen didn't tell you about her idea."

"No, absolutely not."

"Good; please keep that to yourself then. Now I can file her will as written and not have any concern that it didn't express her intentions. And Steven will cooperate on getting the money for the building before the estate's settled. He's going to inherit quite a bit, and that prospect tends to put people in a good mood, even though they have to wait a lot longer than they think for everything to settle."

"How long, Mike?"

"Oh, in Maine you can usually get it done in a year. Actually, getting the half-million right away will ease things since that will resolve one of the principal claims. So Steven and Elizabeth will probably be happy to wait, considering what they can expect."

"I know I shouldn't ask, but curiosity is one of the traits required by my job description."

"And discretion is one of mine, Julie," Henry said firmly before she could get to the obvious question. "I've told you more than enough already. When the will's probated, it'll be a matter of public record. For now, just be assured it's a big, big estate. It's fair to say Steven and Elizabeth are going to be rich."

Chapter 12

When the conversation with Henry ended, Julie sat quietly at her desk, intrigued, trying to puzzle out everything they'd just talked about. As a child, Julie could spend hours on a rainy day fitting together the pieces of a jigsaw puzzle. She loved the features in the Saturday newspaper that invited her to find the monkey hidden in the picture, or presented stories that required her to create the correct ending. In school, she couldn't wait for assignments that took her to the library to track down obscure facts. So becoming a historian wasn't exactly a surprising move. Not that it prepared her to solve a murder so much as it honed her sense of putting together pieces to explain a picture. In fact, Julie was strongly visual and tended to convert abstract and verbal problems to pictures. Making doodles and notes on a pad was her preferred method of working through a problem. So she took out a yellow pad from her desk and began to jot her thoughts on it.

The first thought she had was how incredibly naive Henry seemed, especially for a lawyer. That was because Julie saw two huge matters that Henry didn't—or, if he did, he at least wasn't letting on that he did. One was that because Mary Ellen died on the third of July, she could not exercise her right to cancel the land sale to Nilsson and Dyer. Lucky them! The second was that if Mary Ellen hadn't died on the third of July, Steven and Elizabeth might have lost one-third of a very large estate. So lucky them, too! But not so lucky Mary Ellen.

On her pad Julie wrote "Steven" and put a large dollar sign beside it. She did the same with "Elizabeth." Then she bracketed the two names and put a question mark beside the bracket. Motive seemed obvious enough for Mary Ellen's son and his wife, singly or together. Of course Steven merely had to wait to get his, but

Henry's news meant Steven risked losing a third of it. Still, Julie found it hard to imagine a son killing his mother, especially so brutally, and in her conversation with Steven after the concert she had gotten the distinct impression that he was truly mourning Mary Ellen's death. Although she didn't know him well, Julie couldn't avoid the conclusion that Steven was a nice guy but somewhat weak, and that wasn't exactly surprising since his mother was so domineering.

As was Elizabeth, too, Julie thought, though she knew her even less than she knew Steven. Julie had met her once or twice and sensed she was stronger than her husband, more self-possessed. About Julie's own age? Maybe a few years older. Slim and good-looking. Her career seemed to be flourishing. Henry said she was not maternal. But how well did he really know her? And, well, Julie wouldn't have exactly rejected that description of herself. But Henry and Howard Townsend had both seemed vaguely negative about Elizabeth, and both had made it clear that Mary Ellen was not a fan of her daughter-in-law, either. Certainly Mrs. Detweiller had more than hinted at the same thing. But that was hardly unique in the history of family relations. So what did Julie know about Elizabeth? Not nearly enough to make any further notes beside her name.

Julie looked at her watch and saw it was noon. She should probably have lunch before her tour at one, but instead she returned to her yellow pad. She flipped to a new page and made another large dollar sign and beside it wrote "Nilsson" and "Dyer" and gave them a bracket and question mark, too. Since Mary Ellen had till today to back out of the land sale, getting rid of her before would have some kind of financial value to the two developers. How much? Julie had no idea of the magnitude of the project, but everyone who talked about it implied it was a big deal. Who was at risk if it didn't go through? Apparently both Nilsson and Dyer, but Howard had said Dyer had a small part of it, except of course for the construction. Okay, both men would gain something by making sure Mary Ellen didn't cancel the sale. That was motive.

Julie wrote "Find out," underlined it, and then wrote "value of Birch Brook," and "Nilsson share" and "Dyer share." She really didn't know much about either man, let alone about the condo project they were involved in. She had talked to Nilsson yesterday and remembered meeting him sometime in the past year. Dyer she had been dealing with over the excavation but didn't know much beyond her impression that he was abrupt and not particularly warm. Oh, there also was the matter of the land itself—Howard had said Dyer's father had sold it to Dan Swanson. Julie noted that next to Dyer's name.

The yogurt she had brought for lunch was in her drawer, and though she still didn't feel hungry she knew she should have something now since the tour would occupy her until after two. As she was taking small spoonfuls of it, a thought struck: I can find out more about Frank Nilsson because I have his résumé! She jumped up and went to Mrs. Detweiller's office and found the file labeled TRUSTEES—PROSPECTIVE. Howard had asked her to start a file last summer, when Worth's death left the Ryland Historical Society's board short of members. Howard had asked other trustees to suggest names of potential new members, and someone had suggested Nilsson. It was Mary Ellen! She had proposed his name and had asked him for a résumé. And there it was in the file. Thank heavens Mrs. Detweiller is organized, Julie said to herself when she returned to her desk with the résumé.

It wasn't long. He had probably put together the one-page summary in response to Mary Ellen's request because it emphasized his community involvement: former president of the Ryland Chamber of Commerce, chair of Rotary's Christmas appeal for children, board member of Community Hospital, founding member of Western Maine Scandinavian Heritage Society. Under

"Education" he had listed a high school in southern Maine and Bowdoin College, though without a degree or dates of attendance. Occupation was simple: developer. Married with two children.

There was nothing revealing in the résumé about the man, nothing that would help her figure out if he were capable of murder to prevent Mary Ellen from canceling the land sale. But then, Julie thought as she laughed out loud, you wouldn't exactly expect someone to include a line on his résumé like "capable of murder under the right circumstances." She would have to find another way to learn more about Nilsson.

"They're here, Dr. Williamson." Julie jumped when Mrs. Detweiller issued her statement from the door separating their offices. "The bus tour. I saw them pull up when I was coming from lunch. You have a one o'clock tour, you know," the secretary said sternly.

❧

"Polyester," Julie said to herself as she hustled across the lawn toward Holder House. The bus tour was a quilting group from New Jersey, making a summer tour across northern New England in search of inspiration for their hobby. Three-quarters were women, all but one in hooded sweats, and the rest were bored husbands. Julie sometimes worried that her easy labeling of visitors led her to do canned presentations, pulling out the sentences and ordering them in a certain way more in response to the label she had placed on the participants than to their reality. On the other hand, she often found that stereotypes were useful, offering shortcuts that made her comments appropriate if not precisely fresh. About quilts she was a rank amateur, but given their importance to visitors to history museums she had diligently read quilting books and talked with volunteer guides who themselves quilted. As a result, she could sling the lingo—Grandmother's Flower Basket, Hands of God, Weeping Willows—that impressed tour groups a lot more than such modest knowledge warranted.

But it usually worked, and today it did, too. The seniors were delighted with her, asked soft-pitch questions that she returned with force and grace, expressed appropriate wonder at the collections, and—Julie was especially pleased to see—headed back to the gift shop before boarding their bus.

Returning to her office in Swanson House, Julie cut behind the crafts shed to see how the digging was progressing. The yellow backhoe that had sat quietly the last several days was anything but quiet now. Like some prehistoric animal, the machine extended its long proboscis straight out, then brought it down with a thud and scooped and dropped a load of soil beside the lengthening gash that would eventually be filled with concrete to form the foundation. Julie was pleasantly surprised to see that one of the long trenches was complete and that the machine now was attacking the second. When that was done, the two would be connected with short trenches at both ends to form the rectangular outline of the Swanson Center. Amazing! Julie said to herself. Only yesterday she feared the whole project would be delayed, and now the excavation was almost half done. She stood there for a few minutes to observe the work.

"Coming right along," a voice said from behind. Julie turned to see Luke Dyer, incongruously enough carrying a leather briefcase.

"It sure is," Julie agreed. "I'm surprised how fast you work."

"Not me," he said with what Julie thought was a first-time occurrence: a friendly laugh. "That's Benny, my best backhoe man. I put him on this because I know you were getting antsy. Don't see no problem now getting the foundation dug by tomorrow."

"That's terrific. Thank you so much. And I suppose now you'll be able to get your other project started."

"Should start on Monday, soon as we close."

"I understand it's quite a big project—lots of condos?"

"Biggest development around here."

"And a beautiful site, I hear."

"Gorgeous. Ever seen it?"

"No. It's called Birch Brook, right?"

"Yeah, Birch Brook runs right smack through it, down to the river. You should come out and take a look. Maybe you'd be interested in a condo."

"Thanks, but I'm living in Worth Harding's house here now. He gave it to the historical society."

"Oh, right. I heard that. Well, it's a nice place, and the condos will have every convenience and great views. Maybe you know someone who'd be interested. Anyway, come out and have a look sometime."

"I'll do that." Looking at his briefcase, she wondered if he had come to see her about business. "Are we all in order here, Mr. Dyer, about the project? Any more paperwork?"

"You can call me Luke. All set for now. We'll send an invoice." He noticed Julie's gaze still on the leather briefcase. "Oh, you thought I was looking for you, I see. No, I was just over to your library. Pretty crowded place. I can see why you need this new building."

"It's going to really help us a lot. The library can expand and all the papers will get the special care they need," she said, forgoing the nearly automatic line she could deliver about humidity control, spacious surroundings for researchers, proper lighting, and all the benefits the new Swanson Center would offer. She was too intrigued by Dyer's visiting the society's library. "Hope you found what you wanted," she said.

"Still looking. But I'll be back. Good to see you," he added and walked toward the backhoe, the briefcase swinging at his side an odd accessory to his flannel shirt and work pants.

Chapter 13

Of course I'm indulging in stereotypes, Julie admitted to herself when she was back in her office. But stereotypes work for visitors. So why shouldn't I find Luke Dyer's visit to the Ryland Historical Society library out of character?

Well, it was easy enough to find out what he had been doing. All Julie had to do was walk up the stairs and talk to Tabitha Preston, the earnest woman who served, for free, as the society's librarian and archivist. And that's what she would have done, immediately, had not Mrs. Detweiller come to the door to tell her Steven Swanson was on the phone.

"I know Mom's attorney talked to you," Swanson said abruptly after Julie picked up the call. "I told him it was okay to, because I needed to be sure she hadn't talked to you about giving more money to the historical society in her will. It's not that I was against that, but it seems to me the money she's already given for the building in Dad's name is quite a bit."

"It's a wonderful gift! We're all so grateful to your mother for her generosity, and we certainly weren't expecting more."

"I didn't think so, but it was important for me to know that. I think Mom was just playing one of her games that morning—trying to get Elizabeth riled up as usual. And as usual, it worked. But anyway, the reason I called is to thank you for telling Henry that she hadn't talked to you about changing her will, and to say that I agree with him about the fact that you folks were expecting the rest of Mom's gift. I'll do whatever I can to help out there. It's only fair, because Mom would have given you the money next week when she sold the land. Henry asked me to sign a statement about that so he can present it to the probate judge and see if the money can be released. Like I say, that's fair, and I'll be happy to do it."

"Thanks so much, Steven. That's very generous of you, especially now at such a difficult time."

"That was the other reason I called," Swanson said. "About Mom's funeral. Her . . . her body has been released now, so the funeral can go ahead. Next Monday, at the church. I hope you can come, and tell the others if you will—the trustees, Mom's friends at the society, whoever. I don't really know who to invite, but if you'll just pass the word I'd be grateful."

"That's no problem at all, and I'm sure everyone here will want to attend. What time will it be?"

"Eleven. On Monday."

After the call ended and Julie was sitting at her desk, she smiled at the high-context nature of Steven's description: "at the church." Last year, Julie would have asked "What church?" Now she knew better. "The church" meant the United Church of Christ—or as locals referred to it by its old name, the First Congregational—the Gothic white church that stood on Main Street just below the Town Common. Among the trustees, volunteers, and staff of the Ryland Historical Society—indeed, among almost every Ryland resident Julie had met—it was simply called "the church." The town had five, but the Methodist, Christian Alliance, United Baptist, and Catholic churches were merely places where members went for worship. "The church" was the site for community musical and dance performances, senior citizen discussion groups, Girl and Boy Scout meetings, candidate forums for local elections, and weekly church suppers. It was also the favored site for funerals and memorial services for prominent citizens, whether or not they were communicants. So Julie was hardly surprised that Mary Ellen's funeral would be held there.

"The trustees know," Mrs. Detweiller said when Julie asked her about the best way to inform them of the funeral. "I think everyone here does, too," she added. "Monday at eleven at the church. Should we close the society?"

Instead of responding to her secretary's question, Julie asked one of her own: "How does everyone know? I just found out from Mary Ellen's son."

"Well, I can't really say, but my cousin told me this morning, and I suppose she heard it from someone at the church. This is a small town, Dr. Williamson."

"Yes, I think we should close Monday morning, Mrs. Detweiller. I'll write up a notice we can distribute tomorrow. I'm going up to see Tabby now, before she leaves."

"Too late," the secretary said. "She leaves at 4:30, you know." Julie indeed knew Tabby's schedule, and knew also that Mrs. Detweiller also left at 4:30 and was obviously signaling that Julie's impertinent questions about informing the board of the funeral were delaying that ritualistic event, too. "I lost track of the time," she said. "Sorry to hold you up, Mrs. Detweiller. I'll work on the notice now and have it ready for you in the morning. Have a nice evening."

Writing the notice consumed a mere few minutes, and then she was back to the notes she had made during and after the conversation with Henry. She reviewed them, and added to the list under "Find out" the curious fact that Luke Dyer had been looking at materials in the society's library. *Why?* she wrote. Had he suddenly become interested in town history? Howard Townsend had said Dyer was part of an old Ryland family. Maybe he was doing some genealogical research. That was the favorite activity of users of the society's archives, and there was no reason to think Luke would be an exception. In any event, a talk with Tabby would provide the answer, but that was for tomorrow.

Looking at her notes, Julie found herself focusing on Nilsson and the brief conversation she had had with him at the concert. He was eager to have Julie talk to Steven Swanson about Mary Ellen's plan to contribute the remainder of her gift this summer.

Nilsson seemed to be seeking her help to get Swanson to move quickly on the land sale, but Henry had made it clear that he, as executor of the estate, had the authority to complete the deal. Maybe Nilsson was just looking out for the Ryland Historical Society's interests, which in this matter did overlap with his own. No harm in that, Julie decided.

But Nilsson continued to interest her, and she began to formulate a way to learn more about him. She would phone Nilsson to set up a meeting. Hadn't Howard encouraged everyone to work on the expansion of the board of trustees? Hadn't Mary Ellen requested Nilsson's résumé with exactly that goal in mind? So why shouldn't Julie now talk to the man to inquire about his possible interest in joining the board? She would be carrying out her job as director, and if she learned anything about Nilsson that cast light on his dealings with Mary Ellen—including, of course, whether he might have murdered her—well, that would be an additional benefit. She located Nilsson's phone number on his résumé and called him.

"Good to hear from you," he assured her confidently. "Thanks for talking to Steven Swanson. He's happy about everything going ahead, and Henry LaBelle is handling the closing on Monday. So everyone wins: Our project goes forward, and, most important, you'll get the rest of Mary Ellen's gift right away."

Julie considered pointing out that not quite *everyone* won, since the day of the closing of the land sale would also be the day of Mary Ellen's funeral. Instead, she told him that she hadn't really encouraged Steven, who seemed quite content for things to proceed.

"Well, it's settled anyway, and I'm glad the society is going to benefit as Mary Ellen wanted. That new building is going to be quite an addition for you, isn't it?"

"As a matter of fact, Mr. Nilsson—"

"Frank, please," he interrupted. "And I hope I can call you Julie. Even though we haven't talked much, I feel very positive about you and what you're doing over there. Mary Ellen did, too."

"Well, Frank, thank you for saying that. As a matter of fact, I was wondering if we might get together when it's convenient for you to talk a little about Ryland Historical Society. Mary Ellen had mentioned to me that she thought you would make an excellent trustee, and we're always looking for strong new members."

"Sure, I'm very interested. Mary Ellen did talk to me about this last fall sometime. I think I gave her a résumé."

"That's right. I have it right here, and I'd like to talk to you about what we're doing and whether you'd be able to get involved. Of course it's up to the board to elect new members, but part of my job is to help gather information for them, so if you'd be interested, I'd enjoy sitting down and talking a bit."

"Absolutely," he said. "Things are going to get pretty busy with the closing and starting the project, so maybe we could get together before that. How would tomorrow be? Say, breakfast at The Greek?"

"Let me just check." Julie knew her schedule tomorrow included more tours, but the first wasn't until ten. Still, she didn't want to appear too eager. "Yes, that's fine," she said, after what she hoped he would interpret as a dutiful review of her schedule for the day. "What time would be good for you?"

"Seven-thirty?"

"Great, I'll meet you at the diner then. I'm looking forward to it."

"Me too," he said before ending the call.

What Julie called the diner and what Frank Nilsson called The Greek was the same small restaurant just north of town on the way toward Ryland Skiway. The first time she had had breakfast there—with Mike last year during the investigation of the historical society's missing artifacts—Julie had learned the evolution of the diner. In Mike's early days in town it had been run by a Greek family, and the name was still current with old-timers. Julie honestly couldn't recall its official current name—even though a sign out front said Bert's Family Restaurant and the coffee was served in mugs that said The Food Place—but if you made a date to meet at The Greek or the diner, the result was the same. She wondered why Nilsson, whose résumé indicated he wasn't a Ryland native, used the old-timers' name. Something to ask him, she decided, an icebreaker to open the conversation. After that, she would focus on what really interested her: Did Nilsson play any part in Mary Ellen's death? Of course I could just cut to the chase and ask him, she said to herself with a laugh as she closed her office, locked the door to Swanson House, and headed home to Rich.

CHAPTER 14

At dinner, Rich had told Julie that the person who had waited on him at Holdsworth's hardware store was certain: The latest frost ever in Ryland had occurred in early June, and that had been nearly fifty years ago. So the odds of a frost two days after the Fourth of July were simply overwhelming. But around two o'clock on the morning of Friday the sixth, when Julie got up to rummage for a third blanket, she would have been willing to bet against even those odds. Now, at six, when Rich came back up to the bedroom dressed in a sweatshirt and long pants, he reported that the thermometer outside the kitchen window read 40 degrees.

"And you're going to run?" she asked.

"I do it in Orono when it's freezing, so this isn't a problem, though I did decide on pants instead of shorts. Sure you won't join me?"

Julie said that she was taking a break from their early-morning runs.

"Then I'm off," Rich said. "Have a good breakfast."

"I don't have to meet Nilsson till seven-thirty. You'll be back by then."

"Not today. I'm taking a long one."

"Not slowed down by me."

Instead of responding, Rich asked what she wanted for dinner and said he'd take care of shopping. Knowing she wasn't going to go back to sleep, Julie luxuriated in just lounging under the covers. But when she began to preview the breakfast meeting with Frank Nilsson, she decided to give up and take her shower and dress.

Julie found a table for two by the window at the back of the diner, a spot where she and Frank could talk without being overheard. But not without being seen. Between 6:30 and 8:30 every weekday, the diner served as Ryland's principal business center. Carpenters and plumbers and builders constituted the first wave. They were gone by 7:30, replaced by shop owners and professionals, who in turn left by 8:30, their tables taken over by retirees and tourists. The time Frank selected, 7:30, seemed to Julie to match his status. As she saw the clock behind the counter registering exactly that moment, Frank entered the diner, spotted her at the table in the back, and waved.

It took him some minutes to reach her, however, as he stopped to exchange words with other diners—here a painter, marked by the swatches on his cap, on his way to the door; there another arrivee known to Julie as an insurance agent; finally, with the manager of Ryland Savings Bank, who was seated at the large table that combined the early and late crowds. Frank's progress reminded Julie of watching the U.S. president make his way up the aisle of the House of Representatives for his State of the Union speech and pausing to glad-hand all along the way. At the large table, the bank manager turned to look in Julie's direction as he spoke with Frank.

When Frank at last reached her, he said, "Would have been on time if I hadn't stopped to talk, but it's good to keep in touch with town opinion. Hope I didn't keep you," he added as he took the seat opposite her.

Frank Nilsson was a trim, well-built man. From the date of his high school graduation on his résumé, Julie made him out to be forty-five, though his athletic body could have belonged to someone ten years younger. He had dark black hair cut short and carefully brushed. Everything in his appearance was careful, she noted as they ordered breakfast—his crisply pressed tan slacks, long-sleeved cotton dress shirt with cuffs just visible under his green cashmere sweater, well polished tasseled loafers. The only thing surprising was his gray mustache. Facial hair seemed out of place in someone so carefully done up, and the color was surprising given his black hair.

"Of course everyone's talking about it," Frank said, interrupting Julie's contemplation of him. "Two murders in such a short time, and both such prominent Rylanders. Natural curiosity. But then you've heard all this, I'm sure."

"I don't know so many people the way you do," Julie answered.

"Well, it takes a while to get comfortable in a little town like ours. Just one, soft-boiled," Frank sharply corrected the waitress, who had come to the table to say the special was two eggs and toast. "And whole wheat, no butter," he added.

Julie felt embarrassed that she had ordered two eggs over easy with sausage and home fries, but she had eaten at the diner enough to know that if you didn't take advantage of their high-cholesterol offerings, you might as well stay home and indulge in yogurt with berries.

"Have to watch it," Frank said to her when the waitress left them. "Every ounce counts at my age," he added as he tapped himself just above his belt—an area that looked to Julie as flat as the table they were sitting at. Instead of flattering him by saying so, Julie decided to use her icebreaker: "Funny that this place has so many different names, isn't it? When you suggested meeting here you called it The Greek, the way old-line Ryland people do."

Frank laughed. "Afraid I'm not 'old-line Ryland,' but my wife is, and that's what she always calls it. What *is* it called now, by the way?" he added, looking around the room for an answer.

"Actually, I have no idea," Julie replied, "and no one else seems to know, either. So your wife is from Ryland?"

"Born and bred, quite a few generations. Patty's maiden name was Oakes—you've probably seen the name in the archives."

"I think so. Where did you grow up?"

"York; that's in southern Maine if you're not familiar. So I'm not from away, but I'm certainly not old Ryland. Patty and I met in Portland. I was at Bowdoin, and she was at Westbrook. Bowdoin was all-men then, and Westbrook was all-women, so there were lots of mixers. We got married the year she graduated and lived in Wells for a couple of years, and then in Portland when I was doing projects down there. But she always wanted to return to Ryland, and frankly, I was happy to. It's such a great little town and a perfect place to raise kids. Both of ours graduated from Ryland Academy. Great school. They're in college now, but they like to come home anytime they can."

"Do you live right in town?"

"Not anymore. After the kids graduated from the academy, we rented our place in town and built a new one out at the skiway."

"I lived up there last year," Julie said. "In a condo. It was really nice."

"Ski?"

"Afraid not, but everyone tells me it's a great ski mountain. I'm going to take lessons next year and get started."

"I can recommend a good instructor when you're ready. I helped develop the ski area and the condos and keep my hand in things there."

Their breakfasts arrived, and they both began to eat, letting the conversation slide as they did so. After he had crushed his boiled egg into small bits, Frank continued. "So tell me about your plans for Ryland Historical Society, Julie. I hear you're really doing a great job there, by the way. Mary Ellen was so happy. What a shame!"

"Mary Ellen was a great supporter of the society, as you know," Julie said in the automatic way she had learned to talk about major benefactors. Mary Ellen's intrusive and inconsistent behavior during the planning of the new center wasn't pertinent now. Julie elaborated on Mary Ellen's gift, the many ways the society would benefit from the building, her hopes for increased programming and activities to increase attendance. "So it's a pretty exciting time for us, and as you know, we couldn't do any of it without the trustees. Mary Ellen certainly thought you'd have a lot to contribute."

"Mary Ellen was always looking for more money for her causes," Frank replied.

"Oh, I don't mean money. Or not *just* money, though the trustees do support the society financially." Or *some* do, she said to herself, thinking particularly of Clif Holdsworth's notable lack of generosity. "There's so much to do in setting directions, developing policy, overseeing operations. It's a very good board, but as you probably know, we lost two other trustees last year, and now, of course, Mary Ellen."

"Worth Harding and Martha Preston, right," he said. "Tell me, do you really think I could offer something on the board, really help out? I don't do things halfway, and I don't enjoy just sitting on a board for the sake of it. If I came on, I'd get pretty involved."

"That's exactly what we need, but as I said before, the decision to elect new members is up to the board."

"Understood. But you're the director, and I'd come on only if *you* thought I could be helpful."

"From everything I know, you'd be very helpful. With the new project, for example, Dalton Scott's been such a big help because he's an architect. And we need additional skills like that. You've done so many real estate projects that you could really add to the board's expertise."

"I do know a little about developments, but I don't have any experience with historical societies. Before I moved here I was mostly in retirement communities, in York County and down the coast. Ryland Skiway was my first project up here."

"Birch Brook sounds pretty big," Julie prompted him.

Frank finished his egg, which he had been slowly nibbling at as Julie tucked into her decidedly larger breakfast, which she was a little embarrassed to see was now finished. The waitress refilled their coffee cups, and Julie sipped from hers as she waited for Frank to talk about his new project.

"It's big for Ryland," he said after their plates were removed. "Thirty-five townhouses to start with, but that's only phase one. We've got over four hundred acres there—lots of room for more units if things go as we hope. Terrible shame Mary Ellen won't be around to see the project."

"She was happy about it?"

"Happy to sell the land," Frank said. "Who wouldn't be? She didn't have any plans for it. She struck a hard bargain, but it was fair."

"I'm sure it was, but I sort of got the impression that Mary Ellen wasn't entirely sure about it." Julie didn't consider a small lie too high a price to pay for drawing out Frank on the subject of the land sale, but she was surprised by the vehemence of his reaction.

"Where'd you get that idea?" he asked bluntly, and locked directly on her eyes with a look Julie thought almost menacing.

"Oh, nothing in particular. I just seem to have the impression that she was maybe having second thoughts." Okay, Julie said to herself, if you get started with a small lie you have to be ready to keep going.

"She never said anything to me about *second thoughts,*" Frank said firmly. "We're paying a high price. She couldn't have done better. And she was pretty eager to get that cash so she could finish off her gift to you."

Julie realized she couldn't continue down the path she had put herself on without risking a confrontation. Moreover, she had absolutely no reason to believe that Mary Ellen was planning to cancel the deal, and if pressed by Frank—who seemed perfectly capable of pressing her—she'd end up with an unsustainable story. "You're right about that; she was eager to complete the gift. So I'm sure whatever else I might have heard was just gossip."

"Not a good thing to listen to, especially in a small town where people think they know a lot more than they usually do about other people's business."

Julie nodded.

"Well, I shouldn't keep you any longer, and I should also get out to Birch Brook and see if Luke's getting ready to start next week. I enjoyed our talk, Julie, and if your board is interested, you can tell them I'd consider it an honor to become involved with the Ryland Historical Society. This is mine," he added as he scooped up the check. "Good to talk," he said again as he rose to leave. "It's been very interesting."

Indeed, Julie said to herself as she rose to follow Frank toward the door.

Chapter 15

Julie's first call when she got to her office was to Howard Townsend for what she recognized as a cover-your-rear tactic. Knowing how things happened in Ryland, she could imagine Frank and Howard running into each other and comparing notes, and she didn't want the board chair to think she was working behind his back. As it turned out, the conversation was easy. Howard said he was glad she was following up on the matter and happy to know Frank had expressed interest. "He's a go-getter," the board chair said. "Got his hands into everything. And on the money."

The second call was to Rich. She was so excited about the breakfast with Nilsson that she had to talk about it, even though she knew Rich didn't share her interest.

She recounted the breakfast conversation, emphasizing Frank's sudden and strong denial that Mary Ellen had been having second thoughts about the land sale.

"I didn't know she was," Rich said.

"It was a bluff—to see Frank's reaction. And, boy, did he react! I think that's pretty suspicious."

"Julie, I thought you said you weren't going to get into this."

"I'm not *getting into* anything. Just, well, trying to figure out if . . ."

"If Frank Nilsson had a reason to kill Mary Ellen Swanson to keep her from backing out. I know what you're up to, but you need to let the police handle it."

"Mrs. Detweiller's here. I can hear her stomping around out there. I have to go. We'll talk more about this over dinner, okay?"

After sorting out some work with Mrs. Detweiller, Julie was surprised to see it was already 9:30, and she had no time before the tour at ten to talk to Tabby Preston in the library or to jot down notes on her meeting with Frank. Distracted, Julie felt unable to throw herself into the tour with the energy she customarily deployed. Although the dozen summer visitors of varying degrees of uninterest in Ryland's history seemed not to notice, Julie felt she had let them, and herself, down. As they trooped off to the gift shop after the tour, she was content to return to Swanson House to talk with Tabby.

Not that a talk with Tabby would raise anyone's spirits. She had been volunteering as society librarian and archivist for several years before Julie arrived as director. A Ryland native, Tabby had left town for college and then for a career as a school librarian in a small town on the coast. Julie assumed that she had retired early because she was still in her early sixties. What motivated Tabby's return to Ryland wasn't a topic Julie could ever have broached with the woman, but she guessed it had to do with Tabby's sister, Martha. Martha, too, had gone off to college and then worked at a fairly high executive level in some retail business in southern New England. The two spinsters had returned together to live in the stately Federal house they had grown up in below the Common and just behind First Church of Christ, Congregational. Martha, too, had become involved with Ryland Historical Society, first as the volunteer manager of the gift shop, a job befitting her retail career, and then as a trustee. Julie had heard the stories of Tabby's anger that it was Martha rather than she to whom the board had extended the latter honor. But the sisters remained close in the antagonistic, cat-and-dog way typical of small-town family relationships.

And then their lives took a terrible turn just when Julie entered the scene. Julie could never bring herself to inquire about Martha's state, and Tabby never mentioned her sister. Tabby continued to work diligently in the library, and she and Julie maintained a perfectly correct and productive professional relationship. As Worth Harding had often remarked, Tabby was a great gift to the Ryland Historical Society because she did for free the work that would have cost a good deal if she were a paid staff member. Both for that reason and because she genuinely sympathized with Tabby, Julie always went out of her way to be pleasant to her.

And so she would be this morning, Julie resolved, as she climbed the stairs behind Mrs. Detweiller's office to the second-floor library and archives room. Tabby was sitting at her desk in the center of the large room, squinting through bifocals at a pile of papers and at first too absorbed to notice Julie's entrance. No one else was in the room. Julie cleared her throat and said good morning.

"Sorry, Dr. Williamson," Tabby said as she looked up to locate the source of the sound. "I didn't hear you come in."

"You're working too hard, Tabby," Julie said, deciding to skip her usual correction of the librarian's formal manner of address. For a year Julie had called her Tabby and tried to get her to reciprocate with Julie, but she had made no progress on that front and resigned herself to it.

"These papers just seem to grow. Every time I finish cataloging a batch, another one springs up. And I've put some more letters in that folder for you."

"The Tabor papers?"

"Yes. I found some more of Dr. Tabor's letters from the thirties. What a letter writer he was! No one bothers today."

The papers had been donated, a year before Julie's arrival at the historical society, by descendants of Dr. Samuel Tabor, who had practiced in Ryland for the first four decades of the twentieth century. Julie learned about them last winter when Tabby had, just like today in her usual timid way, apologized for spending so much time cataloging them. To show Tabby that she endorsed the work, Julie had spent some time then looking through the papers, fascinated by their random nature: copies of prescriptions; papers torn from medical journals and fiercely annotated by the doctor, as if he were engaged in a heated argument with the author; long personal letters describing life in rural Maine to family members in Tabor's native Connecticut; notes and minutes from various selectmen's committees on which he served. Surveying them briefly, Julie saw then that the Tabor papers were a rich lode from which she could mine articles—perhaps even a book—that would enhance her professional standing while, of course, contributing to public knowledge of Ryland's history.

It had seemed like a great idea, and Julie still remembered her excitement when she first described it to Rich. Practical as he was, he had suggested she should focus on one aspect, an idea she eventually came around to, settling on a period—the Depression. "I'll call it 'Down and Out in Ryland, Maine,' " she joked to Rich, but instead of finding it funny he warmed to the notion. "Everyone knows about the Depression in the big cities," he had said. "But what was it like in a small town in rural Maine? That's a terrific idea." So Julie began sorting the papers and asking Tabby to do the same as she cataloged, setting aside those from the 1930s.

"Some new ones?" Julie prompted Tabby.

"Yes. More letters to his brother in Connecticut during the Depression and some others. They're over there, in the green folder."

"I'll take them downstairs if that's okay. I can't seem to get big stretches of time to work on them, but if they're on my desk I can read them in between."

Since she had first learned about the Tabor papers and settled on her project of researching his description of the Depression in

Ryland, she had rarely found uninterrupted time to work on them. Mundane tasks that represented the reality of the job of director consumed her time. Those and the monthly meetings of the board—to say nothing of the endless meetings with Mary Ellen, with or without the rest of the building committee. She really did enjoy her job, but it certainly didn't leave time to be a scholar, too.

"I was wondering if we'll be closing on Monday for the funeral," Tabby said as Julie was distracted by her own thoughts about the papers.

"Yes, of course. Mrs. Detweiller will be bringing around a notice about that soon. We won't open until two, but you don't need to come in that afternoon. Things should quiet down next week after the long holiday, so why don't we just agree that the library will remain closed all day Monday."

"I'll be in after the funeral, Dr. Williamson. I just wanted to be sure I could get to it. Mary Ellen will certainly be missed. What a terrible tragedy."

Tabby's anguished look as she said that made Julie aware of how awful the woman's life had become because of her sister. It was better, she felt, to respond with only a nod and then to change the topic. "I'm really eager to read these," she said as she held the green folder in front of her. "Thanks for collecting them for me." Tabby acknowledged the thanks with a slight nod.

"And one more thing," Julie continued, trying to sound casual. "Luke Dyer told me yesterday he was working here, and I was sort of surprised because I didn't realize he had an interest in local history. But then I really don't know him except in connection with the construction project. He's from an old Ryland family, I understand, and I just wanted to check to make sure he's finding what he needs here." Julie knew the story was lame, but it apparently didn't bother Tabby.

Chapter 16

Julie felt strongly that it was neither professional nor appropriate to monitor the work of researchers. What people asked to see they should be given, assuming of course that the donors had not restricted access. No, it wasn't up to the archivist to say who could see what. The society's role was to conserve and provide access, making sure that any documents or books were treated properly and never removed. Copies could be made if the material was not fragile and lent itself to duplication without damage. So if Luke Dyer wanted to consult papers from the Swanson family, and if Tabby supervised their use to prevent damage (ink pens for note taking, for example, were anathema; Tabby kept a drawer of pencils to offer to those who came unprepared), then it wasn't a fit topic of interest for Julie.

Except that she was surprised and fascinated, two emotions she tried to disguise when she responded to Tabby's announcement that Dyer had been looking at papers from the Swanson family. "Oh, I see," was the best Julie could do.

"He only looked at the ones I've cataloged, of course," Tabby said. "I've got a couple more boxes of Swanson materials in the vault that I just haven't gotten to, what with the doctor's papers to deal with first. But there's plenty of cataloged material from the Swansons, and Luke isn't an experienced researcher, so I think there's quite enough to keep him busy till I get to the rest."

"Mary Ellen never mentioned that she was donating papers," Julie said, "but then she was generous in so many ways."

"That's certainly true, Dr. Williamson."

"Are these her husband's?"

"Not so far. The ones I've been through are mostly Dan's grandfather's. I started with the oldest ones. Most of the letters and bills are from the eighties and nineties."

"Then they must be Mary Ellen's husband's," Julie observed.

"No, not *1980s*—1880s and '90s."

"Oh, of course; sorry. So those were Mr. Swanson's grandfather's."

"Herbert. My father always called him Herbie. Of course I didn't know him—he died when I was quite young—but he and my father were friends. Old Dan was also a friend of Father's. He sort of spanned the two generations."

"*Old* Dan?"

"Herbert's son, Dan's father. He was Daniel O. Swanson I, and Mary Ellen's husband was Daniel O. II, but everyone called them Old Dan and Dan."

"You know so much about all this, Tabby. Did you know Mary Ellen when she was growing up?"

"Mary Ellen? No, she's from Connecticut or somewhere. Not a Ryland girl."

"Right, I think she told me that. She met her husband during the war, didn't she?"

"In Boston. Dan was in the navy, and I guess Mary Ellen was one of those girls who . . . well, you know."

Wow, Julie said to herself. One of *those* girls. But to Tabby she said: "And they got married and moved to Ryland?"

"Not right away. Dan came back after the war, and Mary Ellen came to visit, but Old Dan didn't take to her, and so it was a long engagement. I don't think they got married until just a few years before Old Dan died. Let's see, that would have been in the mid-fifties—*1950s*, of course."

Julie nodded. "So Mary Ellen's not from Ryland, but she lived here for about fifty years." Julie was silently doing some calculating. "Then Steven must have been born quite a bit later. He's in his mid-thirties, I think."

"Probably. A lot of people thought Dan and Mary Ellen would never have children, but then Steven finally came along."

Came along pretty late in the marriage, Julie thought. And Mary Ellen was disappointed that Steven and Elizabeth didn't have children yet? Interesting.

"Would it help, Dr. Williamson, if I just jotted down the dates for you? I had to make a little chronology for myself when I started on the papers."

"That would be great! I really need to understand the family since we're going to be having a second Swanson building soon. Have you seen the excavation work?"

"Haven't been back there. Not something I wanted to look at."

"Yes, of course. Sorry." Julie silently rebuked herself for the insensitivity of forcing poor Tabby Preston to contemplate the scene of Ryland's second bloody murder in a year. "Well, I should take a look at those Swanson papers, too, one of these days. You say Luke Dyer was looking at the ones you cataloged—that would be the grandfather's, Herbert's?"

"Yes. But you know, I don't keep track of exactly what researchers look at, just the general description, the box number and so forth."

"Right. Just curious." There, she had given herself away. Or maybe a little more than *just* curious. "I'll ask Luke myself when I see him. He's probably looking into some town history. Well, if you do have time to jot down those dates for the Swanson family, that would be really helpful. Sorry to keep you from your work on the doctor's papers."

"I'll do that today. And I'll see you Monday, I'm sure."

"Good. And thanks, Tabby."

Tabby returned her attention to the papers piled on her desk, and Julie quietly exited from the library and returned to her office downstairs.

It was late in the afternoon when Mrs. Detweiller entered Julie's office and handed her a piece of paper: "For you. From Tabby. She said you asked for it."

Julie had immersed herself in paperwork all afternoon and had lost track of time. She looked at her watch and saw that it was 4:30. Probably Tabby had dropped off the note on her way out. Mrs. Detweiller would be following immediately. And that meant Julie had the office to herself and could put away the business of the Ryland Historical Society that had occupied her for the last few hours and privately return to her notes. From the top drawer of her desk she pulled the manila folder in which she had placed the notes she had made after talking to Henry. She was ready to add to the folder some items she wanted to note from her conversation with Frank Nilsson this morning. But first she looked at Tabby's chronology:

Herbert Oakes Swanson, 1863–1932
Daniel Oakes Swanson I ("Old Dan"), 1888–1953
Daniel Oakes Swanson II ("Dan"), 1918–1997
Married Mary Ellen Leighton, 1951
Steven Leighton Swanson, 1965
Married Elizabeth Myerson, 1995

Julie noted again the odd parallel between the last two generations she had picked up from Tabby's comments. Old Dan had apparently not approved of his son's choice of wife, just as Mary Ellen didn't like Steven's, yet both marriages had occurred, Mary Ellen's and Dan's two years before the father's death. And then there was the fact that Mary Ellen and Dan had not had a child until well into their marriage, fourteen years, and Mary Ellen had been unhappy that Steven and Elizabeth, who hadn't been married that long, hadn't yet produced an heir. So unhappy, in fact, that she was considering changing her will. To put pressure on the couple? Or to punish them?

None of this seemed especially relevant to the question that Julie's talk with Tabby had presented: Why was Luke Dyer reading the Swanson papers? Julie placed Tabby's chronology in the manila folder and took out her yellow pad to record what she hoped she hadn't forgotten from the conversation with Frank over breakfast. She had certainly succeeded in finding out more about him and a little about the condo development he was involved in, and then there was his sharp response to her suggestion that Mary Ellen had considered canceling the deal. Julie noted that very interesting fact on her pad and then started to jot down what she had learned about Nilsson's earlier work in developing retirement communities and his involvement with Ryland Skiway. The bare facts of his life she had already on his résumé. Early life and high school in southern Maine, attendance at Bowdoin (but still no sense of whether he had graduated—she was willing to bet he hadn't), meeting and marrying Patty. What was her name? Oh yes, Oakes—Nilsson had said she was from an old Ryland family and that Julie no doubt had seen the name.

Indeed she had! And just a few moments ago. She pulled Tabby's chronology from the folder, and there it was: Herbert, Daniel I, and Daniel II all carried the middle name of Oakes. Were Frank's wife and the Swansons related? And if so, did it matter?

The growling of her stomach reminded Julie that in the midst of tours, phone calls, talking with Tabby, and paperwork, she had completely forgotten about lunch. She was starved. It wasn't yet 5:30, but she felt the need to head home to see what Rich had decided on for dinner. The green folder with the Tabor letters sat unopened on her desk. Julie glanced at it and felt guilty. But less guilty than hungry.

Chapter 17

Julie was especially glad Rich was such a good cook. She felt weak in the knees when she spied the ceramic dish holding two gorgeous swordfish steaks in a marinade. Next to it was a low bowl holding asparagus covered with lemon juice and black pepper. Big slices of fresh tomatoes and red onions were in a third dish, also marinating. A bowl of strawberries completed the picture. Julie really wondered if she would faint.

"I can grill the fish outside," Rich said from behind her, "but I think we should eat inside. It's still pretty chilly." He embraced her before she could turn and moved his hands gently from her waist up to her neck. "But unless you're in a hurry . . ."

"I'm starved!" she said as she wiggled around to face him. "I skipped lunch."

"Oh," he said with obvious disappointment. "I guess I could start the fire."

"How long will that take?"

"Half an hour."

"Just enough time," she said and took his arm to lead him out of the kitchen. "I should take a shower anyway," she added. "Go light the fire. I'll be upstairs."

The dining room seemed too formal to Julie, or maybe she was put off by its location right across the hall from the living room where she had found Worth's body. Whatever the reason, she and Rich had avoided it so far. The kitchen was cozy, and without consulting Rich she set up for dinner there after she came downstairs. Rich was placing the asparagus in the oven to broil. "A little heat in here isn't such a bad idea," Rich said as he stepped back from the oven. "How about some wine while the fish grills?"

"God, you're good," Julie said as she chewed the first bite of the swordfish.

"I aim to please," Rich said, raising his eyebrows in a mock-wolfish way. "Everything tastes great when you're hungry. You really shouldn't work so hard."

"I just got so involved in things that I forgot. This really is terrific," she said as she took another forkful of the swordfish and then complemented it with the asparagus.

"What *things?* Historical society business, I hope, rather than—just to pick a topic at random—solving a murder?"

"What makes you think they're not connected?"

"What's not connected?"

"The Ryland Historical Society and Mary Ellen's murder?"

"Julie, you promised!"

"Well, they're obviously connected," she continued. "Mary Ellen was killed *at* the historical society, and I'm beginning to think that it had to do with her gift. So . . ."

"There's no way I'm going to stop this, is there?" Rich asked. "Short of agreeing to do a jigsaw puzzle or something equally exciting."

"We could do that."

"Think I'll pass on that. Go ahead, tell all."

"Well, if you really want to know," she began. "Of course I told you a little about breakfast with Frank Nilsson, but here's what's really fascinating . . ."

❧

"I'm afraid it's just strawberries for dessert," Rich said nearly an hour later when both Julie's report and the main meal were done.

"They'll be perfect. Local?"

"I got them at that farm stand on River Road. Tomatoes, too, though they're obviously *not* local. Or not local to Ryland, Maine. Soon though."

"They were fine. Everything was, Rich. I don't deserve you!"

"True, but what's a girl to do?"

"Well, I could end my report with a list of conclusions," she offered.

"Why does that not surprise me? Okay, your conclusions, please."

"My conclusions, in no particular order: One, Frank Nilsson is definitely a suspect. He was really ticked off that Mary Ellen might have hinted to me that she had second thoughts about the land deal."

"Your reasoning?" Rich interrupted.

"Simple. If Mary Ellen backed out, Nilsson stood to lose a lot of money, or at least not *make* a lot. So he had a motive to kill her before the deadline, July fifth. And he's unhappy that someone—me—might know she was thinking about doing that. Ready for number two?" Rich nodded. "Luke Dyer is interested in the Swanson family, at least enough to start reading their papers in our archives, which isn't the sort of work he normally does. He's in the condo development with Nilsson, so he was also at risk if Mary Ellen canceled. Remember that it was Luke's father, Paul, who sold the land to Dan Swanson in the first place. Maybe he's trying to find out why, because if he owned the land instead of having to buy it back from the Swansons, he'd probably make a lot more money. And Frank Nilsson's wife may be related to the Swansons—her maiden name is Oakes, and that was the favorite middle name for Swanson men."

"Pretty weak," Rich said.

"Just because I don't have it figured out yet. But there's something funny about Luke Dyer's interest in the Swanson papers."

"So you suspect Dyer, too?"

"For now, because like Nilsson he had a motive to kill Mary Ellen before the fifth of July. Remember when we were talking about this right after the murder? You said—or maybe I did—that the question isn't just *why* Mary Ellen was killed, but why at the excavation site. Maybe that's wrong; maybe the real question isn't *where* she was killed but *when*. If the timing's important, then Nilsson and Dyer had a motive—each of them individually, and even together—a shared reason to do her in before July fifth."

"I see what you mean about timing, Julie, but don't you also have to add Steven Swanson to the list for the same reason?"

"Absolutely! Both Steven and Elizabeth had a reason to kill her before she changed her will, which she told them Tuesday morning she was going to do. So they're definitely on the list."

"Beyond the list, do you have any more conclusions?" Rich asked as he stood to begin clearing the table.

"Two more, actually. First, that I don't know nearly enough about town history, and especially the families and how they're connected. I've got to find out more about local genealogy. And second, I don't know enough about the condo development."

"I can't help you with the first one, but I might be able to help with the second," Rich said. "Coffee?"

"Think I'll skip—it'll keep me awake. How can you help about the condo development?"

"Indirectly. Are you still off tomorrow?"

Julie said she was. It was Saturday, after all, and she had arranged with volunteers to handle tours.

"Good," Rich continued, "because I've been looking into routes for a hike. It's supposed to warm up tomorrow but still be cool enough for hiking."

"I could do with a hike."

"Me, too. So I found a trail that runs from the river back to the west over Sutter's Mountain. Let me get the map." Rich went to the shelf along the window, rummaged through some items, and extracted a large topographical map. "See, it's right here." He pointed to the trail marked on the map he spread on the kitchen table. "It follows the ridge to just above a brook, and then you drop down beside the brook and come back in at the river, about three miles west. We could just walk back on the road by the river, or we could leave a car out there and drive back. Anyway, it looks pretty good to me—nice views, and probably four to five hours if we use two cars."

"That looks great, but what does this have to do with the condo development?"

"The brook you follow down to the river at the west end is Birch Brook. Isn't that where the development's going to be?"

"You're a genius! Let's do it."

"Early start," he said. "Why don't you head to bed and I'll clean up down here?"

Although their custom was to rotate cooking and cleaning up, and Rich's delicious meal certainly kept his end of the bargain, Julie didn't require additional encouragement.

Happy and content, she even felt brave enough to glance on the way at the living room as she left the kitchen and headed up the stairs. But it was a brief glance.

Chapter 18

Dropping Rich's car at the end of their hiking route would save them a long and flat road walk back to the beginning of the trail. It also gave them the chance to be certain the Birch Brook on Rich's topographical map was the site of the Nilsson-Dyer development. So when they started out Saturday morning, Rich led, and when Julie, in her own car, stopped behind him at the turn-off from the main road by the river she was pleased to see the sign:

Birch Brook
Luxury Townhouse Development
Model Open This Fall

"Think it's okay to leave it here?" she asked when Rich opened the door to her car and slid into the passenger seat.

"Don't see why not. I'm sure they expect people to stop to look over the site. Besides, they won't be working today. They don't technically own the land yet."

"That's true. The closing isn't until Monday. I guess it will be okay."

They retraced their way back along the river in Julie's car, turned north at the highway, and parked in the lot just across from what Rich insisted on calling the recycling center, but that Julie, in line with local custom, thought of as the town dump. The trail began at the parking area and almost immediately ascended sharply to the right across ledges. It was steeper than Julie had expected. Rich paused at the first clearing in the trail, ostensibly to catch the view but more likely, Julie realized, to give her a chance to catch up.

"What a view!" he said as she leaned against a tree and followed his gaze out to the east, over the river and to the low hills beyond. "From the top we should be able to see to the west, to Mount Washington and the northern Presidentials. Ready?"

Replying that she needed a few more minutes to catch her breath didn't seem like a good idea to Julie. It wasn't exactly that she felt competitive with Rich, but it wasn't exactly that she didn't, either. "Lead on," she said.

"Probably a false summit," he said an hour later when they reached an open area at what seemed to Julie like the absolute top of the world.

"Who cares?" she asked. "Just look!" To their left, toward the southwest, two high peaks were visible above the river.

"Nice," Rich replied. "But I'm sure we can see Mount Washington from the top. See how the trail cuts across those rocks over there? Probably another fifteen or twenty minutes will take us to the real summit, and the views to the west. Should be a good spot for lunch."

When they reached it, she agreed it was indeed perfect for lunch, and well worth the challenging climb. The view wasn't quite 360 degrees, but it was very close. To the east was the river and the low hills, but the best sight was to the west, where Mount Washington dominated the horizon with its volcanic peak.

"Still some snow in Tuckerman's," Rich said, pointing to the Mount Washington ravine. "But I think we should go a little farther to get the best view."

"This looks pretty good to me."

"Just a bit more. But we can take a breather here. We've got to climb Washington this summer, Julie. I haven't done it in years."

"Think I could handle it?" she asked.

"No problem. But it's an all-day hike, so we'll have to work up to it."

"We ought to hike every weekend this summer, Rich, and then we'll be ready for Washington in the fall. I wish you were here all the time. It'll be great in August when you can come for the month. You remember that my folks will be here that second week, right?"

"You told me."

"And that's okay?"

"Why not? You don't see much of them."

"You sound like my mother."

"All I meant was they live in Ohio and you're here in Maine, so you don't see much of each other."

"They were here last August, and I went to Marietta for Christmas. I'm thirty-five years old, for God's sake."

"Sorry I said anything. Let's get going."

As Rich resumed the hike, Julie noticed he didn't hesitate to reach and keep the fast pace he had earlier slowed for her. So, she told herself, seeing him disappear momentarily ahead around a turn, he's mad. She well understood by now that Rich O'Brian didn't yell and throw things when he was mad. He just went silent, but in a way that made his silence a weapon to hit you with. Fortunately, that hadn't happened often, and Julie felt bad that she had set him off since their time together was so precious.

Still, she considered as she pushed herself to close the physical gap between them, the matter of her family and her relationship with them, which was good, shouldn't make Rich quarrel. He got on fine with them last August, the longest they had all been together, and they seemed to like him. Or at least her mother did. Dad had been pleasant enough, and told Julie later that Rich seemed a fine young man, but she recognized that in her dad's eyes, no man would ever be worthy of her, his only child. A math professor at the college in Marietta, he appreciated Rich's academic career, though he did ask Julie if the University of Maine was the best Rich could do. Julie had gotten mad at that, and Dad had tried to joke his way out of it by saying that he himself didn't have much to talk about since there he was at little old Marietta College on the banks of the Ohio River. Unsaid was what Julie knew: that he had turned down offers at far more prestigious places because he and her mother liked the small-town life of Marietta.

"You back there?" Rich yelled from where he had stopped at the top of the trail.

"Just trying to keep up with you, in my usual slow way."

"Hey, turtle," Rich said as he stepped back down the trail to her and put his arms around her. "We hares don't always get to the finish line first," he said. "I'm sorry I went off in a huff."

"What did I say?"

"Nothing you said. Just me. I'll be happy to see your parents next month. No problem. I like them, and at least they put on a good face about me."

"They like you, too, Rich."

"Maybe your mother, but let's not kid about your father, Julie."

"Rich, he does like you. He told me that several times. But, face it, I'm still his little girl. No guy will ever measure up. I can't tell you what he was like when I was in high school, inspecting every guy I dated like they were at the bottom of his class. You're from a big family; being an only child is different, and being a girl with a strong father, well . . ."

"You survived it. Pretty decent interpersonal skills. Noticeable but not dysfunctional self-centeredness. Spoiled, yes, but not beyond redemption. I could go on."

"Don't," she laughed, "because if you do I'll start in on some of your less-than-admirable traits."

"I have some?"

She laughed. "Let's eat," she said. Rich took off his backpack and Julie began to sort through it to set out their picnic lunch.

When they finished their sandwiches, Rich jumped up and said, "It's all downhill from here!" A half-hour below the summit they reentered a thick forest of birches and lost the view, but the trees themselves and the occasional waterfall provided equally pleasant sights.

"This has to be it," Rich announced as he stood by the bank of a brook. "I thought it would be wider, but it probably opens up as it goes down."

"You're sure this is the famous Birch Brook?" Julie asked as she looked at the three-foot-wide body of water that seemed more like a marsh.

"The trail turns here." Rich pointed to the two yellow paint swabs on the tree that indicated a turn. "So if the map's right, this has to be Birch Brook. The head of it. The trail's pretty clearly marked along this side, and the timing's right, so let's head along here."

As they descended, the brook widened to six or seven feet, and the water was deeper. To both sides of the brook the land flattened out, and then ahead was an opening. And the sound of car engines.

"Are we close to the River Road?" Julie asked.

"Must be."

Within a few more minutes, they saw the source of the sounds. A Ford Explorer and an oversize pickup, both with their engines running, sat side by side on the flat grassy area just in front of them. Rich's car was in the smaller area just below them.

"Pretty good planning," he said as he pointed down to his car. "We came out exactly where we should have. I wonder what those other guys are doing here?"

"Julie," a loud voice said from just off to their right. "I'm a lucky man, seeing you twice in two days," Frank Nilsson added as he walked toward them, Luke Dyer by his side.

"Glad you came by," Frank said after Julie had introduced Rich to the two men. "Lucky Luke and I are here so we can give you a tour. If you have time to look around?"

Julie explained that they had just hiked through from the eastern side of Sutter's Mountain.

"That's quite a trek," Frank said.

"That your car then?" Luke asked. Until now he had said nothing beyond a crisp "Nice to meet you" to Rich; Julie warranted only a nod.

"We parked it here so we didn't have to walk back on the River Road," Rich explained. "Hope that's okay."

"Fine," Frank answered. "The road's pretty enough, but not exactly what you want to do after coming over the mountain. Good advertising for us—people'll drive by and see your car and think everyone's rushing to buy a condo! In fact, Luke and I did have a couple of potential buyers out here earlier. Tourists, probably just looking for something to do on a pretty July day, but then you never know. We just gave them the tour—not much to see yet, but a little imagination goes a long way. Anyway, care to do the same?"

"If it's no problem," Julie replied.

"Well, let's start right here then," Frank said, pointing to the flat areas on either side of the brook. "That's phase two over there, and phase three that way. Phase one, the first twenty townhouses, is over there." He pointed off to the right and down closer to the main road. "We need to get a structure in place so we can do a model for next ski season. The plan is to have phase one done in sixteen months, but next fall and winter is really the selling season. That's why we need the model."

He led them across the flat area so they could better appreciate the view. Luke followed behind, silently, like a schoolboy on a historical society visit. Julie noted Rich holding back to walk beside him, and she took the cue and moved closer to Frank. From behind she heard Rich asking questions and Luke's monosyllabic answers. So she concentrated on Frank.

"I know you told me yesterday," Julie said, "but I'm surprised it's so big. Did you say four hundred acres?"

"Actually four hundred and thirty. We're aiming for upscale folks who don't want to feel cramped. The clusters will be limited to four townhouses, and even when it's fully built out, you won't see more than one other cluster. Mostly you'll see views like that." He pointed up the river, to the west, where the first range of mountains was visible.

"That's pretty impressive," Julie said. "I enjoyed my condo up at the skiway, but they're right on top of each other. Not like this."

"That's the idea. Of course this isn't going to be ski-in, ski-out, but we think the kind of people who will buy here want space and a view and won't mind driving up to the skiway."

Luke and Rich had caught up to where Frank and Julie were standing in time to hear the developer's last comment. "How much?" Rich asked.

"In phase one, $299,000 for the middle units, $350,000 for the end ones, plus fees—but as we build out, the fees will drop because more people will be sharing them."

"Wow," Julie said, making a quick calculation: The first phase would bring in over $6 million.

"Of course we have to sell them," Frank said, and laughed. "And before that we have to build them. All top-flight construction, high-end interiors. It's a pretty big investment."

"Including the land," Julie said.

"Exactly. Luke and I have to put in quite a bit before we see some returns, but that'll happen. Right, Luke?"

"Not doing it for fun," Luke answered. "I need to get going, folks, if you'll excuse me. Want me to turn off your ignition, Frank?"

"I forgot we left them running. Thanks." Luke nodded and mumbled a good-bye to Julie and Rich and headed toward the spot where the two vehicles were sitting with their engines on.

"Want to go around to the other side and see the views?" Frank asked. "Up above phase three, it's really pretty spectacular."

"If you're sure you have time," Julie said.

Frank led them across the flat area by the brook and up through a stand of birches to an open meadow high enough to command views to the east and west.

"We're still not sure about this," Frank said as they took in the views of the river and mountains. "We call it phase four, but I'm kind of thinking it will be different—individual houses rather than townhouse clusters, three-acre plots. But that's a long way off. Right now we have to concentrate on getting enough of the townhouses up and sold to finance the purchase and construction."

"Pretty impressive," Rich said. "I can't imagine planning and doing something like this."

"It's my biggest project," Frank said, "but I've done enough others to know how it works. And Luke is a great contractor. And partner—we're in this together; he's got a fifth of the equity, but he'll be making most of his on the construction itself."

"I didn't realize you were partners," Julie said.

"When you develop projects, Julie, you have to have *lots* of partners. You just have to keep them all straight! And make sure you protect everyone. But Luke's a good partner, easy to work with if you don't mind long periods of quiet."

"I noticed he's not too talkative," Rich said, and laughed.

"Not Luke. But he brings plenty to the table. He just wishes his father never sold the land!" Julie's quizzical look prompted Frank to continue. "You wouldn't know about that, being new, but Birch Brook used to belong to Luke's dad. He sold it to Dan Swanson."

"As a matter of fact, I think I did hear that, Frank. I guess the financial part of this would be a lot different if the Swansons didn't own the land."

"You got that right. Luke and I would be getting rich here if his old man hadn't sold to Dan. Or hadn't sold so low. That really bothers Luke, and I can't say I blame him. Paul, Luke's dad, got

$700,000, and we're paying almost four times that, but of course, land does appreciate. Try to tell Luke that, but it still bothers him. Well, I shouldn't bore you with all these details, but that's it in a nutshell. Help yourself if you'd like to look around more. I should be getting home."

Rich and Julie accepted Frank's offer of a ride in his Explorer down from the clearing to the parking area where Rich's car sat. Frank gave them a final wave and drove off, and Rich and Julie got in the car and drove east on the River Road to pick up Julie's car at the trailhead in Ryland. "Thinking about our hike?" Rich asked to break Julie's silence.

"It was wonderful, wasn't it? Such incredible views. This is a really great area, isn't it?"

"Sure is. But somehow I get the impression you're thinking about something else."

"Okay! I'm thinking about the hike, but I was also thinking about Birch Brook. Pretty interesting."

"How so?"

"How about money? This is a *huge* deal, Rich—the first phase alone is $6 million or more, and if they do the next two, then the lots for private homes at the top, we're talking big bucks here."

"But not necessarily big *profits*. They have to buy the land and then build the townhouses before they get a penny back. Plus taxes, financing costs on the land and the construction, and . . ."

"I know, I know. But you heard Dyer say he wasn't in it for the fun. They're going to make a bundle here."

"Probably they will, eventually, but it's not like they're going to get rich overnight. And what if they can't sell those places? They're stuck with all the carrying costs. I just think you're making too much of it."

"Another interesting thing," Julie continued, instead of trying to rebut Rich's obviously rational analysis, "is that Luke Dyer is a partner with Nilsson—not just the contractor. Howard mentioned that, but Nilsson confirmed it—Dyer will own a fifth."

"So?"

"So he had more to lose than just the construction business if Mary Ellen had backed out of the deal. And then there's the fact that the land went from his family to Swanson's and now back to him and Nilsson. At a *much* higher price. No wonder he's looking into those Swanson papers!"

"But not Dan Swanson's. You said it was the grandfather's papers."

"For now, but that's because they're the ones Tabby's cataloged. Maybe Luke is just biding his time to get at the more-recent ones."

"Why?"

"I bet he's trying to find out why his father sold Birch Brook so cheaply to Dan Swanson. Dyer has a fifth of the equity. Let's say they paid two and a half million—Frank said it was nearly four times what Luke's father sold it for, which we know was $700,000. Then Luke's share of that is about a half-million! If the land was still in his family, he could get a pile from Nilsson and be so much better off. Wouldn't you be bothered by that? Nilsson said Luke is."

"Of course I'd be bothered, and I can see why Dyer is. But—"

"I wonder what Frank meant about protecting everyone when you work with partners?" Julie interrupted.

"Probably just what it sounds like—some way to make sure no one cheats, or to share the ownership if something happens to one of them."

They pulled up to Julie's car. "Here you go," Rich said. "I assume you plan to continue this conversation after a hot shower and a drink."

"Your assumption's right on the shower and drink," Julie said, "but I think I'll cut my losses with you and drop the topic for tonight. It's our last night before you have to go back to Orono, and I'd like to spend it doing something other than talking about who killed Mary Ellen."

"Scrabble?" he asked.

"Maybe a jigsaw puzzle?"

Chapter 19

Children know the feeling of waking with excitement, anticipating a full day of freedom and fun, and then suddenly being hit by the realization that it will not end as it began. As appealing as Sunday seems at seven or eight in the morning, when it lies before you, it always carries the seeds of its own destruction: Monday, the beginning of the school week, the price you pay for weekends.

Far from being a child, Julie was nonetheless as affected by the mixed and melancholy character of Sunday morning as when she had been a schoolgirl. Sunday had taken on new melancholy over the past two years. One year was devoted to long-distance commuting, between Delaware and Maine, and the expense of that usually limited it to monthly visits back and forth, always ending on Sunday. The past year was so much better because she and Rich spent almost every weekend together, either in Ryland or in Orono, but the frequency and ease of that made Sundays even worse because the weekends together were so good, seemed so natural, that the prospect of their ending was more poignant.

As Julie lay in bed contemplating the cruelty of Sunday, she wondered if they could, or would, continue this way. Rich had gotten angry yesterday when the topic of her parents had come up on the trail, but she suspected that the real reason was the uncertainty of their relationship. She could feel the issue coming to the forefront, hanging in the air between them. Was marriage in the cards? How would they make it work if it still required commuting? And if it didn't, what did that mean for her career, or his? They had avoided a serious and lengthy discussion of the topic and today, with all Sunday's sad aching, was not the time for it either.

They took a long, challenging run that Rich said was necessary to stretch the muscles that had carried them up and across Sutter's

Mountain yesterday. It was warmer today, already near fifty degrees and heading toward the more-seasonable prediction of low seventies, but still perfect for their run. After a late brunch, Rich worked in the garden, pruning and weeding, and trying to impress on Julie the need for her regular attention to such tasks.

"You can't leave it all to the weekends," he said, "especially since you're coming to Orono next weekend, and that means I won't be able to work on this for two weeks." Julie listened patiently to his detailed instructions about which plants needed what kind of care, but she found herself losing focus and then getting angry. As he was describing the proper way to deadhead the rhododendrons, she interrupted: "You know I'm hopeless about gardening. I'm happy for you to do it, happy you actually enjoy it. I don't. So can we just leave it at that?"

Rich stood up from crouching over the plant and looked at her. "Why are you angry?" he asked.

"I'm sorry; I'm not really angry. It's just that you know so much about gardens and cooking and woodwork and, well, all those things. But I don't. And I really don't want to learn."

He was silent for a few moments. Julie turned and walked to the other side of the garden. He joined her. "Look," he said, "I don't mean you *have* to do these things. I was just trying to explain what you could do while I'm away, but you don't have to. Sorry if I come off as being bossy."

"It's not that. I'm sorry I said anything. It's just that sometimes I feel like you're trying to take over my life—like the garden. Tend me. Prune and fertilize. Sometimes I just want you to back off."

"That's your problem," Rich said sharply. "If we're different, lots of people would think that's a *good* thing—a kind of balance. You don't. Anyway, I should be getting ready to leave now." He turned from her and headed to the house. She stayed in the garden. She could hear him inside the house, slamming drawers, packing. She walked to the kitchen door and was there when he emerged with his two boat bags and backpack. "Rich," she said, reaching out to hold him. "Come here. I'm sorry—I really am. I'm really rattled, and, well, the truth is that I just hate it when you leave. I'm sure I'm making a fuss because I'll miss you so much, and maybe it makes the parting easier if . . ."

"If we fight?" he finished for her. "That's a pretty weird way to say you'll miss me."

"So I'm weird. Big surprise?" she asked and laughed.

"Not too big," he said, smiling. "You know I'll miss you, too. It's only five nights. We'll still be together on Friday, right?"

"You still want me to come?"

"I don't think you really have to ask."

"Thanks. Really, I'm sorry. Please say you forgive me, that you'll forget everything I said."

"I'm just going to put on a Stones tape and wind my way to Orono. Can't remember anything bad that happened this weekend."

"I love you, Rich."

"I love you, too. Be safe. I'll call when I get in. You'll be here?"

"That's the plan," Julie said.

"So is it a busy week?" he asked, delaying.

Julie was glad to change the topic and the tone. "More than usual," she said. "Tomorrow's the funeral, and Wednesday Dalton is having a building committee meeting, and there's a lot of cleanup from last week. And now that the excavation's done the builders can pour the foundation and get started. Probably good that I can keep busy and not think so much—about how nice it was to have this week together, about how stupid I can be sometimes."

He laughed. "Not very often. And you can think about August. We'll have the whole month! And by the way, I notice your list of the week's work didn't include solving any murders."

"I'll just slip that in between the other things," she teased.

"Julie . . ."

"I said I'll let Mike do his job, but that doesn't mean I won't think about the murder."

"And give the chief the benefit of your penetrating insights?"

"If that happens, isn't it my obligation as a good citizen to assist the police?" Rich laughed.

"Speaking of Mike, I wonder what he's been up to," she continued. "Haven't talked to him since he gave the go-ahead on the excavation."

"Probably doing his job. Sticking to your job—now that sounds like good advice for everyone."

"How does your week look?" Julie asked.

"Same old, same old. I've got to spend some time tonight prepping my lectures and writing an exam. I thought I'd work on that stuff this weekend, but it was actually nice not to."

"I really appreciate all your help, Rich. I'm sorry I seem to just gobble up your time and then be so ungrateful."

"Gobble away," he said, and leaned over to encourage a kiss. "When I'm in Orono I have more than enough time to think about colonial history, so don't apologize for keeping me otherwise occupied here."

They hugged and kissed, neither referring to the words they had exchanged, and he put his gear in the car and backed out of the driveway. She followed and waved from the street. Then she took a walk through the garden, thinking she should try to perform some of the tasks he had described as a way of making it up to him. She felt even more at loose ends than usual on a Sunday. The holiday week together had been so good, and she hoped she hadn't spoiled it by telling him to back off. That wasn't really what she wanted at all, and she knew she had been bitchy just to make his leaving easier. But there was another reason: Tonight she would be alone again in Worth's house. To take her mind off that, Julie decided to walk to the historical society and try to concentrate on some work.

She walked through the garden and down the back street to check on the construction before going to her office in Swanson House. For some reason, the site of Mary Ellen's death didn't produce the same feelings that Worth's did. The yellow backhoe was gone, though the image of it sitting there idly several days ago immediately came into her mind. The deep trenches that formed the outline of the new structure looked as if they had been magically transferred from the building plan and imposed on the ground. She walked around them, imagining the building that would rise from the foundation to be poured this week. It wasn't going to be huge or grand, but the new Daniel Swanson Center, sixty feet long and thirty-two feet wide, would nearly double the space available to the Ryland Historical Society for the proper storage of library and archive materials. Overseeing its planning and construction truly excited Julie, and aside from Mary Ellen's constant interference, the experience had been satisfying. She credited Dalton Scott's patient and informed guidance of the building committee for that. He was such a pleasure to work with, and though he occasionally lost his cool when Mary Ellen got itchy, he managed her pretty well, Julie had to say. So strange to think of the committee's next meeting, on Wednesday, the first time without Mary Ellen. Julie sighed. Poor Mary Ellen; she truly would miss her, no matter what.

I wonder what *is* happening on that front, Julie thought as she finished her circuit of the trenches. Mike certainly had been distant, but then, as Rich said, he was obviously at work on the investigation. Julie knew the State Police were involved, too, but exactly who did what she didn't know. Anyway, maybe she'd call Mike in the morning. Meantime, she thought, after she'd let herself into

Swanson House and settled into her office, it would be a good idea to make a few more notes in the file so as not to forget the details of Birch Brook she had learned yesterday.

"Almost 7:30," she said out loud when she looked at her watch. How could the time have gone so fast? Rich always called when he got back to Orono, so she would have to move fast to be home for his call. Locking up Swanson House and activating the security system didn't take long, nor did the short walk, and when she entered Harding House and went to the phone, she saw the blinking light that meant a message. She listened with a mix of pleasure and sadness to Rich's report on his trip and realized there was a note of something between anger and concern in his last comment: "I thought you were going to be home. Give me a call as soon as you get in. Love you."

She was just about to pick up the phone to make the call when it rang. "Just went to the office," she explained. "To take my mind off you and the week. I miss you already, Rich, and I'm so sorry about what I said. Don't back off—I don't want that at all." He didn't respond directly, but they talked a bit more about what a nice week it had been, and then Rich reminded her to lock the house tightly. "You're not worried about me, are you?" she asked.

"I'm always worried when we're not together. And I know *you* worry about being there alone. Just be sure everything's locked."

Later, in bed, Julie replayed the conversation. Rich was certainly right. She had locked and double-checked all the locks. Harding House was perfectly safe. So why couldn't she fall asleep?

Chapter 20

Just because you feel like you haven't slept all night doesn't necessarily mean you haven't, Julie told herself around five o'clock Monday morning when she decided that getting up couldn't be worse than lying in bed. Surely she had slept. It was just that she couldn't remember it. What she could remember were the sounds of creaking steps, opening doors, and footfalls downstairs in the front parlor. No. To be precise, what Julie remembered was *thinking* she was hearing such sounds and then realizing they were the results of what she readily admitted was her active imagination.

The sun was already above the eastern horizon as she sat at the kitchen table to await the coffee she had set to brewing. Actually, she told herself, it hadn't been that bad, this first night in a week alone in Harding House without Rich. She had just gotten spoiled with him there for so long. Her memories of finding Worth's bloody body and the red stains on the floor under it were not as persistent as they once were, after all. She poured her first mug of fragrant coffee and walked into the parlor. It looked perfectly normal, even familiar with her white sofa covering the spot where Worth's body had lain. Rich had sanded the spot last week and refinished it to match the rest of the floor, even though he said the bloodstains were nonexistent. "Humor me," Julie had implored him, and Rich being Rich had done so. She went back to the kitchen to refill her mug. Deciding that so much coffee would make a run impractical, she opted for breakfast instead. But a healthy one, she told herself as she boiled water for oatmeal.

Since Mary Ellen's funeral was at eleven, Julie had reasoned that opening the historical society at its usual hour and then closing again so soon wasn't sensible, so no one would be in until the afternoon. That fact made working around the house this morning appealing, but Julie quickly found herself distracted and thinking about the folder in her office desk that contained her notes on the murder. At 9:30 she walked to Swanson House, punched in the secuity code, and let herself into the building with her key. Listlessly turning the pages of the folder, she found herself able to concentrate on the murder no better than she had been able to concentrate on finishing putting her books in the shelves at Harding House earlier. She had time to take a walk through town and end up at the church enough in advance of the ceremony to assure herself a good seat. After a loop around the Common and through the residential section behind the church, she found herself in front of the beautiful Gothic structure just as the hearse pulled up. She held back as the men from the funeral home carried the coffin into the side entrance. She felt as if she were at the theater ahead of the performance, watching the stage being readied and the actors assembling before the audience took their seats. She looked at her watch and saw it was 10:15, and decided on another transit of the Common so she wouldn't be first in the church.

"Warmed up?" a voice said from behind as Julie came onto the sidewalk at the lower end of the Common. She turned to see the police chief.

"Mike, sorry I didn't see you. I was early and thought I'd just take a walk. It's such a beautiful day."

Mike didn't speak for a few seconds, and Julie had the impression he was taking a photo of her with his eyes. Was her black skirt and dark-blue blazer inappropriate for the funeral? Mike certainly was formally attired, but Julie thought she was, too. "Something wrong?" she asked and ran her hand through her hair, wondering if perhaps it had become untidy because of what had turned out to be a longer walk than she had planned.

"Wrong?" the policeman repeated. "Not that I know of. Your hair's always been light red, hasn't it?" He laughed and continued. "I know I'm a cop and should remember things, but I was just wondering if—"

"If I changed my hair color?" Julie completed his question. "No. This is natural. You think I should?"

He laughed again, uncomfortably. "Of course not. It's very nice."

"Thanks," Julie answered, looking at Mike questioningly. "What's up? I haven't talked to you since late last week."

"Pretty busy," he replied, moving quickly away from the conversation about Julie's hair that neither of them seemed to want to pursue. "Working on the case, of course."

"How's it coming?"

"Making progress, though working with the State Police isn't my idea of fun. They've got a detective on this, but of course he doesn't know the scene here, so I end up having to tell him who's who."

"So are they getting close to figuring it out?"

"It's moving along. And I guess we should be, too. Looks like the crowd's gathering." He pointed to the church, where a dozen or so people were standing on the sidewalk.

"Mike, what's the deal with my hair?" Julie asked as they moved down the street toward the church.

"Nothing. Hey, you'd better get in and find a seat. I need to stay out here and help direct folks," he added, turning away quickly before Julie could pursue the topic.

"Want to join us?" Dalton Scott asked as Julie fell in the people moving up the short flight of stairs. Nickie was beside him. "That would be great," Julie replied. "I wasn't sure of the protocol."

"Well, you could always join Howard in the family pew," Dalton said, and pointed to the second row of pews where Howard and his wife were already seated.

"Is that really a family pew?" Julie whispered to Dalton after the three of them had settled into a pew halfway between the front and back of the rows of cream boxes. Dalton had opened the door to theirs to usher Nickie and Julie in before him.

"Only for the past century or so," Dalton whispered back. "Of course you wouldn't know that if you looked—nothing as vulgar as signs or anything, but that second pew is the Townsends', and if you ended up there by mistake no one would say anything, but you would feel out of place pretty fast."

"Is this one okay?" Julie asked, worried now that her ignorance of the complicated business of family pews was another aspect of Ryland's culture that would embarrass her.

"Well, it's not the Scott family's," he replied, "but after the first few rows it's okay at a funeral for folks like us to take it. Until someone comes along and stares at us," he added. Julie glanced up to see if indeed someone was, but then realized Dalton was kidding.

"Don't worry," Nickie whispered in her other ear. "We're fine here."

Relieved by Nickie's assurance, Julie began to take in the scene. She'd popped into the church a few times to check it out, and had attended a few events there, but felt today as if she were really seeing the church for the first time. It was so beautiful in its simple, understated, New England way, so very different from the Lutheran churches of her youth and the Catholic ones she accompanied Rich to. The walls, for example, were practically empty, whereas in the churches she had frequented the walls were often more full than the pews. Here was a plaque with numbers on it off to the left of the altar, and on the right, a small cloth banner embroidered with a cross. And the altar itself was more like the podium at a Rotary breakfast meeting, nothing ornate about it at all. The walls and ceiling were somewhere in color between cream and eggshell—bright, clean, hygienic, and terribly discreet.

"Of course we're white," she amused herself by imagining the walls and ceiling as saying, "but it's not just any ordinary white that any ordinary church might be painted; this is a white as special and as understated as everything in this church."

Caught up in the visual delights of the building, Julie was nearly unconscious of what was happening around her until Dalton and Nickie rose beside her. She jumped up to join them, then noticed that everyone else was already on their feet. She wondered how long she had been the lone sitter. A woman wearing a green stole had entered from somewhere and was now standing in front of the congregation, not at the podium but at floor level, in the middle of the central aisle. She bent down to speak to Steven and Elizabeth, alone in the front pew, and then stood up again to face the rest.

"Welcome to the House of the Lord," the woman said. "We are here to thank Him for the life and good works of our beloved Mary Ellen Swanson," she continued as she looked to the right where the coffin sat on a low stand. "This service of thanks will be as ecumenical as a Congo preacher like me can make it," she added, and smiled as hearty laughs arose from the congregation. Although at first surprised at the levity—both the preacher's and those who replied with laughter—Julie quickly felt a sense of comfort she hadn't expected. When the minister said, "We'll begin with number thirty-seven," gesturing to the small board off to side that contained three sets of numbers, thirty-seven being the first, Julie followed Dalton's lead and reached for the hymnal in the wooden pocket in front of her. She surprised herself by lustily joining the singing, grateful that the words came back so readily from her childhood churchgoing days.

The minister spoke briefly but very touchingly of Mary Ellen's life and her many contributions to Ryland, noting that only God could understand why the woman had been taken before she had

had the chance to see the fruits of her latest gift in the form of the new Swanson Center of the Ryland Historical Society. The reference made Julie uncomfortable as she recalled the location of Mary Ellen's death, and she was grateful when Nickie reached over to give her hand a gentle squeeze. Another hymn followed, and again Julie joined the hearty singing. When it ended, there was an awkward silence as the minister stood at the podium and looked expectantly toward Steven and Elizabeth. She finally broke the silence by saying, "Steven, I believe you'd like to say a few words."

Steven rose slowly and walked awkwardly toward the step that led up to where the minister had moved to stand away from the podium. He paused, and then turned back and planted himself squarely in the middle of the aisle and looked down it toward the back door. Julie smiled at him, and she guessed that the others whom she couldn't see did the same, because gradually he made eye contact with people instead of the door. He cleared his throat and said, "I think I'll just stand down here. It won't take long." Julie saw the minister nod her approval. I can't imagine doing that, Julie said to herself as she thought of Steven's task in talking about his mother a few feet from her coffin.

"Many of you knew my mother as well as I did," he began, "especially in the last few years when I wasn't exactly a regular visitor to Ryland." He laughed uncomfortably, but the response encouraged him to laugh again. "Well, Mom put it differently. She said I was practically a stranger here." More laughter seemed to help him along. "But of course I grew up in Ryland, with Mom and Dad, and so I don't consider myself a stranger. Anyway, I want to thank all of you for coming today to honor Mom, and for being her friends for all those years. She was proud of Ryland and everything that's going on here, and happy to be a part of it. She was really excited about the new building to honor Dad, like Reverend Richardson said, and in a way I guess it will be a memorial to her now, to all that she did for the town and the historical society and all."

Julie wondered if Steven was making a suggestion. Maybe they should change the name to the Daniel and Mary Ellen Swanson Center. Maybe she should have thought of that earlier. Steven resumed his speech.

"Growing up here was great, and that was really because of Mom. And Dad, too, but it was really Mom who made my life here so much fun. So I want to say thanks to her for that, and say how very sad I am that she won't be a part of my life now." Steven's voice caught, and he reached into his back pocket for a handkerchief that he used to dab at his eyes. "Sorry," he said. "That's really the best I can do, the most I can say: Thanks, Mom. For everything." He glanced at the coffin and then practically collapsed into the pew beside Elizabeth.

"Thank you, Steven," the minister said quickly as she walked backed toward the podium. "Thank you for those very loving words, words that only a son can offer at a moment like this. Please know that our thoughts and prayers are with you and Elizabeth now, as well as with Mary Ellen. After the singing of our last hymn, will the pallbearers please come to the front, and will the rest of the congregation stand as we carry the remains of our beloved friend down the aisle? Commitment at the cemetery will be private, but Steven and Elizabeth have very kindly invited you all to his mother's house for a reception, beginning at noon—is that right?"

"I knew I was supposed to say something else!" Steven said to the whole church, his composure now back. He rose and added, "Mom would very much want you all to come. Grander Hill Road, I'm sure most of you know it."

The minister gestured toward Steven, who walked up to the coffin. Several other men rose from other parts of the church, including Howard, Henry, several Julie knew only as faces around Ryland, and—to her surprise—Dalton. Nickie leaned over and whispered to Julie, "Dalton was honored to be asked. Figured he was called on because he was one of the few trustees who could actually heft a coffin, but I see Henry is there, too." The group assembled and gathered around the coffin as the funeral director, who had suddenly materialized, as members of his profession do, entered from the side and gave low-voiced instructions. As the coffin passed up the aisle beside her, Julie realized that tears were streaming down her face. But she felt better seeing she was not alone in having that response to saying good-bye to Mary Ellen Swanson.

Chapter 21

"I'm meeting Dalton there," Nickie said to Julie when they reached the steps outside the church. The hearse was gone, but Julie could see the blue lights of Mike's cruiser at the end of the street and knew the hearse and the few cars of the procession were behind it. "I can give you a ride," Nickie added.

"Great, thanks."

"I'd enjoy the company. Did they say noon? It's ten of now. The family won't be back by then, but I guess we're supposed to go anyway. My car's up the street."

It was a comfort to Julie to ride and chat with the cheerful Nickie. And the day was simply gorgeous—bright blue skies, warm but pleasant temperatures, a gentle breeze blowing in off the mountains, which were dramatically visible to the west through the crystal-clear air. As if reacting to the same stimuli, Nickie said, "Seems like a cliché, but she sure had a great day for it, didn't she?"

Julie agreed, and went on to say what a lovely service it was. "There's another cliché for you," she added.

"I know what you mean, but a lovely day and a lovely service just have to be better than a gloomy old sermon on a rainy day."

"The minister was great," Julie said.

"Annie Richardson? She sure is—funny and with-it, but serious in her way."

"I'm still not used to that abbreviation, by the way," Julie said. "*Congo* for Congregational—but no one seemed bothered by it."

"Standard, I guess," Nickie said.

"Like knowing which pews you can sit in. Sometimes I think I'll never figure out how things work here."

"Don't be silly, Julie! You've figured out everything that matters."

"Not quite." Julie said. "I mean, who would murder Mary Ellen?" She was silent for the rest of the short drive.

Mary Ellen's house always seemed incongruous to Julie. The Swansons were one of Ryland's oldest families, and their homestead on Main Street was a huge Victorian four doors above the large but by contrast modest Harding House. Worth had pointed it out to her when he gave her a walking tour of Ryland, so the first time Mary Ellen had invited her to dinner just a few weeks after she arrived, she was prepared to make the short walk up the street. But the morning of their dinner date, Mary Ellen had dropped into her office to remind Julie of the time and that her house was at the very top of the hill. To Julie's puzzlement, Mary Ellen had explained that they had sold the family homestead to a couple from Boston and built a new house on Grander Hill Road several years before Dan Swanson's death. "We just love the views," Mary Ellen had said then.

It was easy to see why. As Nickie pulled into the driveway below the house, the views out toward the Presidentials made Julie gasp, despite her having been here several times before. "I always forget how great this is," she said to Nickie.

"It is pretty grand, isn't it? Dalton says that if he'd come to Ryland earlier and gotten the commission to design a house for the Swansons on this site, he probably wouldn't have given up architecture to run an inn. Of course he would have done a better design," Nickie added as they walked up the drive and around to the front entrance. "Though this isn't too shabby."

Indeed, Julie thought as she looked up at the high shingled wall that formed a screen against the traffic of Grander Hill Road. Four irregularly placed sash windows, small like gun slots in a castle, provided the only break in the facade. The entrance was nearly hidden under a gable. The door was opened by a young woman Julie didn't recognize—a college-student waitress from the Ryland Inn, hired for the event, she guessed. As Nickie and Julie walked through the narrow entrance hall they heard subdued voices, and then they entered the great room. The house was all about views. The entire wall of the great room consisted of glass panels, running close to twenty feet from just above the floor to the ceiling. A couple of dozen guests had positioned themselves at intervals along the glass, staring out and exchanging quiet words. Loretta Cummings, Julie was happy to see, was one of them.

"What a gorgeous view," Julie said when she walked over to join Loretta.

"Mary Ellen always had the best, didn't she? Wasn't it a lovely service?"

"Very nice."

"Mary Ellen would have been pleased," Loretta continued. "So simple and dignified, but light enough. And Steven's eulogy . . ."

"Must have been awfully hard for him."

"I'm sure, but I thought he did a good job of catching Mary Ellen's spirit—like that comment about how his mother got after him for not coming home much. Couldn't you just hear her saying that? She didn't mince words, as you know. But I'm sure she really missed her son."

More people were arriving behind them, and Julie turned back and saw the family and party from the cemetery weren't among them. "He seems very nice," she said. "What's his wife like?"

"I've only met her a couple of times," Loretta said, "but from what I gathered she and Mary Ellen didn't get along. I suppose that's easy to understand: Elizabeth took Mary Ellen's golden boy from her, and both of them are strong women. Bound to clash."

"I wonder how Steven felt about that."

"Caught in the middle of his strong mama and his strong wife, like a lot of guys. Not an unusual story, I guess. Now I was lucky—my husband's one of six kids, and his mother was happy to see him get out of her kitchen and into mine!"

The low murmuring came to an abrupt end just as Loretta was finishing, and everyone pivoted as if on command to see Steven and Elizabeth come down the entrance hall into the great room. Behind them were Reverend Richardson and the pallbearers. Steven stopped at the long table serving as the bar and poured a glass of something Julie couldn't identify but was sure wasn't the white wine she and Loretta were sipping. He took a long gulp and then looked around at his now-silent guests.

"Thank you all for coming," he said. "The circumstances of Mom's death are tragic, but today, let's put aside our questions and concerns and celebrate her life. Mom would be happy to have all her friends in the house today. Elizabeth and I are happy you're here, too." He turned his head to the right to confirm this, but Elizabeth was already moving away, toward the windows. In fact, she was headed toward Julie, who stepped back, hoping the other woman's path would change. When it didn't, she found herself face-to-face with Elizabeth.

"I'm so sorry for your loss, Mrs. Swanson," she said.

"Myerson," the woman corrected her. "I didn't take Steven's name, but please call me Elizabeth. You're Dr. Williamson from the Ryland Historical Society, aren't you?"

"Yes. Julie. We met briefly a couple of months ago."

"One of those interminable get-togethers about the building! She certainly enjoyed all the fuss. Too bad she can't enjoy the building."

Julie didn't know how to gauge the sincerity of Elizabeth's regret. "It certainly is" was all she said, hoping that would prompt further commentary. When it didn't, Julie continued: "I think your husband's point about the new building being a monument to both his parents was really good. I'm sure the board of trustees will want to pursue that."

"You'll be getting the rest of the money, Stevie said, so your board ought to do something."

Stevie! Julie thought. Mary Ellen was so insistent on calling her son Steven; Mary Ellen's daughter-in-law obviously didn't agree.

"Yes, I understand from Henry LaBelle that Steven is going to ask the probate court to release the rest of the gift right away. That's very generous of you."

"Oh, I have nothing to do with it. It's Stevie's money, and he's welcome to use it however he likes."

Julie didn't think it would be worth pointing out that the $500,000 was Mary Ellen's pledge, not her son's gift. "He'll get plenty," Elizabeth continued. "Of course you would have gotten more if his mother had changed things, but then."

Julie's mouth, quite literally, dropped open. She wasn't sure what words should come out of it. Was she supposed to know that Mary Ellen considered changing her will to give more to the Ryland Historical Society if Steven and Elizabeth didn't produce an heir? She wasn't going to fall into that trap, but she couldn't resist an indirect try. "I'm not sure what you mean, but then, it's really none of my business."

"No, I suppose not, though I assumed Stevie's mother had told you. Well, it doesn't matter. Excuse me, please, I guess I should circulate."

Julie watched her walk away—not, as she had indicated, toward other guests but toward the left side of the house where, Julie knew, the bedrooms and baths were. Probably needs to use the bathroom, Julie told herself as she studied the woman's retreating form. Elizabeth's was a lot like Mary Ellen's, Julie realized: slim, taut, elegant. Of course she was a lot younger—probably early thirties—and her hair was a dazzling blonde (too dazzling, Julie thought, to be entirely natural, but very striking). She didn't seem too interested in Steven's apparently large inheritance. Or had

Elizabeth deliberately brushed that off because she didn't want to be seen as a gold-digger?

"I thought Elizabeth was here," Steven said in a lost-boy way.

"Oh, she was," Julie replied. "She went that way." Julie pointed toward the door that led to the private part of the house. "I thought your speech at the service was just right," she added. "It must have been so hard for you, but what you said about your mother really evoked her spirit. It was good."

"Thanks. Yeah, it wasn't easy, and like always I said too much and too little. Shouldn't have said that about Mom saying I was a stranger here. And I should have mentioned the reception."

"It was just right, really," Julie assured him.

"Mom never really understood her," Steven continued as if Julie's presence was a fortuitous opportunity for him to work out something that was bothering him. "Mom never worked—outside the home, I mean," he continued, "and she just couldn't get it into her head that Elizabeth does. And she works very hard, with long hours. It was hard for her to get away to come here, even if she had really wanted to."

"What does your wife do?"

"She owns a mortgage company. That's how we met—I'm a broker, and when she was getting started she had a party for people in the business to introduce herself. She's very good at her job, and I still recommend her to my clients, but of course I tell them we're married, even though the business is entirely hers."

"Of course," was all Julie could say.

"Mom would have been a great businesswoman herself, you know, so maybe not having the chance to do something on her own grated her. Well, I should go talk to some others. Thanks for coming, Julie. I know Mom liked you very much. By the way, Henry LaBelle has all the papers ready for me to sign, the petition to the court, so as soon as the land sale closes he'll file them.

He said it might take a couple of weeks, but you should get that money pretty soon."

Before Julie could thank him, Steven walked away and joined a group of old women standing by the window. Of course I should thank him, Julie said to herself, but the way he puts it, it sounds like *I'm* getting the money. And after all, it was what Mary Ellen had wanted. How grateful was she supposed to be?

Chapter 22

Post-funeral receptions were not at the top of the list of social events that Julie felt knowledgeable about, but as she looked around the crowd in the Swanson great room she realized she would soon need to overcome that deficiency. Given the average age—somewhere north of seventy, she guessed—and the fact that so many of the people in the room were connected with the Ryland Historical Society as trustees, volunteers, or members, she imagined a string of post-funeral receptions in her future. One of the things she would have to learn was when to leave. Without a program, or cues from the host, it was hard to know. She decided to follow the crowd, making for the door when others did, but so far there was no sign a mass movement was about to commence. Maybe it was the food, both very good and very abundant, that held them. Certainly Julie was not alone in making lunch, a rather full lunch, out of the provisions heaped on the table and being passed by young men and women in white jackets.

"Pretty good spread," Henry said to Julie as the two of them stood over the food table trying to decide what to add to their plates. "Mary Ellen would have approved—nothing but the best."

"I'm amazed how many times people have said things like that today," Julie said. "About how Mary Ellen would have been pleased."

"Sorry. I guess it's one of those time-worn clichés you revert to at a time like this," the lawyer answered soberly.

"I wasn't criticizing," Julie quickly assured him. "Just an observation. I'm pretty new to this kind of thing."

"Funerals and receptions?"

"Right."

"Get used to it, Julie. Your job is sort of like mine—courting the elderly. Eventually it ends up like this." He gestured around the room. "But it's better to have a nice send-off than a bad one, or none at all. And that's something Mary Ellen would definitely agree with."

"I'm sure she would."

"And speaking of that," LaBelle said quietly, as he added some small quiches and a couple of bacon-wrapped scallops to his plate and then indicated to Julie they should move to a more private spot, "the closing is this afternoon at four. Steven is going to sign the petition to the probate court, and I'll present it tomorrow. I've already talked to the judge, and I don't see a problem. I think he'll release the funds in a couple of weeks at the latest."

"You really think it'll be so fast?"

"There are plenty of assets in the estate, and the pledge is just about the only debt to satisfy, certainly the only big one, so I don't see a problem. Judge Childerson is a life member of the Ryland Historical Society, by the way. He understands. Has Steven mentioned anything more about renaming the building?"

"No more than he said at the funeral. You think that's what he meant?"

"Probably. I can ask him if you like. I'm sure the board would go along with calling it the Daniel and Mary Ellen Swanson Center. Why not?"

"Mary Ellen would really like that," Julie said before she caught herself.

Henry grinned. "Far be it from me to say a word. Fact is, you're right. I suppose we should have thought of that before Steven raised it."

"I guess *I* should have."

"You've got plenty to think about. We trustees need to take some responsibility. But no harm done. We can consider it at the next meeting. I'll suggest it to Howard, though I'm sure he's already thinking about it. What did Elizabeth have to say? I saw you talking to her earlier."

"She said she didn't care what Steven did with the money, as if it were a gift from him instead of Mary Ellen's pledge."

"Doesn't care about the money? That would be a surprise."

"But Steven said she owns a mortgage company. He gave me the impression that she does quite well."

"She does indeed. Very successful, from what I hear. But did you ever hear of anyone having too much money, Julie?"

Before she could answer, Frank Nilsson, who had moved in behind them in their corner, did. "No one I know has that problem," Frank said heartily. "Hello, Julie. Let me introduce my wife, Patty."

A woman who could only be described as frumpy in a loose black dress smiled and reached out her hand to shake Julie's. "Frank's told me about you, Dr. Williamson," she said. "Welcome to Ryland. I'm afraid I'm a little late in that since I know you've been around awhile. I've been meaning to come by and meet you, but you know how the time just flies."

"Julie, please. And I'd love to have you come in to the society. I gather your family's been in Ryland for a long time. I'm sure we have lots of artifacts and papers about them."

"Not as many as you will when Patty gets around to her dad's stuff," Frank said. "She's got boxes of his things. I'll bet there's lots of important stuff relating to Ryland. You ought to get going on that, Patty. I'm sure Julie would be glad to look it over and see what might be valuable to the society."

"That would be great," Julie said. "Any time at all."

"Can't be too soon," Frank said as much to his wife as to Julie. "We're paying to store all those boxes, you know. Might as well get the good stuff to the historical society where it can be useful."

Patty laughed, seemingly oblivious to—or purposely ignoring, Julie thought— her husband's stern and even condescending tone. "I know, there are lots of letters and papers," she said. "I should make that my summer job, going through the boxes. If Frank would be so good as to fetch them back to the house, of course."

"Anytime you like, sweetheart," Frank said. "Except right now." He looked at his watch. "It's almost two, and we've got the closing at four, right, counselor?" He looked over at Henry, who had moved off to the side while Julie talked with the Nilssons.

"That's right," the attorney said. "But I've got the paperwork ready, so there's no rush."

"Well, I don't have everything in order. Luke and I need to meet our lawyer and finish things up, so I'd better head along. You want a ride, Patty?"

"I'm sure I can catch one with someone," she answered. "Go ahead."

"I'll just find Luke; anyone seen him? I'll probably have to pull him away from the food."

"Over there," Julie said, and gestured toward the window where Luke was standing alone without even a plate or glass in his hand.

"Excuse me, then," Frank said. "See you at four, Henry."

When Frank and Luke left, it had the effect on the crowd of a ringing school bell. People shuffled to the buffet table to return used plates, said their thanks and condolences to Steven, and then formed a steady line down the entrance hall and out of the house.

"It's like we were all just waiting for permission," Julie whispered to Dalton, who was behind her in the line. Nickie had to get back to her shop, so Dalton offered to drop her off at her office.

"I didn't see Elizabeth," Dalton said as Julie was fastening the seat belt on the passenger side of his Volvo. "Did she come back after the funeral?"

"Yes; I talked to her, in fact. But she sort of disappeared after that."

"No love lost there."

"I guess not," Julie said. "I didn't know she ran such a successful business."

"Meaning she didn't have a motive to kill her mother-in-law?"

Julie laughed. "I guess most daughters-in-law think they do. All I meant was that she's apparently well off on her own. She told me she really doesn't care what Steven does with his mother's money."

"And you believed her?" Dalton asked as he pulled out of the driveway and turned left down Grander Hill Road.

Julie paused, and Dalton glanced over to see if she had heard his question. "Yeah, I did," she finally responded. "But, still, that doesn't mean she didn't have anything to do with Mary Ellen's death. It's all so complicated. I promised Rich and Mike I wasn't going to keep thinking about this, by the way."

"So why are you?"

"Because I'm involved, Dalton. And the historical society is involved. And it's just such a big puzzle. Who would do such a thing?"

He pulled up in front of Swanson House, and Julie thanked him for the lift. "See you Wednesday," she said as she opened her door.

"Wednesday? Oh right, the building committee. It would be nice if we could go ahead and authorize the next phase at that meeting. But we can't do that until we know about the $500,000 from Mary Ellen."

"I'll check with Henry tomorrow to make sure the closing went through today, and that the judge will let us have the money soon," Julie replied. "It would be nice if at least one part of all this got settled."

Chapter 23

Julie had intended to spend Monday afternoon in the archives to see if the Swanson papers Luke Dyer had been looking at offered any clue to his interest. But catching up on paperwork at her desk consumed the afternoon, and when she had finished it was six o'clock already. So she had gone home instead, vowing to get in early on Tuesday to begin her search. Alone, the night seemed long, and she slept poorly, waking at least three times that she could remember to assure herself the house was empty and the sounds she heard were from outside. A long run at dawn helped, and when she reached her office at 7:30 she felt refreshed and eager to start on the Swanson papers before Tabby arrived.

Opening the vault to retrieve them revived unpleasant memories—distant ones about her fear of being locked in the bank vault when as a child she had accompanied her father to put items in his safe box, and more recent ones about being briefly but mysteriously locked in this very vault last year. While she didn't consider herself particularly courageous or tough, Julie resented the weakness her claustrophobia represented. Small, tight, dark spaces scared her. No, more than that—they caused her to panic. And that's what bothered her: losing control.

She took a deep breath, assured herself there was no danger, and used the two keys to open the door and then swiftly stepped inside. Just as swiftly, she retrieved the Swanson box and carried it to the large worktable in the center of the room, placed her yellow pad at her side, and began extracting papers from the box.

By 8:30 Julie had filled four pages with penciled notes, mostly questions she needed to answer to understand the people referenced in the letters. By beginning with the items on top, she assumed she was following Luke's trail through the papers. His interest was now obvious: Birch Brook. Although the letters referred sometimes to "the river property" and sometimes to "the brook land," Julie was sure from the context that the subject was the 430-acre parcel of land on Birch Brook. Now this is getting interesting, she said to herself.

She jumped at the sound of Tabby's voice.

"Oh, it's you, Dr. Williamson!" Tabby exclaimed. She was standing in the doorway at the top of the stairs. "I couldn't think of who would be here at this hour of the morning!"

"Sorry to startle you," Julie said, despite the fact that she was startled, too. "I came in early to look at these papers, and I guess I lost track of the time."

"I'm early," Tabby said. "I'm sorry if I bothered you."

Julie decided she had to bring this round of apologies to an end. "I'm glad you're here because I'd like to make copies of some of these. Do you think they're too fragile?"

Tabby put her oversize purse on her desk and came to the worktable to look at the papers Julie had put in a separate pile. "I don't see any problem. These are fine. Do you want me to copy them for you?"

"Please. But there's no hurry. I should get to work downstairs. Should I just put this box back in the vault?" Julie turned to look at the open door of the vault, hoping Tabby would agree to do the task herself.

"Why don't you just leave the box here on the table, and after I've made the copies I'll put the originals back in and return everything to the vault at the same time."

"That's great," Julie said with genuine relief. "I'll pick up the copies later."

"I'll bring them down."

Julie could hear voices in the outer office when she reached the bottom of the stairs from the library. Mrs. Detweiller and Henry LaBelle were standing by the secretary's desk.

"Her door's open, so I assume she's around somewhere," Mrs. Detweiller said.

"I'll wait a bit and see if she turns up," Henry said.

"And here she is," Julie said as she entered the office. "I was upstairs in the library."

"She's early," the secretary said in her customary accusing tone.

"Do you have a few minutes?" Henry asked in Julie's direction. "We can do it later if you like."

"This is a good time," Julie said. "I was going to call you this morning anyway."

"Ah, great minds! I just wanted you to know the closing went fine yesterday," he said as they entered her office. "The money's in the estate account, and I've got an appointment with Judge Childerson at eleven this morning to formally present Steven's petition. I'll give you a ring when I get a reading from him, but I wanted you to know everything's moving along. Dalton told me the building committee's meeting tomorrow and he's anxious to get the next phase authorized."

"We all are. But I have another question."

"Shoot."

"About Birch Brook. I've been looking through some of the Swanson family papers that Mary Ellen donated. It looks like that property had a funny history. I just wondered if you know about that."

"Welcome to New England!" Henry said. "Real estate is our major industry, and every piece of land has a 'funny history.' I know all about the Birch Brook parcel since I just handled the closing. We researched the title back to the Abenaki, or so it seemed. What did you want to know?"

"It looks to me like the Swansons and the Dyers sort of traded that land back and forth."

"That's one way of putting it. Herbert Swanson—that would be Mary Ellen's husband's grandfather—owned an adjoining parcel farther west along the river, and Luke's great-grandfather—Leonard, if I'm remembering right—had an adjoining parcel east of there. So they had a dispute about the land in between—what became the Birch Brook property. That was in the 1890s. They went to court over it, and Swanson won, based on some sort of survey."

"But I heard that Luke was mad about having to buy the land from Mary Ellen because his father had owned it."

"That's right. It changed hands in the Depression. Old Dan was pretty stressed financially, like a lot of folks around here who were land-rich but otherwise poor."

"I'm reading some stuff on that," Julie said. "We got all these papers from a Dr. Tabor, who practiced here then, and I thought it would be interesting to see what the Depression was like in a small town like Ryland."

"Not very pretty, I'll bet."

"Well, I'm just getting started," she said sheepishly, thinking of how little she had actually accomplished—and seeing on her desk the green folder that Tabby had given her with some additional Tabor letters. "But I'm sure things were tough."

"Probably why Old Dan sold the land to the Dyers then. But then Paul—that's Luke's dad—sold it back to Dan—Mary Ellen's husband—in 1997. That's why Luke's mad. If his dad had kept it in the family, Luke wouldn't have had to join up with Frank to buy it yesterday so they can do the condo development."

"Why did Paul Dyer sell it?"

"I have no idea. I came to Ryland that year, but I didn't represent the Swansons until two years later, when their old attorney died. Maybe that's in the Swanson letters you mentioned."

"You think Luke didn't know, and is trying to find out now?"

"Hard to say. Maybe you should just ask him."

"Or find out by reading the rest of the papers," Julie mused. "I was having trouble sorting it all out. Hold on a second."

Julie quickly jotted notes on a yellow pad and then placed it in front of the attorney.

> 1890s: Herbert Swanson (Dan's grandfather) owned land west along river; Leonard Dyer (Luke's great-grandfather) owned land east along river; current Birch Brook parcel was between and disputed; they went to court, Swanson got Birch Brook.
>
> Depression: Old Dan Swanson (Dan's father) sold Birch Brook to Paul Dyer (Luke's father).
>
> 1997: Paul Dyer sold it back to Dan Swanson for $700,000.
>
> This year: Frank Nilsson and Luke Dyer buy from Mary Ellen Swanson for $2.5M.

"That looks right to me," LaBelle said. "But why is this important?"

Before Julie could respond, there was a knock at the door. "It's for you, Mr. LaBelle," Mrs. Detweiller said when Julie opened the door. "Mr. Swanson's calling. He said he tried you at your office and they said you were here. He says it's urgent."

"You can use my phone," Julie said.

"Good morning, Steven," the attorney said after Mrs. Detweiller transferred the call to Julie's phone. The look on his face told Julie something was wrong. "Just now? That's strange . . . But I'm not a criminal lawyer. I can recommend one, but do you think that's necessary? Maybe it's just routine."

Julie felt uncomfortable listening in, but her curiosity trumped that feeling.

"Okay, I'll stop by and see what's happening. I'll call you from there—you're at the house, right? Okay. Don't worry; I'm sure there's a simple explanation. I'll talk to you shortly."

Henry returned the phone to the cradle and sat silently for a few seconds, apparently collecting his thoughts. Julie asked, "Something wrong?"

"Not sure. Seems strange to me: Mike went to the Swansons' this morning and asked Elizabeth to come to the police station to answer some questions. Steven's upset. As I told him, I don't do criminal law, although I am the family lawyer, so I think I'd better go over to the station and see what's happening. I'll get back to you later about the probate situation," he said as he left.

"Probate?" Julie said aloud. "What about Elizabeth?"

CHAPTER 24

"Tabby left these for you," Mrs. Detweiller said after Henry left and Julie was sitting at her desk thinking. The secretary handed over a pile of papers.

"Thanks, Mrs. Detweiller. Tabby didn't need to rush; I told her not to."

"Oh," the secretary added as she walked toward the door, "your friend called—Mr. O'Brian. While you were with Mr. LaBelle. I told him you couldn't be disturbed."

Having a secretary for the first time ever had seemed to Julie a wonderful perk when she started the job last year. Since then, she had every reason to be pleased with Mrs. Detweiller's typing and filing skills; yes, on the whole, Julie had to admit, Mrs. Detweiller was just fine. But why, then, did the secretary drive her to distraction with her implied criticisms, her innuendos, her formality that made "Mrs. Detweiller" and "Dr. Williamson" their customary forms of address? Maybe those reasons are enough, Julie thought angrily as she punched in Rich's number on her phone.

What had just happened made Julie even more eager than usual to talk to Rich, so when his message came on she was both disappointed and irked. Instead of relaying the recent news she left a short confirmation that she was returning his call. Which is pretty obvious, she said to herself after hanging up. Then she decided it was just as well he wasn't available; she knew he was becoming impatient with her involvement in the murder. And maybe he's right, she thought. Maybe . . .

"It's almost noon, Dr. Williamson," Mrs. Detweiller said sharply after knocking on the door to Julie's office. "You have a tour. In case you forgot."

Julie walked quickly to Holder House and arrived just as the first several people were coming out of the bus. She really hated to think she was already putting her tour talk on autopilot, but she was grateful that she had enough of a script in her head. Unfortunately, it was the wrong script. The tour was a garden club from Medina, Ohio, a fact Julie would have known had she spent a few moments looking over the booking form before she left her office. It was doubly unfortunate that Julie neither knew nor cared about flowers. But if she didn't have flowers in common with the group, she did have Ohio. And she made the most of it; but somehow telling the thirty people assembled for their tour about growing up in southern Ohio didn't seem to make up for not knowing the flowering dates of the shrubs that several asked her about as they walked around Holder House before going in.

"It's a different zone, anyway," one of the women said curtly. "Medina is way far north of the river. Zone five. You must have grown up in Zone six."

Having not the faintest idea what the woman meant, Julie smiled and hurried the group inside to the welcome area that displayed artifacts of various Ryland's history. She was relieved to see Mabel Hanson, a volunteer, in the gift shop. Mabel was also responsible for the society's gardens. "After I do the general introduction, Mabel, maybe you could take them through our gardens? You know everything about them, and that's what they really want to hear about."

Mabel agreed, and Julie finished off the local-history bit of the tour in record time and turned the group over to the volunteer, relieved but still disappointed in herself for neglecting to prepare. On top of that, as she walked back to her office she continued to have doubts about whether she should pursue her growing interest in Mary Ellen's murder investigation. Preoccupied with her thoughts, she was extremely surprised to find Steven Swanson pacing in front of the secretary's empty desk, looking, as seemed usual for him, lost and uncomfortable.

"I'm sorry if you've been waiting long," Julie said. "Mrs. Detweiller is out to lunch, and I was doing a tour at Holder House. What can I do for you?"

"These are for you," he said, pointing at four large cardboard boxes stacked outside the door to her office. "Last night after the funeral seemed like a good time to pack them." Julie looked puzzled. "Mostly just old papers, letters, and documents," Steven said. "Mom had gathered them up but hadn't boxed them yet. I figured she was planning to give them to the historical society."

"Oh! Of course. Your mother had already given us some, and I knew there were more. That's very kind of you, especially under the circumstances."

"Circumstances? Which one do you mean—Mom's funeral, or Elizabeth?"

Julie knew a plea for help when she heard it. "Do you have a minute to come in, Steven?" She gestured toward her office door, he meekly followed, and she closed the door behind them.

"I really appreciate your bringing in the papers," she said.

"Well, I know that's what Mom wanted, and last night it was pretty hard to concentrate on anything, so I just boxed them up. I was planning to call you to see when I could bring them in, but then Elizabeth . . . well, I guess you've probably heard."

"I hope everything's okay."

"Elizabeth's back at the house. Mind if I sit down?"

"Please."

"I don't know what Barlow was thinking. But maybe it was the state cops. They said some kid saw someone who looked like Elizabeth—a blonde woman, anyway—talking to Mom at the construction site. Before . . ."

"Last Tuesday?"

"Right. Before Mom was killed." He paused. "Anyway, it couldn't have been Elizabeth, because she was at the house with me. Well, she told them that, and then Barlow asked me to verify it. Which of course I did. So Elizabeth's back at the house, but they told her to stay in Maine for twenty-four hours because they need to do some more checking. This is all nuts. And Elizabeth's fit to be tied."

"I don't blame her," Julie said. "But it sounds to me like everything's straightened out now."

"I hope so. Elizabeth just wants to get back home and back to work. She doesn't want to set foot in this town—or state—again." Before Julie could think of a response, Steven stood up. "I shouldn't keep you. Just wanted to leave off those boxes."

"Thanks again, and if there's anything I can do, just let me know."

He extended his hand and shook hers weakly, then walked distractedly out the door before Julie could ask him if he wanted a receipt for tax purposes for the papers. Well, she decided, she could do that later. Julie found it hard to believe Steven was essentially her own age. She thought of him as a boy, a boy reeling now that his mother was killed and his wife seemed so unsympathetic. But that wasn't her concern now; the boxes were.

She was opening the first one when Mrs. Detweiller returned from lunch. "I'll get someone to take them upstairs," the secretary said after Julie explained them. "They shouldn't be cluttering things up here."

"I'll just put them in my office for now," Julie said. "I should look them over quickly anyway."

"If that's what you'd like."

Julie was sliding the last of the four boxes into her office when Mike walked into the reception area.

"Thanks," she said to the policeman's offer to help with the box. "This is the last one." She decided not to tell him about the boxes' contents. "But I suspect you didn't come by to move boxes."

"Not quite," he admitted. "Mind if I close the door? It's been a busy morning."

"Really?"

"Frankly, I'm pissed, if you'll excuse my French. Those stupid staties!" he answered. "But forget I just said that. Look, if you have a few minutes I need to ask a couple of questions."

"Shoot."

"Okay, I know we went through this last week, and everything checked out, but I have to ask you again about the morning Mrs. Swanson was killed, between nine-thirty and ten-thirty."

"I was at the Inn, checking on arrangements for the lunch. You confirmed it."

"Right. But let me just ask again: When you were over at the construction site putting those shovels out, did you happen to notice a woman around—not Mrs. Swanson, a younger woman, blonde?"

"So your interest in my hair color wasn't exactly personal?" Julie asked with a sly smile.

Mike blushed. "Sorry about that. I got it straight now, but I had to check."

"Why the interest in a blonde?"

"Let's just say someone thought there was a young blonde woman at the construction site that morning, maybe around nine forty-five or ten, and maybe arguing with Mrs. Swanson."

"And you thought it was me?"

"Come on, Julie, you know I have to check things. The State Police detective interviewed the kid who said he saw them. I know the kid, and he's totally unreliable—a troublemaker, most likely looking for his fifteen minutes of fame—but the detective wanted to pursue it. Of course he has to follow every lead. Anyway, yesterday I just had to be sure the kid hadn't seen you there when you were arranging the shovels. I didn't think you were blonde, but . . ."

"I understand. No, I'm not now and never have been blonde. And, to answer your question, I didn't see anyone at the construction site—no one at all, let alone a blonde woman, let alone Elizabeth Myerson."

"What does *that* mean?"

She explained that Henry had been in her office when Steven called, and then about Steven's own recent visit and his report about his wife.

"Small town," the policeman said. "So you know we talked to her, and Steven confirmed she was at the Swanson house all morning. But he's her husband, so we have to take what he says with a grain of salt."

"And that's why you're questioning me?"

"Just confirming. Absolutely no one around? Not even, say, a kid on a bike, maybe back in the woods?"

"Was the kid in the woods when he saw a blonde?"

"Just take a minute to think about it again. When you were there Tuesday morning, was there any chance that a woman, blonde or not, was anywhere around? Or anyone in the woods? Could you have heard a noise from there?"

Julie closed her eyes. The power of suggestion was strong, she knew, so she tried not to imagine the scene the police had been told about and instead blanked her mind and concentrated on that morning. But, except for the sharp image of the yellow backhoe, the blank remained.

"Sorry. I'm pretty sure I didn't see anyone, or hear anyone in the woods, but I honestly can't be definitive."

"Sure," he said. "You can't rule it out, but you can't remember. That a fair statement?"

"Yes."

"Okay, that'll do as far as I'm concerned. I'll tell the detective. Maybe he'll move on to something else."

"Like the shovel? Any luck on that?"

"Nothing. It's possible it'll never turn up. Anyway, thanks for your statement. And I'm sorry about—"

"About suspecting me? I don't take it personally, Mike. I know you have to check everything. As a matter of fact, I have some ideas . . ."

"Hold it! You said you were going to stay out of this," he said, but then sighed, and added, "If you have any solid information, of course I need to hear it."

"I still think it's about the land, but I don't have any 'solid information.' Just too many loose ends."

"The land?"

"Birch Brook—the condo development. Mary Ellen could have backed out up till the fifth of July."

"LaBelle told me that."

"So isn't that a good motive?"

"For?"

"Frank Nilsson and Luke Dyer had a lot at stake. And the land itself is pretty weird—I mean, as to who owns it."

"I wouldn't go around naming people as suspects if I were you. If Nilsson or Dyer found out, they could—"

"Of course not!" Julie interrupted. "I'm just confiding my suspicions in you."

"I hope so. So what do you know about the land?"

"A little." She proceeded to describe the shifting ownership of Birch Brook as she had sketched it out, with Henry's help. "And Luke's been looking at the Swanson papers here in the historical society," she concluded. "He doesn't strike me as your basic amateur historian. I think he knows there's something funny about the ownership."

"Julie, I think you've learned that land sales in New England are a form of blood sport, but that's not exactly news to folks who grew up here. And you've discovered that maybe Nilsson and Dyer had something to gain—or something to not lose—if Mrs. Swanson was out of the way before the fifth of July. But motive isn't the only thing."

"So maybe you need to find out what Frank and Luke were doing last Tuesday morning."

"Maybe. But you can't rule out Steven and Elizabeth Swanson."

"Myerson, Elizabeth Myerson," she corrected him. "And isn't it strange that he's her alibi for Tuesday morning? That means she's *his*. Or they could both . . ."

"I thought you were interested in Birch Brook, Julie."

"Well, I am. I mean, I think the land's involved in this somehow, which makes Frank and Luke suspicious. At least to me. But you've got to admit that Steven and Elizabeth aren't exactly in the clear. Not that I think Steven could possibly have done it. But you have to look at everything."

"Gee, Julie, I'll try to remember that. Meantime, maybe you could go back to playing director of the Ryland Historical Society and I'll keep playing at being a cop. Which I'm off to do right now. See you later, I'm sure."

"And then there's the shovel, Mike. We've got to find that."

"Drop the *we* . . ."

"But don't forget about Frank and Luke. If you could just find out where they were last Tuesday . . ."

"See you."

CHAPTER 25

"Mr. Townsend for you," Mrs. Detweiller said through the door left open when Mike went out.

Damn that man! Julie said to herself when she finished the phone conversation with the chairman of the trustees. Of course it made sense to have another board meeting. There were two big items of business: to review whatever the building committee recommended about proceeding on the project, and to consider renaming the new center for both Dan and Mary Ellen. Obviously Howard needed to call a meeting. But why did he have to do it for four o'clock on a Friday afternoon? Julie hoped to be on the road to Orono then. Howard hadn't even asked if it was convenient for her.

She'd have to let Rich know. If the meeting didn't run too long, she could still be in Orono Friday night. But how long would the meeting last? Even under the best of circumstances, the twisty highway between Ryland and Bangor was slow going, but on a late Friday afternoon in the middle of summer, it would be really slow because of all the recreational vehicles and sightseeing tourists. To take her mind off her anger at Howard and off the frustrating trip she was already imagining, Julie decided to move the four boxes of new Swanson papers to the archives. A little physical exertion would feel good, she decided.

"I think she's free, Mr. Dyer," she heard Mrs. Detweiller say.

Julie quickly moved to stand in front of the boxes to keep Luke from seeing them—not that he'd know what they were, but better not to take a chance.

"Hello, Luke," she said as cheerfully as she could when he came through the door. Would he wonder why she was shielding the boxes?

"I just brought the bill by," he said. "For the excavation. Left it with your secretary, but since you're here I wonder if we could talk for a moment." Julie closed the door and beckoned him toward a chair—one facing in the other direction from the four boxes. "I've been using your library," he said after he sat. "But you know that. Tabby Preston told me just now that you were looking at the letters I read. I'd like to know why."

It was a perfectly reasonable question, Julie realized, but Luke's tone heightened it. She couldn't really describe the tone as menacing, but it was far from friendly.

"Well, I'm the director here, and I try to know what we have in our collections and how they can be useful to the community and to researchers, and so of course I'm interested in the papers that you—"

"Well, let's just cut the crap. You knew I was looking at the Swanson letters, and you went in there and read the ones I looked at. When I realized someone else had been in the box, I asked Tabby about it. And now I'm just asking you a simple question: What's your interest in those letters?"

"The Swanson family is very important to the historical society, especially now, and I just wanted to see the nature of the papers, see if there was material we could use when we open the new center." Julie congratulated herself silently on such a clever answer. Luke, unfortunately, didn't share her view.

"So what took you so long? How come you didn't look at them till you knew I was?"

"Luke, really, I'm sorry you're upset about this. It really is just a coincidence. I should have looked at them before, but to be honest I wasn't aware we even had them until Tabby mentioned you were using them. I should have told you that up front, but, frankly, I'm new here, and I didn't want to look silly for not knowing what we have in the collections."

Julie had often heard people say that honesty could be disarming, but she wasn't prepared for the immediate effect it had on Luke. "That makes sense," he said in a much friendlier tone. "People here can be tough on folks from away. I can see your point. But you could have told me that when I asked."

"I'm sorry. But really, that's all there is to it." No reason to test the old proverb a second time, she decided.

"Okay then. Thanks for your time." He moved for the door, apparently satisfied.

"I hope you're finding what you want," Julie couldn't help adding.

"Not yet. But I will. Invoice is with your secretary. No hurry, but we charge interest if you don't pay in fifteen days."

Had she imagined it, Julie pondered, or did Luke glance at the four boxes when he said he'd find what he was looking for? How could he know? Mrs. Detweiller was an obvious source. Steven could be, too, for all Julie knew. Or maybe she really had just imagined that Luke was interested in the boxes. But she knew her own interest was real. Unfortunately, so was her watch, which told her it was past 4:30. Tabby would be gone, and Julie could hear Mrs. Detweiller closing drawers to signal she, too, was ready to leave. And that would mean all the volunteers were gone and the Ryland Historical Society was about to shut down for the day. So if Julie planned to secure the new Swanson papers in the vault, she was going to have to do it herself. Of course, she could just keep them in her office. She knew it was bad practice, but it was perfectly safe with the security alarm on and all the doors to Swanson House locked. Tomorrow she would talk to Tabby about them and get someone to do the heavy lifting. She locked Swanson House, set the security alarm, and walked home.

Chapter 26

A nursing student who was Julie's dorm mate in college had told her that hospital staff dread the period from three to five o'clock in the morning because that's when weak patients tend to die. Something about body temperature, or heart rate, Julie couldn't remember exactly. But the fact—if it really was that—stuck with her the way odd bits of information always do.

The clock beside her bed read 3:20. It would be nice to think her waking was the result of body temperature or pulse, but she knew the cause was more direct: the soft but insistent scraping of the lower branches of a large pine tree against the house just below the window of her bedroom. Rich had identified the noise last week when it had awakened her then, and she had in turn awakened him. Now, the branches kept rustling, swishing, hitting the siding, waking her, and then keeping her awake.

This was the worst night Julie had ever spent alone in Harding House. As on the other nights, before going to bed she had dutifully made the rounds downstairs, checking and double-checking windows and doors until she was satisfied that the house was secure. From eleven until three she had actually slept deeply, but the pine branches put an end to that. For the next thirty minutes or so she turned and tossed, telling herself that at any moment she would slip back down into sleep. But then the birds arrived, encouraged by the breaking dawn. After another quarter-hour spent trying to identify the sounds of individual birds, she gave up and decided to join them in greeting the day. It was still too dark to run safely, but the absence of full daylight didn't deter her from breakfast.

As she ate her cereal, she fiddled listlessly with the jigsaw puzzle she had started the night before—the map of Maine, which Rich had given her along with the grill as a housewarming present. She was working her way north, from York County to Aroostook County, and hadn't yet gotten to Ryland. She couldn't concentrate and got up to pour a second cup of coffee. She stood at the counter and thought about her less than brilliant performance as a tour guide yesterday with the garden club. She had become more and more confident, learning about Ryland and its history, picking up interesting stories from volunteers and her own reading of documents and old newspapers, developing an entertaining and informative line of patter for visitors. But yesterday's experience had thrown her for a loop. Had she just glanced at the booking form, she would have known it was a garden group, and while she couldn't make herself expert on the society's plantings, she could have made sure Mabel Hanson would be available to handle the flora. Luckily Mabel had been there, but luck was something Julie knew she couldn't count on.

Instead of concentrating on her job, she was spending too much time thinking about suspects, speculating about motives, digging into town history not so she would be a better tour guide and director, but so she could figure out who killed Mary Ellen—and why. And she couldn't say her efforts were paying off. The murder was already more than a week old, and Julie knew that as more time passed the odds of identifying the killer waned. If Mike and the Maine State Police were unsuccessful in that time, what hope had she of sorting it all out?

Maybe, she decided, it was a good thing that those pine branches woke her. The boxes of Swanson family papers Steven had brought in yesterday were there waiting for her in her office. She abandoned the puzzle, left the dishes in the sink, showered and dressed rapidly, and entered her office at five-thirty, feeling that early hours were becoming too common. And it was going to be a long day; the building committee didn't meet till four.

The boxes were where she had left them, just inside the door of her office. She lugged the first one to the long table and began her search. Bills, newspaper clippings, more bills, some canceled checks. The second box contained more of the same. The third box was all letters to and from Dan Swanson. Julie was pleasantly surprised that he had been so orderly; he kept copies of his letters and attached them with paper clips to their responses. Most dealt with business matters of one kind or another—dunning letters to renters tardy in paying up, appeals to the town tax board about assessments, instructions to brokers about buying and selling. Near the bottom of the box was a handwritten letter to Paul Dyer, dated October 12, 1997:

Dear Paul,

Considering the tangled web surrounding the ownership of the river property, I would be pleased to make an offer to you to purchase the land outright and end once and for all the disputes and bad feelings that have arisen over the years between our families because of it. Naturally, once I obtained free and clear title to the land, I would have no further interest in pursuing the matters we discussed on Saturday. You have my word as a Christian and a gentleman that any and all disputes, including the clouded nature of the 1883 survey, would, from my point of view, be put behind us and forever buried in history—a history neither of our families need ever revisit.

Please let me know your intentions. I will instruct my attorney to draw up the necessary papers as soon as I've heard from you.

Sincerely,

Daniel O. Swanson II

It was a copy, not the original. Had the letter ever been sent? There was no appended response. But she knew Paul Dyer had sold the land to Dan Swanson. She extracted from the manila folder the sheet of notes she had written after talking to Henry LaBelle.

> 1890s: Herbert Swanson (Dan's grandfather) owned land west along river; Leonard Dyer (Luke's great-grandfather) owned land east along river; current Birch Brook parcel was between and disputed; they went to court, Swanson got Birch Brook.
>
> Depression: Old Dan Swanson (Dan's father) sold Birch Brook to Paul Dyer (Luke's father).
>
> 1997: Paul Dyer sold it back to Dan Swanson for $700,000.
>
> This year: Frank Nilsson and Luke Dyer buy from Mary Ellen Swanson for $2.5M.

After the 1997 entry, she inserted:

WHY? "Clouded nature of the 1883 survey"; what does this mean? How to find out?

Then she turned back to Dan Swanson's letter. What was all this about "disputes," the "tangled web," the "clouded nature of the 1883 survey"? And what matters—apparently discussed in a conversation between the two men—would Dan Swanson be willing to give his word about dropping?

The letter had such a melodramatic tone, especially concerning the promise to bury the past and not revisit it. And it was so flowery. Did people still write like that in 1997? Julie glanced back through several of the other letters and decided they didn't prove much on that score since their content was mostly straightforward. But the handwriting on all of them matched. She felt confident the letter from Dan Swanson to Paul Dyer was genuine. And very important.

Obviously something funny had gone on with the Birch Brook land, something Dan Swanson was willing to overlook, in return for buying the property at what at least Paul Dyer's son Luke considered too low a price. Is that why Luke was spending time in the Ryland Historical Society archives? Did he know—or at least think—this letter existed? Did he have the original? No, because, if so, why would he be looking for this one? Or did he wonder if his father had responded to it, without keeping a copy, and was seeking that? If she could think of a way to do it, Julie would ask Luke. But right now she couldn't.

In fact, right now all she could think about was Dan Swanson's letter and what to do about it. The first thing was obviously to put it back in the box and put that box and the others where they belonged, where Steven intended them to be—in the archives. First, though, a copy, Julie thought. She needed to make a copy. But here her instincts went to war. One side of her, the side that was trying to solve Mary Ellen's murder, was prepared to march out to the copy machine in Mrs. Detweiller's office, wait for it to warm up, and then make the copy. The other side, her museum professional side, told her to wait till Tabby arrived and could make the copy according to standard procedures, which meant allowing Tabby to examine the paper and be sure that copying was safe. But, it was already a copy, Julie reasoned, and a copy of a copy couldn't do harm. Still, it just didn't feel right to her. It was only 7:30, and Tabby wouldn't be in for another two hours. Well, there was another box, and she might as well take a look at it. She went item by item through the final box and discovered more bills, checks, and short business notes, but nothing more related to Birch Brook or to the Dyers. So she read the 1997 letter again. If I keep this up, she thought, I won't need to make a copy of it—I'll have a copy in my head! After the fourth rereading, Julie decided enough was enough.

She was actually pleased to hear Mrs. Detweiller in the outer office. Tabby followed shortly behind, and Julie was happy that Swanson House was coming to life after the long and quiet early morning she had spent alone. The high school boy working on the grounds for the summer came to carry the boxes of Swanson papers to the library. Julie went upstairs to explain the papers to Tabby and awkwardly worked her way around to requesting a copy of the 1997 letter. "If it's safe to copy, of course," she said.

"It's already a copy, Dr. Williamson," Tabby replied as she examined the sheet of paper. "Nothing fragile."

Julie knew that, but she felt better getting the librarian's permission. So she took the page downstairs, copied it, and returned the "original" to Tabby. "These don't seem to be in any order," the librarian said, looking at the box it had come from, "so I'll just put this on top. The boxes can go in there," she added, directing the boy to place them inside the vault.

"Maybe I should put it where it was, near the bottom of that box," Julie said. If Luke Dyer came today, she didn't want to make it too easy for him to find the letter.

"Whatever you say, Dr. Williamson. Luke said he'd be back today. I should tell him about the new ones."

Julie couldn't come up with a good reason to disagree. She knew why she hoped Luke Dyer would not find the letter, but she just couldn't manage the lie necessary to bring that about. With luck, she said to herself, he wouldn't be in today. If she just had a bit of time, she might be able to figure out the letter's significance before Luke read it.

CHAPTER 27

When Dalton stopped by at 3:45 to talk with her about the upcoming building committee meeting, Julie wasn't sure she could keep her eyes open. It had been such a long day, and she was still agitated about the Dan Swanson letter. She had tried to concentrate on her work, and the tour she had given at noon was, she felt, back to her old standard. But she was definitely drooping.

"The excavation's done, and the foundation should be poured next week. We're off and running, and if the committee agrees, we can recommend full steam ahead," Dalton said to her across her desk.

Dalton's enthusiasm gave Julie an immediate burst of energy. "It *is* exciting, isn't it?" she said. "Such a shame Mary Ellen isn't here to enjoy it."

"Really sad, but you have to admit, Julie, the committee will probably be able to actually accomplish something today. I know that's terrible to say, but just think—we can finally get the Swanson Center under way, and Mary Ellen would have been happy about that, even if she had a few questions."

Julie laughed. "I know what you mean, Dalton. Do you plan to take up the issue of renaming the center for both of them?"

"I thought we should, but obviously that's up to the full board. We meet Friday, right? So if the building committee agrees, we could make that one of our recommendations."

"What else do we need to do today?"

"Just confirm the plan and recommend to the board that the project go ahead. Is the money issue settled?"

"Henry LaBelle said it looks good. The probate judge seemed sympathetic, and Steven Swanson's letter asking him to release the

$500,000 was really important. Henry thinks we'll hear within a week."

"That'll keep Clif at bay. I was afraid he'd resist moving ahead because without Mary Ellen's final gift we'd have to borrow so much. This ought to persuade him."

"I hope so. Um, Dalton? Before the meeting, do we have time to talk about something else?"

Dalton looked at his watch. "If it's short, or we can talk on the way to Holder."

Realizing it was five minutes before four, Julie said there wasn't really time and asked if Dalton would be free afterwards for a few minutes. "Assuming we have a nice short one. I've got a busy night ahead at the inn," Dalton said. "We better go."

When the new Swanson Center was finished, the society would have a comfortable conference room for board and committee meetings, but for now it was forced to set up the classroom in Holder House for such purposes. When Dalton and Julie arrived there, Clif and Mabel, the volunteer whose knowledge of plants Julie had relied on for the recent tour, and a member of the building committee, were waiting.

"Thought maybe I'd got the time wrong," Clif said. "Mabel and I were about to leave."

"It's exactly four," Dalton said with exasperation. "And Loretta's not here yet."

"Never knew her to be on time," Clif said. "Might as well begin."

Julie explained that Loretta had left a message with Mrs. Detweiller that she was running late on school business.

"Like I said," Clif repeated, "might as well begin."

"It's so sad not to have Mary Ellen here," Mabel said as they took their seats at the table.

"Dalton and I were just talking about that," Julie said.

"Should speed things up, though," Clif said. "Mary Ellen did like to ask questions."

"Very good ones," Mabel said.

"Well, it was her money, so I guess she had a right. We going to replace her on this committee?"

"That's up to the board," Julie answered. "But I can see that another member would be a good idea."

"Steven would be wonderful," Mabel said. "Carry on the tradition."

"Don't think he'd be interested," Clif said. "Never was. You heard what he said at the funeral—didn't spend much time here because Mary Ellen didn't like that wife of his. I guess they're married—she doesn't use his name, I understand."

"Of course a lot of the issues are settled," Dalton said, ignoring Clif's remarks. "When you think about it, we may not need to add a member since the design questions have all been answered and our role as a committee now is just to supervise the construction and deal with any change orders. Maybe we should bring this up on Friday and let the board decide? That okay with everyone?"

Clif nodded, as did Julie, but Mabel was about to speak when Loretta entered the room. "Sorry to be late, folks," she said in her pleasant but rushed way. "With school over you'd think I'd be on time for things, but the superintendent called a special meeting. I'm glad you started."

"We were just talking about the committee," Dalton said, and reviewed what they had discussed.

"I'm okay either way," Loretta said. "If it would help to put Steven Swanson on, to sort of keep the family tied in, that's fine with me. But like Dalton says, we probably won't have a lot to do now—not the way we have in the past."

"Let the board decide," Clif said. "What's our business here today, Dalton?"

Dalton summarized what the building committee needed to do.

"Then let's do that," Clif said. "I've got my own business to run."

Dalton reported on the excavation work and said the foundation would be poured within a week. "That's the extent of what the board authorized," he reminded them, "because we hadn't given final approval to the construction documents. Our main goal today is to do that—if we agree, of course—and recommend that the board sign the construction contract."

"What about the money?" Clif asked. "I'm not in favor of a lot of borrowing. Do we have enough in hand now to proceed with only the bridge loan at the end?"

Everyone in the room knew what Clif was asking: Could they count on the remainder of Mary Ellen Swanson's gift? "You want to answer that, Julie?" Dalton asked.

"Well, you're all aware that Mary Ellen had $500,000 left on her pledge. Some of you also know that Mary Ellen told me she expected to pay that off in full this summer. Naturally, with her . . . death, there was a question about that. Not about getting the money, but whether we would have to wait till her estate was probated. Steven Swanson very kindly asked the probate judge to release the half-million dollars to the society as soon as possible, before the whole estate is settled, and Henry LaBelle has talked to the probate judge and is pretty confident that will happen. So I think—"

"The cash is there?" Clif interrupted.

"Soon will be, yes."

"Birch Brook closed, I heard. Guess that will take care of it."

"I suppose that's right," Julie continued, "but anyway, my understanding is that we'll be getting the rest of the gift pretty soon."

"Donny Childerson?" Holdsworth asked.

"I'm sorry?"

"Donny Childerson. He the probate judge?"

"I think Henry said it was a Judge Childerson, yes."

"That's okay, then. Donny's a Ryland boy. He'll do what's right. I'm satisfied, Dalton. Move we recommend the board sign the final construction contract."

"Second!" Loretta sang out.

"Okay, it's been moved and seconded," Dalton said. "Any discussion? I guess that really means, are we satisfied, as a committee, with all the plans and the construction documents?"

"Now if Mary Ellen were here," Clif said, "that question would be worth asking. Fact is, the rest of us are satisfied. Have been for some time. I call the question."

"Okay, Clif," Dalton said. "But let's be sure we're all in agreement here. Loretta?"

"Absolutely. It's a great plan, great design. I say let's do it."

"Mabel?"

"All the landscaping seems fine to me. I don't really know much about the rest, but you're the architect, Dalton, and I assume you're satisfied."

"Delighted, really. But I'm only one person. Any other concerns?"

They voted unanimously to recommend proceeding. Julie felt relieved. Then Clif spoke: "Now I assume the board will have to have some assurance about the money. I think it's fair for the building committee to make the recommendation, but I'm sure as a full board we'll need some assurances. Henry going to be there on Friday?"

Julie said that Henry LaBelle would be present. "Maybe he'll have spoken to Donny by then," Clif continued. "We finished, Dalton?"

"Just one more item," Dalton said. "Most of you heard Steven Swanson's comment at the funeral about how the project honored both his father and mother. Would the building committee care to go on record as recommending to the board that we name the building the Daniel and Mary Ellen Swanson Center?"

"Hear, hear!" Loretta Cummings said. "I so move."

"Second," Mabel said. There was no discussion. After a unanimous vote, Dalton declared the meeting adjourned. Clif stood up and walked to where Julie was sitting.

"Don't suppose you've heard any more about those shovels?" he asked in a quiet voice.

"As a matter of fact, I haven't. The police chief still has them, I guess. Or maybe the State Police. I can check again, Clif." Having decided, uninvited, to call him by his first name, Julie was intent on being consistent, even though it required extra effort not to say *Mister* Holdsworth as she had for the past year.

"I'd appreciate that. Don't know why they're so interested in my shovels, but that's cops for you."

Clif walked away, nodded to Dalton, and exited. Loretta and Mabel had already gone. "Pretty fast," Dalton said as he glanced at his watch. "Only 4:35. So I've got time now if you want to talk."

"Maybe we could go back to my office if that's okay. I'd like to show you something. In deepest confidence, I might add, or Mike will have me thrown in jail just to shut me up."

Chapter 28

"Fascinating," Dalton said when he read the copy of Dan Swanson's letter to Paul Dyer. "What a strange way to say things—all that about being a Christian and a gentleman. Sounds like something from the Victorian period, doesn't it?" Julie agreed. "What do you make about this 'tangled web' and family disputes business?"

"That the Birch Brook property created a lot of problems between the Swansons and the Dyers," Julie answered.

"You told me that the other day, but aside from confirming what you knew, what does this letter add?"

"Well, not much, I guess. But when you put everything together, doesn't it seem like this land deal is at the center of things?"

"Center of what things?"

"Mary Ellen's murder."

"Whoa! That's a big leap! You'll have to walk me through this."

She did, pointing out that Mary Ellen Swanson's murder occurred conveniently two days before the cancellation provision expired, and that both Luke Dyer and Frank Nilsson had a lot to gain by the expiration.

"Sure, you said that before, and I don't disagree. But what's the point about the dispute over the land—and this letter?"

"Luke Dyer wasn't happy that he and Nilsson had to buy the land from Mary Ellen. If his father hadn't sold it back to Dan Swanson, Dyer would have pocketed a lot more money."

"But they *did* buy it. What good is it going to do now if someone finds out there was something funny about the deal between Dan and Paul?"

"So you agree there *was* something funny?"

"It's a strange letter, I'll grant that. And I suppose if there was some kind of pressure—blackmail or whatever you want to call it—when Paul Dyer sold to Dan Swanson, then maybe Luke would have some kind of case. I don't know; I'm not a lawyer. I agree there's something funny here. I just don't see what good it does to pursue it now."

"Luke Dyer *is* pursuing it." Julie explained that Luke was reading the Swanson papers in the archives.

"Well, *that* is interesting," Dalton said. "Okay, for the sake of argument, I'll concede that Luke may have smelled a rat. But the fact is that if he did—if he thought he had some chance to claim the land for himself and thereby save having to buy it from Mary Ellen—then Luke would have no interest at all in preventing Mary Ellen from exercising her option to cancel the deal. On the contrary, he would have had a lot to gain—delay the deal, find out about the sale back in '97, and then get title to it himself. If he could."

"That's true. I see what you mean. But Luke is in this with Frank, so both of them would have a good reason to question Mary Ellen's ownership. If Luke could lay claim to the land, Frank might have benefited, too—paid a lower price, worked out a different split on the equity, whatever."

"It's one thing to question her ownership. It's another to kill her."

"I know. I just haven't figured that out. Mike is going to check their alibis for last Tuesday morning. At least then we'll know if either of them could have done it."

"What about the son and daughter-in-law? You were thinking before they might have done it."

"Steven already provided an alibi for her, which also covers him—kind of convenient."

"How do you know that?"

"You didn't know the police questioned Elizabeth?"

"Hey, I run an inn; it keeps me busy. What happened?"

Julie explained about Elizabeth's being questioned and about Steven's alibi for her.

"So you're back to Luke and Frank?"

"I guess so; I don't really know. Thanks for listening, anyway. I guess I sound a little loony about all this." When Dalton didn't immediately disagree, Julie continued: "I should probably just forget all this and wait and see what the police determine."

"I couldn't say it better. I've got to get going. Thanks for showing me the letter. I'll give it some thought."

It was five-thirty when Dalton left her office, and Julie dutifully checked to see that the building was empty—Tabby and Mrs. Detweiller both gone for the day, no volunteers working in the back office. She was ready to lock up but went back to her office to retrieve the folder with her notes. She had added to it the copy of Dan Swanson's letter to Paul Dyer. After setting the security code, she walked behind the building to take a look at the construction site. A pile of metal forms had been placed by the far trench. Tomorrow they would be inserted into the excavation, and within a few more days the cement would be poured. That phase would be complete, and the next phase would, she was sure, be approved by the board on Friday, making it likely that the structure would be up and closed in by the late fall. At long last the Swanson Center was on its way to becoming a reality!

As she walked across the site toward the street, Julie saw a pickup truck pull away from the curb and drive out to Main Street. Pickups were hardly rare in Ryland, but she was sure she recognized it as the one she and Rich had seen at Birch Brook on Saturday—Luke's. Well, that too was hardly a surprise. He might have been making a final inspection of the excavation that his company had been responsible for. Then again, it might have been someone else.

At home, Julie put the folder on the kitchen table and poured a glass of wine. She took the wine and the remote phone into the garden. Over the last few days the temperature had gradually returned to normal, but it was still pleasantly cool. Julie's talk with Dalton had temporarily revived her, but sitting down with a glass of wine she suddenly felt exhausted. She reminded herself she had started the day around four a.m. A quick call to Rich, a light supper, and an early bedtime sounded just right. Rich had been so good last night when she had called to tell him about the late-afternoon board meeting on Friday. He had immediately suggested he come to Ryland for the weekend, but Julie had felt guilty enough about not holding up her part of their deal that she suggested they wait till tonight to make plans. Nothing today, though, had made her driving late Friday to Orono seem more attractive. She was happy then, during their phone conversation—brief because Rich had to go out to an evening lecture—to hear that he was still willing to come to Ryland. After hanging up Julie concocted a salad from the remains of Rich's cooking last weekend, worked a bit more on the State of Maine puzzle, made multiple rounds of the house to assure herself all windows and doors were secure, and finally dragged herself up the steps to bed at nine, far earlier than she normally did, but it felt more like midnight to her tonight.

She was out at once and slept soundly until she woke with a start. Damn those pine branches, she practically said aloud. But as she emerged more fully into wakefulness, Julie wasn't so sure it was the tree branches she had heard. A door slowly opening or closing? Not possible—she had locked them all. Footsteps? Come on, she told herself, you're just letting your imagination roam.

She sat up in bed and concentrated her hearing. There was no wind, she was sure now, so the sounds couldn't be the result of the swaying branches. She kept concentrating, trying to make out the source. It *is* a door, she suddenly realized—the screen door in the kitchen. A solid wooden door opened from the kitchen to the back garden, but Rich had found a screen door that fit the opening and installed it so they could open the main kitchen door and get air through the room. Like most screen doors, it was a little flimsy and didn't make a perfect match with the opening, but it was tight enough to do the job of holding Maine's armada of bugs at bay. The screen door itself didn't lock, and you had to give it an extra push to close it. But the main one had a standard lock, and she was certain she had checked it before coming to bed. But then she had been so tired; was it possible she hadn't?

Yes, she was sure now the noise came from the kitchen. And it was no longer just the door—it was footsteps, the sound of someone moving on the creaky kitchen floor. Don't move, she told herself. Stay still, wait, listen. The digital alarm clock by the bed read 2:48. By the clock was the phone. Could she turn quietly and reach it to call the police? Would whoever was in the kitchen hear her? And leave? Or come upstairs? Was that creaking coming from the steps—was someone coming up? Surely not!

As her mind alternated rapidly among the possibilities, she couldn't settle on a likely one. Even more than her confusion, Julie felt incredibly cold. Despite the blankets and the moderate temperature, she was shaking, responding to a cold that seemed to reside at the very center of her body, a cold deeper and more penetrating than any she had felt in the middle of winter. Shouldn't she be sweating? she asked herself in an effort to get in touch with her mind, to overcome the icy cold.

As she wrestled with her emotions and pulled the blanket—quietly, slowly—around her, Julie realized the house had gone quiet. She concentrated again. Yes! There were no sounds from below now. But did that mean whoever had been there was gone? Or waiting? Going downstairs would surely be dumb, but how else would she know?

The clock said 2:50. Was it possible so much had happened in a mere two minutes? Could she safely reach the phone? Before she could decide, Julie heard a loud bang—the screen door, she was sure. The screen door *closing!* Without even thinking further, she grabbed for the phone and hit 9-1-1. A voice answered before the second ring. Julie spoke so softly the man at the other end had to ask her to repeat what she said. She was out of bed now, huddled in the corner of the room farthest from the door. The calm voice told her he'd patch the call directly to the local force. Within seconds, she heard Mike's confident response: "Ryland Police. Chief Barlow."

"Mike, it's Julie. Someone's in my house—or was. I heard noises downstairs."

"You okay?"

"Yes, I'm in the bedroom. The noises were downstairs."

"Stay where you are. Keep calm. I'm just up Grander Hill Road. I'll be there in a couple of minutes. Stay on the line, Julie. Everything's going to be fine."

Chapter 29

"I'm going to hit the siren," Mike said. Julie heard it first over the phone, and then the sound was audible from outside.

"You're close."

"I'm at the top of Main now. Stay put. I'll stop in front and leave the lights on, but I'll have to switch to the handheld radio, so I might lose you. I can see your house now."

The pulsing blue lights reflected weirdly on the bedroom window. Julie went to it and looked out to see the Ryland cruiser. Mike leapt out and raced toward the front door, just below her, and then around the house. "You still there?" the voice on the phone asked. She confirmed it. "I'm at the back door. It's unlocked. I'm coming in." Julie was surprised that the handheld radio was so sensitive that it picked up the snap of Mike's holster as he opened it to withdraw his gun.

"Julie," he yelled, and the sound came more from downstairs than the phone. "I'm coming up."

She heard his footsteps as he took the stairs two at a time. Then he came into the room, and she raced toward him and accepted the one-armed embrace he extended as he held his pistol in his right hand, pointed down. "Let me get this," he said, and clicked the safety on. Then he added his right arm and held her tightly.

"God, I was so scared!" she sobbed. "Thank you!"

"It's okay. You're safe." He steered her to the bed and got her to sit. "I think it's clear downstairs, but I want you to just stay here while I go take a better look."

The cold was returning, and Julie pulled the blanket more tightly around her, but she couldn't stop shaking. Mike returned after what to Julie seemed hours but was no more than minutes.

She heard his steps on the stairs again; this time he was taking them one at a time.

"Whoever it was, he's gone."

"You're sure?"

"I went through the place. He's gone."

"But there really was someone, wasn't there? It wasn't just my imagination?"

"No. The screen door was closed, but the main door wasn't locked—wasn't really pulled shut, in fact. Maybe he heard you up here and ran, leaving the light on and not quite closing the door. Come on down and take a look?"

She nodded, then realized she was wrapped in the blanket and under that was wearing only pajamas. "Let me put something on first."

Mike withdrew to the hallway while Julie pulled on jeans and a sweatshirt. She joined the policeman at the top of the stairs and then followed him to the first floor.

"Be careful," he told her as he guided her across the room toward the kitchen. "Let's take a look at the door, but don't touch anything."

Mike stopped at the door. The screen door was closed. He examined the area around the lock. "You're sure you locked this last night?"

"Absolutely. I checked and rechecked everything."

"I'm sure you did. It's not easy, but you can jimmy these if you know what you're doing," he said as he peered at the lock. "You really should have a dead bolt on this."

"I was going to, but haven't had time."

"Well, right after I get the crime lab folks to check this out, you should make the time. Meanwhile, can you just look around and see if anything's missing or messed up?" Julie scanned the room. Could she remember where things had been? It seemed so long ago when she had closed up and gone to bed. "Take your time. Look carefully."

She continued to take in the room, straining to recall what had been where. Then she saw it: the folder with her notes! It was on the counter, next to the sink. She was sure she had left it on the kitchen table. And she was sure, absolutely sure, she had left it closed. But it was open now. She started toward it, but Mike grabbed her. "Don't touch anything," he commanded. "Just look. I'll have to dust it."

"This folder was closed, and it was on the kitchen table."

"What is it?"

"My notes on Mary Ellen's murder. Oh, God, someone went through my notes!"

"Your *notes?*" Julie couldn't help but notice his tone was suddenly less patient and understanding than it had just been.

"Just stuff I jotted down—biographical information, details about Birch Brook, motives, that sort of thing. Oh my God, Mike, there *was* something else. Dan Swanson's letter. It was right on top!"

He reached for Julie's right arm as she extended it toward the folder. "Hold it, Julie!" the policeman said.

She quickly withdrew the offending arm. "Sorry. It must have been that letter he was after."

"Think you could make some coffee?" She nodded. "And you've got to get Oxford in there."

"What are you talking about?"

"Oxford County—in your puzzle." He pointed to the table where the bottom third of the state of Maine was intact next to pieces in piles.

"Too bad he didn't put it in for me," she said.

"Criminals these days—bad manners," Mike said. "Now tell me about this letter."

She finished recounting the contents of the letter just as the buzzer sounded to indicate the coffee was ready. She poured them both a cup and sat back down across from Mike.

"So you think this letter explains about the ownership of Birch Brook?" he asked.

"Not exactly *explains* it. I knew the land had passed back and forth between the two families, and Luke wasn't happy he and Frank had to buy it from Mary Ellen, since Luke's father had sold it to Dan Swanson so recently. I mentioned this before." Mike nodded. "But the letter adds something," she continued. "It mentions disputes and fights. I wish I had the copy so you could see what I mean!"

"You said *copy?*"

"Yes, of course. I had a copy, not the original; I'd never take an original out of the archives. It's still there. Or it *should* be. Let's go down to the office and check. That way you can see for yourself."

"Relax, Julie. We can see about that later. Maybe you've forgotten already, but I'm here, drinking coffee with you in your kitchen in the middle of the night because someone broke into your house. Maybe we could concentrate on that for a minute. Assuming the person was looking for the letter—the *copy*—who would want it?"

"Luke," Julie responded immediately. "He was there today, I'm pretty sure. I saw a truck pulling away after I closed up. We can check with Tabby Preston. If Luke was in working on the papers, Tabby would have told him about the new batch—the boxes that Steven Swanson brought in."

"It's hard for me to imagine Luke breaking into your house, Julie. I've known him all my life. He's not a polished sort of guy, but he's a straight shooter. If he wanted something from you, he'd ask. Not break in."

Julie considered Mike's description of Luke and nodded. "I see your point. But I still think he's a prime suspect."

"For B and E—or murder?"

"For both, I think. I mean, he wouldn't go to the trouble of breaking in to recover the letter if it didn't point to him as Mary Ellen's killer? Would he?"

"You're getting beyond me, Julie." Mike's handheld radio crackled: "Chief Barlow?"

"Barlow," he responded.

"Just checking on that call," the voice said.

"Sorry. Should have closed with you. The perp's gone, and I'm with the woman who called. The house is secure, but I'll need to have a mobile crime lab out to check a few things. Can you put that through?"

"I go off at six, and the crime scene guys don't get in till eight. I'll leave a note, but you'd better check in the morning, Chief."

"Ten-four. Thanks. Sorry about that." Mike added to Julie. "I should have closed with Dispatch. Good to know they keep track. Anyway, what were you saying?"

"Just that whoever broke in here—Luke or whoever—must have thought the letter was pretty important, and that makes me think it's connected to Mary Ellen's murder. Shouldn't we go check the archives to see if the original is there?"

"Why don't you explain that one?" Mike said.

"Well, if Luke saw the letter in the archives, and if Tabby told him I'd made a copy, he wouldn't take such a big risk in coming here to get the copy unless he also took the original."

"Could he do that? I thought you said stuff never left the archives."

"I said that *I* wouldn't take an original. But Luke could have. When Tabby wasn't looking, he could have slipped it into his papers and just taken it. Then if he found out from her I had a copy he would want to get that one, too."

"Why?"

"So no one else would know about the funny circumstances of Dan Swanson buying the land from Paul Dyer."

"I thought you said Luke was mad about that."

"Of course he was. If his dad hadn't sold, he wouldn't have had to pay so much to Mary Ellen to buy Birch Brook."

"So Luke would want the letter known, wouldn't he? Instead of trying to get rid of it, he'd want to make sure it was out in the open, so he could contest the sale or whatever."

Julie finished her coffee and stared silently, remembering that Dalton had made a similar point yesterday. She got up and brought the pot to the table and refilled both their cups. "Or am I missing something here?" the policeman said to break the silence.

"No, you're not. Just the opposite. It's a good point, and I don't know what to say. Maybe it means someone else had an interest in the letter."

"Like?"

"Like Steven Swanson. If someone had grounds to contest the ownership of Birch Brook, Steven would stand to lose some money."

"But you said he brought you all those papers. He could have just taken that letter out before he did."

"True, but that assumes he read through them, and that he saw that particular letter and understood its significance. What if he didn't—I mean, before he gave them to me? Then what if he found out later, came to the archives to take that one back, and then found out from Tabby that I had a copy? That would fit, wouldn't it?"

"Seems like a stretch to me."

"Okay, but it's possible. And then of course there's Frank Nilsson. Let's say Luke found out about the letter. He tells Frank because he's happy that maybe the Dyers can get title to the property. That would save them both a lot of money, but then it would put Dyer more in the driver's seat, or at least give him a bigger piece of the pie. And it would slow everything down while they fought it out with Mary Ellen's estate over the ownership. Nilsson has a lot riding on this project and doesn't want any delays. And of course he wants to keep the biggest share for himself. So he realizes he needs to get rid of the letter. And the copy! That would work."

"A lot of things would work. And so should the chief of the Ryland Police Department. Funny how the citizens expect me to be out driving around at night instead of having coffee with the director of the historical society. I'll get the state crime lab in here tomorrow. Or later, I should say," he added after looking at his watch, which said 3:55. "You going to be okay alone here now?"

"I could always go to the office and check the archives, Mike. It should be safe there—especially if you come along."

Chapter 30

"Hope you keep changing that code," Mike said as he stood below Julie on the steps of Swanson House while she touched keys on the lighted box.

"I did it last year. I'm sure you remember that!" Julie added, reminding them both of the break-in at the historical society that led to the recovery of the lost Lincoln letter. "Statewide Security keeps reminding me that they told Worth Harding to change it regularly for ten years! They thought I'd be better. I did, too, but I will change it."

"One of these days," he finished her sentence.

"Yeah." When the blinking light moved from ARMED to OFF, Julie used her key to open the door. Inside, she switched on the light and waited till the policeman closed the outside door before she started up the steps to the archives and library. "Tabby probably put the new boxes in the vault," she said as she turned on the overhead light.

She found the two keys on her ring, unlocked the vault, and paused in front of it.

"Want me to open it?" Mike asked.

Julie nodded, and the policeman swung the door open. The boxes that Steven Swanson had brought were on the floor.

"These?" Mike asked, and Julie nodded again. "I'll get them," he said. "That table okay?"

"It's fine, but you don't need to get them all. I can find the one with Dan Swanson's letter. I remember the other stuff in it." She leaned hesitantly into the vault, just enough to check the boxes. "Here, it's this one," she said after lifting and briefly examining a few of the letters on top.

Mike carried it to the large table in the center of the room and stood quietly while Julie thumbed through the contents. "No," she said, "it's not here."

"Shouldn't we check the others? Maybe the letter ended up in another one."

"It's possible, but Tabby's so careful I'm sure she returned it to the right one. Do you have time for me to go through them?"

"Yeah. I just need to check in."

Mike's voice and the crackling of his radio comforted Julie as she worked her way through the boxes. "Not this one," she said after finishing the second box.

Mike looked up from the page he was writing on and nodded. "You don't need to rush; I'm just finishing my report," he told her. "Everything's quiet out in the greater world, and they know where to find me if that changes."

"Nope," she said when she finished the next box. "One to go." When she finished it, Julie felt a mixture of relief and anger—relief that her theory about the missing letter was confirmed, anger that someone had taken it. "That's it, Mike," she announced. "I've been through all the boxes. Dan Swanson's letter is missing. And so's the copy. It all fits."

"You've said that before, Julie, but I'm still not sure what the *it* is and what it fits. I'll admit this does look interesting. Unless Tabby put the original letter somewhere else, of course."

"We have to ask her, and also ask her about what Luke was doing here yesterday."

"Did I hear *we* again?"

"Well, I guess I can ask her when she comes in."

"When's that?"

"Nine-thirty. You can set your watch by her."

"That's more than five hours from now," Mike said. "You planning to stay here?"

"No, unless I can persuade you to keep me company."

"Don't think the citizens of Ryland would appreciate that. Let's lock up here and I'll walk you home."

As they approached Harding House, the sun was visible just above the eastern horizon.

"Going to warm up," Mike said.

"I can stand it. I was thinking of taking a run. Before it warms up."

"Mind if I have another cup of coffee first?"

Julie was happy to have the policeman around—and happy that he made it seem like she was doing him the favor rather than the other way around. She went upstairs and changed into her running clothes.

"I've been thinking," Mike said when she reappeared in the kitchen. "Might be a better idea if I handle Tabby. Seems like the missing letter may have some bearing on the B and E here, maybe even on Mrs. Swanson's murder. I should take a statement from Tabby just so everything's on the up and up. I'll stop by her house later, before she comes to work."

"That makes sense. I'm glad to see you agree about the letter."

"It has to be checked out. Now, about you—I'll call the State Police again after eight to make sure they get a crime scene unit out here, but in the meantime you need to be careful. Here's my cell number if you need anything."

"Thanks for everything, Mike. Really. I appreciate it. I'm sorry to be a bother."

As Mike's cruiser headed up Main Street, Julie went in the opposite direction, toward the river. She stayed on the street, avoiding the woods behind the construction site. Another runner, a man she didn't recognize, passed her going the opposite way on the path by the river. She returned his wave, but for the next few seconds she kept glancing behind to make sure he hadn't turned and followed. Don't be silly, she told herself. Why would anyone follow me? Then again, why would anyone break into her house and steal the copy of Dan Swanson's letter? Someone had. She picked up her pace, hard to do when running alone, and glanced behind a few more times just to be sure she really was running alone.

We're going to pay for last weekend, Julie said to herself when she slowed to a walk at the top of the Common. She was dripping, and it was still only six-thirty. It was obviously going to be a hot one, what the locals called a broiler. Maybe even mid eighties. Outside Harding House, she paused to consider whether she should use the front door. She decided against it and went around to the back and through the unlocked kitchen door, being careful not to touch anything. She wondered if the crime scene crew would actually get there today, and even if they did, whether she could get someone in to fix the lock. She was nervous being in the house alone. Just thinking of staying by herself tonight, even with a new lock on the kitchen door, made her shudder. She dialed Mike's cell phone to ask him if it was okay for her to replace the lock.

"You need to wait for the crime guys, and I'm not making any guarantees about when they'll arrive. Any chance you could find another spot for tonight?"

"I'm sure Dalton would rent me a room at the Black Crow Inn."

"Good idea. Let me know later where you'll be in case I need to reach you."

Later, sitting in her office in bright sunshine with the world awaking around her, Julie realized she needed to call Rich. So why was she dreading it? She did want to hear his voice, but he'd want a full description of what had happened. She didn't want to relive it and was afraid she'd get upset if she did. That would frighten

Rich, frighten him enough that he would propose she leave Ryland at once to join him in Orono, or his coming immediately to Ryland. In a way, she would have welcomed either suggestion, but she also knew she wouldn't accept either.

"You can't stay there, Julie!" Rich practically yelled when she finished her brief description of the break in. "This is getting serious."

"I know, I know. I was thinking of calling Dalton to see if I can stay at his inn tonight."

"Call him right away."

"I will, but it's only for tonight, Rich, just till I get the lock fixed."

"No, you have to live somewhere else until this is settled."

"Settled?"

"The break-in, at least, maybe the murder, too. You're right in someone's cross-hairs. If I could just figure out a way to cover things here, I'd . . ."

"Don't. You don't need to trail all over the state to take care of me. You have a job in Orono. I live here."

Rich was silent for several seconds, and Julie was about to repeat her point when he said, "Okay, but call Dalton right away."

"I will."

"How do you feel?"

"I'm fine now, really. It was scary, but Mike got there so fast."

"But having someone in your house, Julie, that's . . ."

"A violation," she completed his sentence. "Funny, I've heard people say that's how they feel when they've been robbed—*violated*. I guess I didn't really understand it, but it's right; I feel dirty and used, knowing someone was in my kitchen, looking through my folder, standing at the counter the way you and I do.

"Still," she continued, "I don't feel as if I'm in, how did you say it? Someone's crosshairs? I think whoever broke in was looking for the copy of the letter, and when he found it he was probably happy to get out without having to confront me.

"I wish I could get there. I'll see if I can get someone to cover my class and maybe I can—"

"No! What if something like this had happened when I lived in Delaware? You couldn't have come down. Just because we're in the same state doesn't mean you have to come be my protector. I'm going to call Dalton, and I'm sure that will work for tonight, and then we'll see. Maybe everything will be cleared up by tomorrow."

"You believe that?"

"Not necessarily, but I also don't *not* believe it. We'll just have to see. So I'll call Dalton right now."

"Okay, but call me back. And keep calling—if I'm in class, leave messages. Just stay in touch. Then we'll figure out something."

"I will, I promise! Okay?"

"Okay. I guess that's all we can do for now—if you're going to be so stubborn. But be careful. I love you, Julie."

"Love you, too. Bye!" She hung up before Rich could say anything else. She heard Mike in the outer office and she wanted to find out what he had heard from Tabby.

Chapter 31

The police chief was talking to Mrs. Detweiller. Tabby was nowhere to be seen.

"I gave Tabby a lift," Mike said to Julie. "She went upstairs. You got a minute?" Julie gestured to her office and shut the door after she followed him in. Then she remembered she hadn't even spoken to her secretary. She apologized to Mike and went back to the outer office. "Didn't mean to be rude, Mrs. Detweiller. I know the chief needs to talk to me. How are you this morning?"

"Fine, Dr. Williamson."

"Great. If Rich calls, you can put him right through."

Mrs. Detweiller paused and then nodded in the patronizing way she used with her employer, her nod implying that if that's *really* what Dr. Williamson wanted, it wasn't up to her to disagree. No matter how wrong Dr. Williamson might be.

"Pretty interesting conversation," Mike began when Julie rejoined him in her office.

"I wish I could have been there."

"I'm sure you do, but I'm only updating you because of your break-in. First," he said as he opened his leather folder and looked at his notes, "Tabby confirms that Luke Dyer was in the library Wednesday—yesterday. She told him about the new Swanson papers. Said he seemed excited and spent an hour or more looking through the boxes. Can't say what he actually saw, or didn't see."

"Or whether he took one," Julie interrupted.

"Right. I didn't exactly ask her that, but I sort of worked around the point enough to get that sense."

"But then Luke wasn't likely to say, 'Oh thank you, Miss Preston, this is exactly what I was looking for; I'll just take it home with me.'"

"Well, no, of course not."

"But it's missing. We know that."

"Right again. Now do you want me to continue, or have you heard enough?"

Mike's tone got Julie's attention. "Sorry. I'll be quiet."

His I'll-believe-that-when-I-see-it laugh eased the brief moment of tension between them. "Okay, then about Frank Nilsson." Mike consulted his notebook again. "Seems Frank also paid a visit to the library yesterday, earlier than Luke, before lunch. Said he wanted to talk to Tabby about how the historical society preserves papers because his wife was thinking of donating some things from her family."

"That's right. The Nilssons mentioned that to me."

"So anyway," Mike resumed after clearing his throat, "Frank asked some questions about how papers are handled now and how that will change when the new center is built. Tabby said she showed him the vault to assure him that anything his wife planned to give would be well protected even before the new storage area is ready."

"Of course the humidity will be controlled in the new area," Julie couldn't help interjecting.

"Tabby told him that. Anyway, Nilsson looked around the vault, and Tabby pointed out the Swanson papers and told him they had just been given by Steven and explained about how they would be cataloged."

"Did he want to see them?"

"Why am I not surprised you asked? It really is a shame you couldn't conduct the interview with Tabby yourself."

"I'm sorry! I *promise* I'll shut up so you can finish."

"To answer your question, yes, he did look at them. Tabby said she thought it was okay for him to go through a couple of the boxes so he'd have an idea of the kind of papers the society collects. He brought two boxes out to the table and Tabby said he spent twenty or thirty minutes looking through them. Then he returned them to the vault and told Tabby he was happy with how things are done here and would talk to his wife again about getting the Oakes family papers. And that's it."

"So I can ask a question now?"

"Just for a change?"

Julie laughed and continued: "Tabby of course can't be sure Frank didn't take the letter?"

"Again, I didn't ask her quite that bluntly, but I satisfied myself that she wasn't aware that he did."

"Of course not," Julie said. "So what do you think?"

"That both Dyer and Nilsson had the opportunity yesterday to take the letter."

"Exactly. But there's another point, isn't there? Did either one know I made a copy?"

"Ah, I figured you'd get to that. Yes, she did mention the copy to both of them. I had to be real careful in asking her that, but I played dumb about your having the copy—in fact, I didn't mention the break-in either. Figured that's best. Anyway, apparently they both asked about copies—Dyer because he wanted to make some himself, Nilsson in his general way of asking about how papers are treated—you know, something like, 'And could we make copies of my wife's papers once we gave them?' So she told both of them that she'd just recently copied one of the letters in the new Swanson materials."

"For me?"

"Yes."

"Did she tell them which one?"

"What she said was that it was a 1997 letter. I gather she was trying to assure them that it wasn't old, fragile, whatever."

"There you are."

"Where?"

"With proof that both Luke and Frank could have seen the letter from Dan Swanson, could have taken the letter, and could have known I had a copy. Giving the date, 1997, would have been enough to identify the letter, don't you think?"

"Yes."

They were silent. Mike glanced at the page in front of him and then closed the leather notebook. Julie looked out the window toward the Common. She was the first to speak.

"But wait a second, Mike. If Frank came in before Luke and took the letter, then Luke couldn't have seen it."

"That's true." The policeman flipped back through his notes. "Here. Tabby said Luke seemed excited about the new stuff and looked through it. I guess that doesn't prove anything; he could have been excited about that particular letter, or just about more Swanson stuff."

"So either one could have taken it."

"I guess we're back to that."

"So what's next?"

"Think I better have a talk with Frank and Luke."

"To check their alibis for last night?"

"Police business, Julie." He stood and left.

Chapter 32

Although she really wanted to tell Dalton everything—about the break-in, about Mike's interview with Tabby Preston, about her suspicions of Nilsson and Dyer—she didn't want to do it on the phone. She wanted to sit down with him at the inn and have a long talk and use Dalton's intelligence and knowledge of the people to figure out what was happening. But first she had to arrange to stay at his inn. Telling him there was a long story behind the short story, she merely said she wanted to stay at the Black Crow for the night.

"Not a problem," Dalton told her. "We're empty. The holiday weekend was wild, but I don't have a single booking for tonight, so please, be our guest, on the house. If you paid, I'd have to treat you like a guest. Nickie will be here, so let's all have dinner. Seven okay for you?"

So that was done. Julie phoned Rich to tell him where she'd be, and then called and left a message for Mike to let him know, too. She'd have to stop by Harding House to get some things for the night, and then she'd have to arrange for someone to come change the lock, assuming the State Police crime scene crew had finished. Which, she decided, was worth checking on right now. She walked the few minutes to the house.

A white van with large black lettering announcing itself as the MOBILE CRIME UNIT was parked in front of the house. A young woman and an older man, both dressed in civilian clothes, were working on the door. She identified herself and talked with them long enough to be sure it was going to be appropriate to have a locksmith come that afternoon. "We're out of here in fifteen minutes," the man told her. "So go ahead and get someone. And get a dead bolt. Every door should have one. Wouldn't have had this problem if you'd had a dead bolt."

Julie decided the presence of the two officers made this a good time to pack a bag. They were gathering up their equipment when she returned to the kitchen with it.

"You could call Holdsworth's—you know, the hardware store here in Ryland. They do locks," the woman said.

When she got to the office and made the call to Holdsworth's, the young man who answered said he'd send someone out by two that afternoon. There were lots of advantages to a small town, Julie told herself after she finished the order by stipulating a dead bolt.

"Always the best idea, ma'am," he said. "It's the kitchen door of Worth Harding's place?"

"Right." She was about to give the address when she realized that if he knew the house as Worth's he certainly knew where it was.

"We'll take care of it. Will someone be there?"

"I can be."

"Don't have to. We can lock up and you can swing by the store to pick up the key."

Another advantage of Ryland, Julie told herself, feeling good about it and realizing how she was settling in.

"Dr. Williamson," Mrs. Detweiller said from the open door. "Mrs. Nilsson's on the line."

Mrs. Nilsson, Julie repeated to herself; not Frank but his wife. What could Patty want? Her husband was much in Julie's mind, but she doubted the wife was calling to talk about his possible guilt in either murder or breaking in to Julie's house.

"Hello, Mrs. Nilsson. I was happy to meet you Monday, despite the circumstances."

"That's certainly true, and please call me Patty. Everyone does," she added pleasantly. "You probably wonder why I'm calling out of the blue like this, but the other day Frank mentioned those family papers of mine—the Oakes papers?"

"Oh, yes, I remember very well."

"Well, I think our conversation shamed Frank into bringing them home—and shamed me into finally taking a look at them. That's why I'm calling, but if this is a bad time I can call later."

"Not at all. I'm very interested in your family's papers," Julie replied.

"Anyway, talking to you the other day finally got us going, and Frank got the papers out of the storage unit. I've been going through them, and I thought that if you'd really like them for the Ryland Historical Society, I could arrange to bring them in. The trouble is there's lots of junk—well, it seems like junk to me, and I'm not sure what to do. I don't want to load you up with old newspapers and things you probably have already."

"You'd be surprised how valuable these things can be to researchers. We'd be really happy to have whatever you'd like to donate."

"Well, I was wondering if it would make sense for you to look through the boxes first, get an idea of what I have, and then you could pick what you want. Would that be an imposition?"

"Not at all. I'd love to. Anytime you like."

"I'm going to be gone for a month. We have a camp down at the coast, and I'm going to spend some time there with some old college friends, and then Frank is coming down for vacation with the kids. I know it's pushy of me, but now that I've started this I'd like to finish. Do you think you could come out in the next few days and take a look?"

Julie didn't want to appear too eager, but the Oakes papers fascinated her, and she didn't want to wait till Patty Nilsson returned. "Would this afternoon be convenient?"

"Perfect. Why don't you come around two? You could look through them and we could have tea."

Julie agreed, and Patty provided directions. Although Julie had lived in a rented condo at the ski area for a year, the Nilssons house was in another part of the development, one of a dozen or so very substantial private residences discreetly tucked in the woods across the road from the main ski lodge. Julie had walked through the area, admiring the houses, so when Patty gave her directions she had no trouble taking them in.

She arrived exactly at two, parked in the driveway, and looked up to see Patty opening the door to greet her. From their first meeting, Frank Nilsson's wife struck Julie as an odd fit with the trim, handsome man. Patty was short and chubby, not quite fat but definitely a contrast with her husband. While she seemed older than him, Julie remembered they had met when they were college students, so she assumed that the apparent age difference wasn't real but the effect of Frank Nilsson's obvious commitment to keeping himself looking fit and boyish. Julie found herself liking Patty Nilsson's easy acceptance of who she was and how she looked as a nice counter to her husband's obvious concern for appearances.

Patty led Julie to a large basement room paneled in pine. Below grade, the room had small windows that let in enough light for Julie to see the bar at one end next to a pool table and some overstuffed chairs and a sofa at the other. Family room in a ski house, Julie told herself as she took it in.

"It's so dark down here," Patty Nilsson said. "Let me get some lights."

Fluorescent recessed lights bathed the room with an unnatural quality. "Here they are," she added as she pointed to five cardboard boxes on the floor in front of the sofa. "I'm sure it's mostly junk, but if there's anything worthwhile you're welcome to it. I can just leave you with them, or I can stay here while you look. Whatever you like."

Julie suggested she could take a look on her own first if the other woman had things to do. "I do have some packing to get ready for the camp, so why don't you go ahead. Just call up if you have any questions. Can I get you some lemonade or iced tea or something?"

Julie declined the offer, and after Patty retreated up the steps set about examining the contents of the boxes. Nothing surprised her. It was the sort of stuff you always got when people brought in boxes of "family papers." There were letters, which qualified, and photos, which Julie always lingered over, trying to imagine why they had been taken. But most of the contents were the typical leavings: old clippings from Portland and Boston newspapers, programs from musical events, receipts, instructions that had accompanied apple corers and washing machines. The boxes were more or less chronological, one containing materials from the late nineteenth century, another with letters and clippings from the period between the two wars, and the last three of more-recent vintage. These contained items like the programs from Patty's high school and college commencements and clippings about her wedding. Someday historians might value them, but Julie wondered if Patty really intended to give them up now or if she had simply gotten tired of examining the boxes' contents and decided to hand over the decision to Julie.

"Dear, you must be tired of sorting through those old things!" Patty said as she stepped into the room carrying a tray. "And bored, too, I'm sure."

"Not at all. There are some very, very useful items here the historical society would be delighted to have."

"And plenty to start a fire with."

"Oh, I didn't mean that. I just meant that some of the more-recent items are probably of personal interest to you now—things you'd like to keep for your own family."

"Actually, I didn't get into the last couple of boxes, I have to confess. Are there recent things?"

"Clippings about your wedding, your commencement program, things like that."

"My kids would think those are medieval! I guess I should go through those boxes again. Now here I am with this pitcher of iced tea and I haven't offered you any." She pointed to the tray with the pitcher and glasses and a plate of cookies.

"Do you have time to join me?"

"Absolutely! If I'm not in your way."

As they were sipping iced tea and nibbling cookies, Julie suggested she could take the three boxes of historical materials and leave the ones with more-recent materials for Patty to review later. She agreed.

"You didn't happen to come across a diary in those, did you?" Patty asked. "A little brown book, maybe four inches by eight inches?" Julie said she hadn't. "That's too bad. I know it was there because my mother pointed it out a couple of times. In fact, when I was in high school I had to do a project on my family, and Mother suggested I use her grandfather's diary. I read it, but it was so boring—dates and facts and names."

"What period would that be?"

"Well, Thaddeus Oakes was my great-grandfather. I think it was probably the 1870s and 1880s."

"I didn't see anything like that. Maybe it got into the boxes of more-recent things. I went through those pretty quickly, but I think I would have spotted something like a diary, especially an old one. That would be of real interest to the historical society."

"I suppose so. Thaddeus was a surveyor—the only one in Ryland in his day, my mother said. He kept records on all the work he did in that diary, which means practically every piece of land in Ryland is mentioned in there."

Chapter 33

Julie nearly lost her grip on her glass of iced tea and had to use her left hand to steady it and lower it to the table. Thaddeus Oakes's diary might contain information about the Birch Brook property. Henry had mentioned that the dispute between the Swansons and the Dyers over the property had been settled by a survey. And it was sometime in the 1880s!

"I should be letting you get back to your packing," she said to Patty. "About that diary—maybe we should take a quick look together and see if it's here somewhere. I'll just go through these things in the three boxes and that way you can also see what materials I'm taking."

Patty agreed, and they spent another half-hour examining the contents of the three boxes Julie planned to accept on behalf of the Ryland Historical Society. Thaddeus Oakes's diary was not in them. Patty suggested they take a quick look at the other boxes to be sure, and again watched as Julie thumbed through the items.

"I guess I shouldn't be surprised my mother kept all these things," Patty commented. "Lord knows I've kept enough memorabilia from when my own kids were young, and it probably will all end up in the recycling one day, just like these boxes should."

"Of course if you should find the diary—t" Julie said. But before she could finish the sentence a man's voice interrupted: "What diary?"

"Oh, Frank, I didn't hear you," Patty said. "Julie and I were just going through these boxes. How was Boothbay?"

Frank Nilsson, wearing a crisp cotton shirt and creased slacks, walked into the room from the steps and extended his hand to shake Julie's. "Everything's fine in Boothbay," he said. "Went down to the coast yesterday to check on a project I have going there," he added in Julie's direction. "Stayed over at our camp. I finished a little earlier than I expected," he said, this time in the direction of his wife. "So what are you two up to here?"

"I told you I was going to call Julie about the papers," Patty said. "She was so great to come right out, and she's been through the boxes and is going to take three of them for the society."

"Glad to hear it," Frank said. "I hope I get some credit for this," he added to Julie. "After I stopped by your place, I went to see Tabby Preston in the archives, just to be sure Patty's family papers would be safe, I encouraged my wife to get a move on with it."

"I appreciate it." Try as she did, Julie couldn't read the look on Frank's face. He paused, looking directly into Julie's eyes. Then he abruptly turned to his wife: "But what diary were you talking about?"

"Thaddeus Oakes's—my great-grandfather. Remember? I think I mentioned that to you when I started to look through these. I figured it was one thing of real value since it's so old, but I couldn't find it. And Julie can't either."

"Oh, right. Well, that's a shame. I remember you said it was, what, a hundred years old or so?"

"More than that. He died early in the twentieth century. I don't know how long he was keeping the diary, but at least twenty years or so."

Julie stood silently as husband and wife talked. Was Frank's interest in the diary a husbandly bit of pleasantry? Or was it more? Julie just couldn't tell.

"Well, I shouldn't be keeping you," she said. "I'll be very happy to take these three boxes, and of course I'll send you a receipt for tax purposes."

"I can carry those up for you, Julie," Frank said. "That must be your car in the driveway? You sure you can fit all these in? I could bring them to town if you'd like."

Julie assured him her Volkswagen Jetta was up to the challenge. She picked up a box, and he took another. "Just leave that one, honey," Frank said quickly to Patty. "I'll come back for it."

"Sorry I wasn't here earlier—didn't realize you were coming out," he said as he placed the box in her trunk next to the one Julie had carried. "I'll just go get the other one."

When he returned with it, Julie said she had been happy to have the chance to talk to Patty. "We should have had you out for dinner already," Frank said. "Patty's leaving Saturday for the camp, and I'm going down later. We won't be back in Ryland full-time till the end of the summer. Let's not wait," he added. "Any chance you could come for dinner tomorrow?"

"Friday?" Julie said, startled by the invitation.

"I know it's last-minute, but if it works for you we'd be very pleased to have you come out." Julie explained that Rich was coming and reminded Frank they had met at Birch Brook. "Nice young man," Nilsson said.

Much as she hated to give up their private time the first night Rich would be there, the prospect of having his help in assessing the Nilssons appealed to her. To the extent that being around Frank frightened her—and she wasn't sure to what extent it did—Rich's presence was an added bonus. So she accepted. "Unless Patty has something else planned," she added. "If you want to check and let me know, just call me at the office."

"It'll be fine with Patty," Frank said in a tone that seemed to Julie to command rather than explore his wife's willingness to have dinner guests. "It's supposed to cool down again tonight. If we have that weather we had over the Fourth," he continued, "we could even have a sauna before dinner. Got a great one here. Ever done it?"

"Taken a sauna? No."

"Wonderful Scandinavian tradition. 'Course you can tell by my name I'm not prejudiced! Why don't you come about six and we can take a family sauna and then settle in for dinner?" Julie explained that Rich was driving from Orono and that she had a trustee meeting, but that they could try to get to the Nilssons' by six-thirty.

"Then it's a date. Of course you know the custom," he added. Julie said she didn't. "Part of the tradition—no clothes in the sauna," he said with a laugh. And then: "Just kidding, Julie. That *is* the custom, but bring a bathing suit. See you then."

Frank's look when he mentioned the custom of nudity in the sauna didn't bother Julie at that moment, but as she drove back to Ryland she decided that it should have bothered her more. It was consistent with what she had seen about the man's character over the last week, and reinforced her sense that she didn't like him or feel comfortable around him. She was glad dinner on Friday would include Rich, and of course Patty, whom she was growing fond of because she seemed so much nicer than her husband.

Thinking further of Frank as she drove, Julie wondered if Mike had talked with him. She thought of calling Mike to find out, but she reconsidered when she thought it through. Despite the good relationship she had developed with the policeman during the past year, she didn't want to push it, because she knew he was trying to maintain the line between them on this case.

Mrs. Detweiller was leaving as Julie returned to her office. She had time before leaving for dinner at the Black Crow Inn to do some work at her desk, and there was plenty of it: bills to be checked and approved for payment, requests for tours, articles for the society's newsletter to be edited. They were the core of her job, the nitty-gritty that she usually found satisfying to deal with as a way of marking progress. But today her heart wasn't in it. She listlessly glanced at one of the tour requests and was about to check the time against the master calendar when she spotted the green folder that Tabby had given her last week. More Tabor papers, she thought—just what I need! She opened the folder and leafed through several items on the top: two prescriptions, some notes from a town committee on which Dr. Tabor had sat, and then two letters. She loved reading the copies of his letters. He kept carbon copies of all his correspondence, she had discovered. The practice of inserting a sheet of carbon between two pages in the typewriter was quaint, but she was grateful that Dr. Tabor had taken the time to do so. Both letters were to the doctor's brother in Connecticut, one of his regular correspondents. She read the first:

> January 7th, 1933
>
> My dear brother Lemuel,
>
> I wish you the very warmest greetings for the New Year. Although I know you did not wish to see Governor Roosevelt go to Washington, let us hope he can work the miracle that those of us who did vote for him earnestly pray for.
>
> I read that another bank failed in Hartford last week. I hope it was not one where you keep your money! Things are quite bad here in rural Maine, too. Just this week one of my patients told me he must sell some land that has been in his family for decades because he needs the money to keep his family and business above water. As he is probably the richest man in Ryland, his news was very distressing. If someone like Mr. Swanson is in trouble, what of the little people? Of course in his case there is another layer, as there always seems to be in these small towns. I understand there has been very bad blood between Mr. Swanson and the man he sold to, going back to some long-ago dispute about the very land he now has to sell.

The letter continued, with comments on Ryland's weather and some sharp observations about a town selectmen's meeting. Julie rushed through those parts to be sure there were no further references to the Swanson land sale and then reread the opening paragraphs. "Amazing!" she said out loud. It wasn't that the letter told her anymore than she'd already guessed about the sale from Swanson to Dyer in the Depression. Rather, it was the coincidence—right here on her desk was a letter from 1933 referring to the very matter she had noted in her chronology of the land's ownership. As a historian, she shouldn't be surprised when pieces of evidence came together, but in this case she took delight in it.

And it did seem like two pieces of evidence were coming together; it's just that the other one—the 1997 letter from Dan Swanson—was missing. No, stolen! But Julie was sure she remembered its reference to the nineteenth-century survey, not some dispute during the Depression. Had it said anything specific about that, about the sale between Dan Swanson's grandfather and Luke's grandfather? No, she didn't think so. But the reference in Dr. Tabor's letter to "very bad blood" between the families going back to the old dispute surely pointed in the same direction as the words in the now-missing letter.

Julie returned to the green folder and flipped quickly through some newspaper clippings—worth reading for her project, she told herself, but not immediately relevant. She came to another letter:

April 25th, 1933

My dear brother Lemuel,

I am so glad to see our President taking action on the banks. Both of ours have now reopened and are taking deposits again, though I doubt they will be loaning out that money anytime soon. Who can afford debt these days?

You asked about the business I mentioned at the New Year—the land sale by one of my patients. Your interest in such a small-town transaction doesn't surprise me. I know you love a good story. So here is what I know.

> Back before the turn of the century, the land—it is a beautiful parcel west of town on the Androscoggin River—was the subject of legal action because the two families who owned land on either side of it disputed who owned the middle parcel. There was a survey, but I do not know more about what it determined. I do know, from my patient, Mr. Swanson, that his family ended up with the parcel in question. He says he had to sell it now—back to the family who earlier claimed it—because he needs the money. But that's not how our Town Gossips see it! I hear that the man who bought it, Mr. Dyer, threatened Mr. Swanson with another lawsuit because of something he found. But then that may just be the talk of the flibberti-gibbets!

"The Oakes survey!" Julie practically screamed. This confirmed it: Something fishy about it must have surfaced and caused the one man to sell to the other. But in 1933? Or 1997? Or both?

She glanced at her watch and saw that she should be starting off to Dalton's. After losing the original and the copy of the 1997 letter, she wasn't about to expose these two to a similar risk, even though she couldn't imagine who besides Tabby knew of them. (Had Tabby read them? she wondered.) The Tabor letters belonged upstairs, in the safe.

Chapter 34

As she drove out of town toward the Black Crow Inn, Julie felt pleased that the few breathing exercises she had forced herself to do before and after entering the safe and placing the letters there had had the intended effect. She was also feeling a kind of high about what she had found; it was the very same feeling she got when she clicked the last piece of a difficult jigsaw puzzle into place or entered the Latin name for raccoon in a crossword. But then, she asked herself, what had she actually learned? That the ownership of the Birch Brook property was contested, tangled in family feuds and perhaps more, was hardly fresh news. Nothing in Dr. Tabor's reports to his distant brother explained exactly what had gone on between the Swansons and the Dyers.

So what had she learned, she asked herself again as she pulled off the highway and entered the drive up the hill toward Dalton's. And more to the point, she reminded herself, what did it all have to do with Mary Ellen's murder? That was the trouble with historical research, she thought as she parked her car: it's so much fun, but a lot of the time you have no idea where it's going. If anywhere.

Dinner was good. Running the Black Crow Inn had turned Dalton Scott into a very respectable cook, another example of Julie's belief that men were taking over in the kitchen. Conversation over dinner was led by Nickie, whose current obsession was what she considered the high-handed approach of Ryland's planning board in the implementation of the town's new sign ordinance.

"It's a good approach," Nickie said. "Dalton was on the committee that developed it, and it's very reasonable. But the way the planning board is handling these cases is just crazy. They're letting the motels put up all sorts of crap—really ugly signs—but then when I present my request they turn it down flat. Too big, wrong colors, too close to the road. I mean, Dalton designed the sign, and he knows the standards better than anyone."

"But you did make some changes in my design," Dalton interjected.

"A few, but still. I just think the planning board is a bunch of idiots."

Neither Dalton nor Julie had a good counter to that observation, and Nickie seemed to realize that her interest in the topic far outpaced theirs. "So you're having the house painted?" she asked Julie, whose blank stare promoted a refinement in the question. "Did you say that, Dalton, or did I dream it up?"

"I think I guessed that," Dalton replied before turning to Julie: "You didn't say, but since you needed a place for the night I assumed you were having some work done at Harding House."

"I didn't want to get into it on the phone," Julie said, and then explained to them about the break-in.

"My God!" was Dalton's response when Julie finished.

"Holy shit!" was Nickie's. "You must have been terrified. You poor thing! What did they take? Do you have antiques or something?"

"Well, that's another story, and sort of a long one."

"To the deck!" Nickie commanded. "Leave these dishes and I'll clean up later, Dalton. And bring us some brandy; I think we're going to need it."

On the deck overlooking the woods behind the inn, Julie told them about the missing letter and her guess that whoever broke into the house took her copy. Although she had talked before to Dalton about her suspicions, she had to go back a bit and bring Nickie up-to-speed. It was a longer story than she meant it to be, but the brandy helped. She didn't mention the two Tabor letters because she still didn't know what they proved.

"So you think Nilsson or Dyer or maybe both of them killed Mary Ellen to stop her from backing out of the land deal," Nickie summarized. "And then one of them, or again, maybe both, found out that the deed to the property was in question anyway. And then that you had a copy of the letter that proved that. Wow!"

"I guess that's it in a nutshell, but there are too many loose ends here. Like whether Nilsson and Dyer have alibis for last night or for the morning Mary Ellen was killed."

"I assume Mike's checking on that," Dalton said. Until now he had listened quietly to Julie's recounting of the incidents.

"He said he was going to, but I haven't heard. I hate to keep bothering him."

"Hell, it was your house that was broken into," Nickie said. "You have a right to know."

"But Mike doesn't want you involved in the murder investigation, does he?" Dalton said.

"Obviously not."

"Which doesn't stop you, of course."

"If the break-in and the murder are connected—and I'm sure they are—well, then, of course I'm involved. I have to be."

"Mike would say you don't *have* to be involved, Julie. And he'd be right."

"And Rich says the same."

"Then there you are," Dalton said.

"Did I tell you Frank Nilsson invited Rich and me to dinner tomorrow night?" Dalton shook his head. "Oh, and about the diary. I didn't tell you that, either." So she filled them in.

"This really is bizarre," Nickie said when Julie finished this new portion of the story. "Fights over land, murder, missing letters, a break-in. Sounds like a TV show."

"Or life in a small Maine town," Dalton said. "Anyway, folks, it's getting late, the mosquitoes are starting to bite even though it's cooling down, and I need to clean up in the kitchen. So . . ."

"I said I'd do that, Dalton. You and Julie can go inside and continue this."

Sitting in the lounge, Dalton repeated that he thought Mike and Rich were right, and that Julie should stop trying to do the policeman's job. "And why would you even want to go to the Nilssons' for dinner when you suspect him as a murderer and as someone who broke into your house?"

"Rich will be there. And you know how I love puzzles, Dalton," she replied. "Besides, this really does involve me."

"I don't know . . ." he said, adding, "Hey, what's happening about the missing shovel? I always heard that you can't solve a murder without the weapon."

Julie smiled. "See, you like puzzles, too. I think you can solve a case without the weapon, but it sure would help to locate that shovel. Mike and the state cops came up empty there. There's got to be a simple explanation. A shovel just can't disappear."

"But the person who used it to kill Mary Ellen—assuming that's what happened—could have taken it. And then hid it or got rid of it somewhere. That seems pretty logical to me: If you just bashed someone with a shovel, you wouldn't exactly place it beside the body, would you?"

"Of course not, but then walking around Ryland with a blood-covered shovel might attract a little attention."

"It might. Then again, Ryland's a funny town."

"Not *that* funny, Dalton," Nickie said as she came in from the kitchen to join them in the lounge.

"Except for the planning board," Dalton pointed out.

"True. Maybe the planning board killed Mary Ellen!"

"I think it's time for bed, Nickie," Dalton said. "Let me show you your room, Julie, but don't feel you have to turn in now just because we are. Stay here if you want to read or something. How about some more brandy?"

Chapter 35

It had not been a good idea to accept that offer, Julie thought when she looked at her watch and saw it was after midnight. Instead of easing her into sleep as she had hoped, the brandy left her feeling both sluggish and restless. But then she couldn't blame it all on brandy. She was exhausted after a very short and very frightening night and a busy day. And she kept thinking about that missing diary. Surely Thaddeus Oakes had done the survey that settled the dispute over Birch Brook back in the 1880s. Dr. Tabor's letters confirmed at least the dispute. And if there had been some hanky-panky, Oakes's diary might prove it. How convenient that it was missing! Like the Swanson letter. Patty Nilsson was certainly surprised. Was Frank?

That was hard to figure out, Julie said to herself as she shifted once more in the unfamiliar bed. Frank had certainly shown interest in the fact that Julie and Patty had been discussing the diary. But she really couldn't read his reaction to Patty's comments. At least she didn't remember anything particularly revealing. So, she considered as she rolled to her left side, what I should focus on is whether Frank had a reason to be glad the Oakes diary wasn't going to end up at the Ryland Historical Society. And he did: If there was a problem in the ownership of Birch Brook that Frank aimed to suppress by taking Dan Swanson's letter and Julie's copy of it, then information in Thaddeus Oakes's diary had to be suppressed, too.

That thought taking firm shape in her mind, Julie rolled out of bed and stood at the window of the guest room. Though only half full, the moon was bright enough to illuminate the woods behind the inn. Julie thought of what effect the light was having on the view from her bedroom in Harding House. The sooner the break-in was solved and the criminal arrested, the sooner she could go back. Tomorrow Rich would be there, so that would be fine. But when he returned to Orono on Sunday she would face the choice of having to stay on in the house by herself or continuing to seek refuge at the Black Crow Inn until someone was arrested for the break-in.

She pulled the wicker chair beside the bed to just in front of the window and sat down to think this through. So much depended on what Mike found out about where Frank and Luke had been last night. Wait a minute, she told herself: I do know where Frank was last night. He had gone to Boothbay Harbor to check on one of his projects and had stayed at the Nilsson camp near there. He got back just as Julie and Patty were finishing up with the papers. If he was there, he couldn't have broken into Harding House this morning. Then it must have been Luke. Mike had greeted that possibility with obvious skepticism, but then he knew Luke a lot better than Julie did. Besides, as both Dalton and Mike had pointed out, Luke had good reason for the truth about the ownership of Birch Brook to be exposed, not hidden. So if the Oakes diary shed some light on the question, wouldn't he want it, too, to become public? Even if for some reason he didn't, Julie couldn't imagine any simple way for Luke to steal the diary if it had been among the Oakes papers that Patty reviewed at her house.

Julie's head was spinning now. There were just too many questions. And she was too restless. She had brought a book with her and decided this was the moment for which she meant it. She located the paperback catalog of New England quilts in her bag, sat down with it in the chair next to the window, and tried to find it interesting. The pictures were the best part—well-done illustrations of brightly colored quilts from an exhibition in Boston. But the prose in the essays just didn't keep her attention. She flipped back to the illustrations. Great images, she thought.

Yes, images. She remembered now how Mike had tried to guide her to recall the scene at the tent when he was investigating whether someone in the woods might have witnessed the murder. He had told her to close her eyes and recapture the scene, not thinking in words but focusing on images. What did you *see?* he *had* asked. She decided she should try again now. She turned off the reading lamp. The moon was still too bright, so she pulled the curtains closed. Sitting back down, she closed her eyes and tried to relax. What did she see? The tent. The patch of earth marked in flags to indicate the site for the ceremonial digging. The table under the tent. The shovels on the table—she couldn't count them, and while she knew she had brought four and later found only three, she really couldn't make out how many were in the scene she was reconstructing. Must be four, she said, because this was at 9:30 and I'd just brought them over. What else could she remember? The woods behind the construction site were there but not vivid—just something she was aware of, but not clear enough for her to answer Mike's question about whether someone on a bike might have been back there. She rotated her mental picture and looked the other way, toward the back of the buildings of the Ryland Historical Society. She squeezed her eyes tighter and there was the yellow backhoe. The machine was sitting there waiting for the groundbreaking to be over so it could dig into the earth and create the ditches in which the foundation for the new Swanson Center would be poured. Julie thought of it almost as an animate object, capable of digging on its own, and eager to get started.

If only it were animate, Julie said as she opened her eyes and sat quietly, trying to find the meaning in this. If it were the animal she pictured it as being, the backhoe would have been a witness to Mary Ellen's murder. And that was just silly, she told herself. But something about the recalled scene troubled her. She was still trying to figure out the source of her unease when she fell asleep.

When she woke to the sound of crows in the trees behind the inn—the birds for whom Dalton had named his establishment—she was at first surprised to discover she was sitting in the chair. Then she remembered the long, sleepless night. She looked at her watch: 6:15. She couldn't have slept for more than a few hours, and though she was stiff from having done that sleeping in a sitting position, she felt oddly refreshed. She recalled the previous night's long conversations with herself about Frank and Luke, about missing letters and a missing diary, about alibis and motives. What stood out was not all her arguments, but a simple, clear, vivid image: the yellow backhoe. But she still didn't know why that seemed important.

Julie had no idea whether Dalton and Nickie were early risers, but she decided to play it safe by staying in her room and reading till she heard them. A perfect chance, she told herself, to learn more about quilting. Around 7:30, when she heard voices in the hall, she decided that what she knew about quilting was adequate for the foreseeable future.

She declined Dalton's offer of breakfast in favor of stopping at the diner on her way to the office. She ordered the "Lucky Day Special" without realizing its meaning until she overheard two customers behind her talking about Friday the thirteenth. Oddly, she did feel lucky—because Rich was coming this afternoon. She had phoned him yesterday about the Nilsson invitation and was pleased he was agreeable. With luck on this supposed unlucky day, she thought, Rich would arrive early enough and she would finish the trustee meeting early enough to allow them time before they had to leave for dinner. And the pre-dinner sauna, she reminded herself, thinking of Frank Nilsson's smarmy look when he'd mentioned nudity. She had warned Rich to bring a bathing suit.

The blinking light on her office phone alerted her to Mike's message: "Had a talk with Frank and Luke," the voice said. "I should probably fill you in. Give me a call when you get in. Oh, it's about seven a.m. You're keeping banker's hours, Dr. Williamson."

"If you've got coffee on, I'll just swing by," the policeman said when she returned his call. Five minutes later he was sitting in her office. The coffee she'd started after the phone call was still dripping.

"Not very helpful, I guess," he began. "They both check out. Frank says he was home with Patty last Tuesday morning, working in his office there. And he was at their place down the coast this Wednesday night. Went down to check on one of his projects at Boothbay Harbor and stayed over."

"Or so he said," Julie said, and then briefly explained about being at the Nilsson house yesterday when Frank had returned.

"Right. I didn't check with people in Boothbay yet, but I can do that."

"And Patty verified that her husband was working at the house the day Mary Ellen was killed?"

"Haven't checked that, either. As to Luke, he said he was out at the Birch Brook site the morning Mary Ellen was killed, and at home this Wednesday. I can check with his wife about that, I guess, but there's really no way to verify his story about being at the condo site last Tuesday."

"So we really don't know," Julie said. "I mean, if their wives support their stories, it looks like Frank couldn't have killed Mary Ellen and Luke couldn't have broken into my house. But Luke could be lying about Tuesday morning, and Frank could be lying about Wednesday night. We can't really confirm either one of those stories."

"We could eliminate Frank as far as the break-in goes if some of his people at the Boothbay project confirm he was there."

"He could have gone down there but not stayed the night."

"True. But if you were thinking the same person who killed Mary Ellen broke into your house, neither Frank nor Luke could have done both."

"Assuming their wives confirm they were home those times. Are you going to ask them?"

"That coffee ready yet?" Mike asked. Julie went to the outer office and returned with two steaming mugs. "It's getting a little awkward," Mike continued as he sipped the hot coffee. "This is a small town, Julie, and I'm reluctant to make waves unless I have to. It wasn't easy questioning Frank and Luke. They were naturally suspicious. I had to make up a little story to cover things."

"How'd you do that?"

"Oh, I can tell a white lie when I have to. About Wednesday night, I made up a story that a driver had been run off the highway and reported vehicles like theirs. Said I didn't really think they had been out in the middle of the night but had to follow up. Just hope they don't talk to each other and compare notes since I told Luke the vehicle was a pickup like his, and told Frank the vehicle was an SUV like his. Probably the driver was confused and said it could have been *either* a pickup or an SUV! Maybe that'll do it."

"You're devious, Chief Barlow," Julie teased. "But how did you bring up the morning of Mary Ellen's murder?"

"Didn't have to lie on that. I just told them that while I was talking to them, I needed to do what the State Police asked me to do and ask everyone I could if they had been near the historical society that Tuesday morning and might have seen anything. Actually, I put a notice in *The Ryland Gazette* along those lines, asking anyone who might have been around there to get in touch with me. Both of them had seen that, as a matter of fact, so it was pretty easy."

"Maybe I'll find out some more tonight," Julie said. "Frank invited Rich and me to have dinner there."

"You sure you want to do that? If you really suspect him, won't you feel a bit creepy?"

"Rich will be there—and Patty."

"At least you're not planning to do any interrogating, I assume."

"Of course not. Frank is being considered to be a trustee of the historical society, and Patty is giving us some of her family papers. So I'm just doing my job. But about those papers, Mike, there's something you might want to know."

"With a refill," he said, and Julie went to get it. Mrs. Detweiller had arrived, and Julie spent a few minutes chatting with her about some tours before rejoining Mike. She explained about the missing Oakes diary and her supposition about what it could mean about Birch Brook. And she mentioned Dr. Tabor's letter describing the sale of the Swanson property in the Depression.

"Which confirms what the 1997 letter said," Mike noted. Julie agreed. "But no details?"

"No, that's true."

"Well, missing letter, missing diary. You do seem to have trouble holding on to things," Mike said. "But all this is getting to seem more like a history project than a police investigation."

"Maybe that's where I come in," Julie said.

"I can't stop you from speculating."

Did the lab people find out anything about the break-in?"

"Haven't heard. Probably won't till next week. Did you get your door fixed?"

"They were supposed to put on a dead bolt yesterday. I haven't been by the house to check yet."

"Good. I need to push off. Oh, by the way, did I mention that I called Steven Swanson, while I was at it, and he says he was in New Hampshire Wednesday and Thursday, showing houses during the day and at home with Elizabeth at night. Anyway, remember not to give the Nilssons the third-degree tonight. Of course, if you do pick up anything . . ."

"You'll be the first to know," she answered.

Chapter 36

When she did not find them terribly frustrating, the meetings of the Ryland Historical Society board amused Julie. The first couple of monthly meetings after she'd started in the job had been sheer torture, but she found she was coming to look forward to them, not so much for the content but for the theatrical experience they offered. She previewed today's meeting as she sat in her office early Friday afternoon, ostensibly preparing for it, but the meetings were so predictable that she had learned there was nothing special required of her.

Trustee meetings were Howard Townsend's show. He wrote the script and orchestrated the dialogue, and the trustees played their roles with admirable consistency. Clif, the treasurer and general curmudgeon, could always be relied on to hint at fiscal doom ahead. Loretta, bright and chirpy, would find something wonderful to contemplate in the smallest matter. Henry, the ironic attorney, was always good for a sharp dig. Dalton confined himself to matters he knew about, which over the past year had been exclusively those relating to the plans for the Swanson Center. Julie was brought up short when she realized that there were no other actors now on the stage called the board of trustees. Today's would be the first official meeting without Mary Ellen. Despite all of Mary Ellen's to-ing and fro-ing, Julie really was missing her.

Howard's role as director of the play began with the stage setting and props. He insisted on an urn of coffee and several trays of cookies. Julie had begun smuggling bottles of water and some fresh fruit into the room, additions warmly greeted by Loretta, Henry, and Dalton but snubbed by Howard and Clif. "Who eats fruit at this hour?" the board chair had asked the first time he had seen the apples and grapes on the tray beside the cookies. In fact,

Loretta, Mike, Dalton, and Julie *did* eat fruit, which the two older men watched with increasing dismay. Julie thought, though, that Howard was secretly pleased with the new menu, since the fruit diverted some of the trustees from the cookies, leaving more for Clif and himself to divide up at the end of the meeting and take home for private consumption.

"Everything's ready, Dr. Williamson," Mrs. Detweiller announced from where she stood in the door between the offices. "I got extra cookies this time. They always seem to go fast."

They did, Julie knew, only when the meetings ended. Gathering her papers, she headed to the classroom in Holder House that was set up for the trustee meeting. Although it was only 3:45, she wasn't surprised that Howard was already present. And having a chocolate-chip cookie with his coffee. Julie opened a bottle of Poland Spring water.

"Everything looks in order," Howard said as he scrutinized the agenda Mrs. Detweiller had mailed to the board earlier in the week. "I expect Dalton will have some backup papers on the project, though. The building committee met on Wednesday, didn't it?"

Julie said it had, and described their discussion and recommendations. "So we'll have to vote on signing the construction contract," the board chair said. "Clif will have some tough questions about the numbers, I'm sure, so Dalton will need some paper on that."

Whether Dalton had prepared "some paper on that" Julie didn't know, so she simply said she was sure that he would be ready. "We had a good meeting, Howard," she continued, "and the building committee is eager to move ahead."

"Assuming we'll be getting Mary Ellen's gift, of course."

"I'm sure Henry will have something to say on that."

"And so I will," said Henry as he joined them. "Good news, in fact. Judge Childerson phoned this morning to say he sees no problem about making the disbursal right away. With the proceeds of the land sale, there's plenty of cash in the estate account, so as soon as the judge puts it in writing I'll be able to prepare a check."

"Good old Mary Ellen," Howard said. "How we'll miss her." And her money, Julie thought the board chair was silently saying. But out loud she simply agreed, heartily and with deep sadness. Being here for the meeting without Mary Ellen brought home her death so sharply, though Julie continued to wonder how many of the others shared that view.

"Well, that should satisfy Clif," Howard continued.

"Seeing Clif satisfied will be worth the ticket of admission," Henry observed.

Loretta and Dalton entered just in time to catch Henry's comment, and after Henry explained it, Dalton said, "Anyone care to wager on it?"

"I don't think that would be appropriate," Howard said sternly. "And here's our treasurer now." Clif walked stiffly across the room, headed directly for the cookie tray.

"You must have been talking about money," Clif said between bites of a large peanut-butter cookie. "I didn't think I was late; it seems like you already got started."

"Not at all," Howard said. "We'd hardly begin without you, but as we're all assembled now . . . let's be seated."

Howard called the meeting to order and asked, as he always did, for a motion to forgo the reading of the minutes since they had been mailed. And, as always, Clif so moved. Dalton seconded, and it was duly authorized that the minutes would not be read aloud. They never were, but Howard always insisted on accomplishing that obvious convenience with a formal motion.

"Corrections or comments?" the chair then asked. "Hearing none, I call for a motion to approve the minutes."

"One moment, Mr. Chairman," Clif Holdsworth said. "You didn't hear my correction because you didn't give me a chance to say it before your call for approval."

"I'm sorry, Clif. Please proceed."

"In the third paragraph of the second page," Clif intoned, "the word 'approve' should be deleted and the word 'accept' introduced in its place. That refers to the treasurer's report, as you may know."

Indeed they did, because each time Clif gave his treasurer's report, one of the trustees would inevitably try to end the agony by moving its approval. And each time that happened, Clif would point out that the report didn't need to be *approved* but *accepted.* The difference between those two actions was of considerable importance to him, but no one else cared, let alone understood. Clif always said he stood ready to explain the vital distinction, but, at least in Julie's year of meetings, no one had been foolhardy enough to take him up on the offer. Yet Henry, in preparing the minutes, invariably used *approved*, and with equal invariability Clif had the correction made before the minutes were approved. Julie strongly suspected that Henry took some impish pleasure in what he always apologized for as his "terrible error."

Howard said the minutes were ready for approval as amended orally by Clif, and Loretta promptly moved their approval. "Or should that be *accepted?*" she lightly queried Clif.

"I believe the minutes themselves—unlike a report—do require formal approval. Though of course I would defer to our learned colleague Mr. LaBelle for confirmation of that."

"You've got me, Clif. I'm just a lawyer. We didn't study Roberts' Rules of Order at Yale Law School."

"Not surprised," Clif said. "Perhaps our distinguished chairman should rule on this."

"I'm afraid I didn't bring my copy of Robert's," the chair answered, "but I'm prepared to rule in favor of *approval* if there are no objections. Then hearing none, I call for a vote on Mrs. Cummings's motion to approve the minutes."

"As amended orally," Clif added.

"Quite. All those in favor? Opposed? Then the minutes are approved as amended."

"Orally," Loretta offered, drawing laughter from everyone except Clif.

Julie glanced at her watch. When Henry had said before the meeting that the rest of Mary Ellen's gift would now be forthcoming, she had entertained the hope that this news would lead to a short meeting. But since it took ten minutes merely to get the minutes out of the way, that hope was fading.

"Next order of business," Howard announced, "is the report of the building committee, which met two days ago. I believe, Dalton, you can summarize the meeting and the recommendations of the committee. If you have any paper on that, this would be a good time to distribute it."

"No paper, Mr. Chairman," Dalton said. "I think this is pretty simple." He quickly described the committee's discussion and its two recommendations: to approve the contract for the construction of the Swanson Center, and to rename the building to include Mary Ellen.

"Are those formal motions?" Howard asked.

"Sure. I present both as formal motions. Do I need to rephrase anything?"

"We understand, Dalton," Loretta said before Clif or Howard could object. "I second Dalton's motions."

"Perhaps the clerk could read them for us?" Clif suggested.

Without looking down at his notes, Henry spun out some formal language that captured the building committee's recommendations. Julie was impressed; she hadn't known until a few moments ago that Henry had gone to law school at Yale, but she wasn't surprised.

"Those your motions?" Clif asked Dalton, who replied, "Better than mine, but Henry got them just right. I call the question."

"I believe, Mr. Chairman," Clif said to no one's surprise, "that an opportunity for questions and discussion should precede the vote. Calling the question now precludes that."

"I withdraw my motion, Clif," Dalton said patiently. "I was just using the words casually, to mean that I'm ready to move ahead."

"So we understand, Dalton," Howard said, "but Clif is of course correct that we need to discuss these matters. Both are quite critical to the future of the Ryland Historical Society. Questions or comments on the motions?"

This, Julie said, is going to take the rest of the day. She was resigned to forgoing some private time with Rich before dinner with the Nilssons. But she was pleasantly surprised. Clif, as expected, focused on the financing of the construction, but Henry's assurance about the $500,000 gift from Mary Ellen quite easily convinced him that approving the contract would not lead to immediate insolvency for the Ryland Historical Society. Clif knew, to the penny, how much money was in the bank already and how much the contract required, and that the additional cash from Mary Ellen's estate was more than enough to bring the two figures into balance. "Of course, down the road a piece," the treasurer noted, "when we fit out the building and put up the signs and all, we'll need some more cash, but we have pledges scheduled to come in this fall. So I believe we can proceed to approve the contract based on Henry's assurances."

Although Henry paused for a moment on the word *assurances*, understanding it more narrowly than the others, he resisted comment. "Ready for the question, then?" Howard asked. The motion to approve the building committee's recommendation and sign the contract for the construction was promptly approved. With almost no discussion, the second recommendation was also approved: The new building would be officially called the Daniel and Mary Ellen Swanson Center.

"Think there's room for all that on the signs?" Clif asked.

"We can squeeze it in," Dalton replied. "Of course we might have to come back to the board for approval if the extra letters cost too much."

"I don't think anyone here will object," Clif answered with such seriousness that it was impossible to grasp whether he recognized that Dalton was pulling his leg.

"Fine," Howard said. "We've done some very important business here today, and I'm sure you all understand how significant this moment is. We all feel very deeply the absence of Mary Ellen Swanson at this time. Which brings me to a last piece of business. If the board is prepared to spend a few more moments?"

Julie checked her watch again and saw it was just 4:50. If the discussion about new trustees didn't take too long, she would have forty-five minutes or so alone with Rich. Others looked at their watches, and there was a general murmur of agreement that they could withstand another item of discussion.

Howard reminded them that with Mary Ellen's death the membership of the board had declined by three over just a year. "Of course you're a fine group. A fine group," Howard continued. "And numbers aren't everything. But I think you'll agree that we could benefit from an enlarged board—bring us up to full complement. Certainly one more member, perhaps up to three. With that in mind, you'll recall, I asked you last year to recommend names of potential new trustees. With all our other business this year we didn't make much progress, but I don't think anyone will be surprised that it was dear Mary Ellen who took this matter in hand. She suggested Frank Nilsson, and at my direction Julie has had a talk with Frank about this matter. Julie, could you bring us up-to-date?"

Julie knew very well what Howard wanted her to report on: her breakfast meeting with Frank a week ago, the highlights of his résumé, his interest in serving on the board. There was so much more she knew about the man—and even more she could speculate about without completely knowing. If she was right, this man wouldn't come within ten feet of sitting on the board. But she had to focus squarely on the matter at hand. She gave the facts.

"Excellent report, Julie," Howard said when she had finished. "I believe most of us know Frank in one capacity or another, but our director has provided a fine overview from an outsider's perspective. What comments do you have about the prospect of asking Frank Nilsson to join our board?"

The comments were neither numerous nor passionate. Julie sensed a general willingness to invite Frank to become a trustee—not because he was an outstanding candidate, but because he *was* a candidate, one willing volunteer whose appointment would reduce the number of vacancies. And—here Julie was in agreement—electing him would end this meeting. But she had not reckoned on Clif Holdsworth.

"We need to be careful about Frank Nilsson," the treasurer said.

Chapter 37

"Careful?" Loretta asked. "What's that supposed to mean? My impression is that Frank's a solid citizen."

"Suppose so." Clif responded. "I've known Frank since he married Patty and moved to town. Knew her from when she was born, and her folks—the Oakes family goes back a long way in Ryland. But there are matters I don't think the rest of you are aware of."

Clif's grumpiness and negative perspective were well known, but Julie sensed something more lay behind these comments. Could he, she wondered, suspect Nilsson of Mary Ellen's death? Or know about the break-in at her house and see him as responsible for that? But aside from Dalton, Julie didn't think anyone on the board knew what had happened. What could Clif be getting at?

"Maybe you could explain what you're getting at," Dalton interjected; Julie wondered if he was reading her mind. "Perhaps you could spell it out for us newcomers," he added.

"It's not a case of newcomers," Clif answered. "I feel rather reluctant to go on, frankly, since I might be compromising my duties here."

"For heaven's sake, Clif," Henry said, "if you know something important about Frank Nilsson, tell us. If you don't, or can't say, then you shouldn't have brought it up."

"All right, since I opened my mouth I suppose I should go ahead and use it. I think you all know I sit on the board of Ryland Bank and Trust." In fact, Julie didn't know, but she guessed she was the only one who didn't. "If you want to conclude what I'm going to say is privileged information, you can ignore it. But, mind, I'm not saying this comes from my role at the bank. It's the sort of thing anyone with open eyes and ears could know."

"Clif, please!" Howard said. "If you have information we should know, then by all means go ahead and tell us. This is a private discussion, and I'm sure we all recognize that nothing said here should go beyond this room. But if you feel you're revealing something you shouldn't, then let's drop it."

"Like I said, Howard, anyone paying attention can see Frank Nilsson is up to his neck in debt. He's got a couple of projects for old folks going down the coast, and he and Luke Dyer just went deep into it to buy Mary Ellen's land and finance the condo project."

"You're saying he's in trouble?" Dalton asked.

"Didn't say that. Just noting that he's not the moneybag a lot of you might think he is. He's highly, highly leveraged, and I don't see when and how he's going to get square. This Birch Brook thing—well, it's hard to imagine they can make that fly."

"Let me see if I understand this, Clif," Loretta said with the sort of patience Julie imagined her bringing to a parent-student conference. "Frank Nilsson has a lot of debt associated with his projects?"

"Correct."

"Okay, then what?" the principal continued. "What impact does this have on his role as a trustee here?"

"Not saying it has *any* impact. Just feel we ought not to buy a pig in a poke."

"Meaning?" Loretta continued.

"Meaning he's not in a position to give a lot of money to the historical society. If the rest of you think he's a golden goose waiting to be plucked, think again."

Julie enjoyed Clif's mixed metaphors, but it wasn't either a pig or a goose Julie would compare Nilsson to—more like a weasel.

"One's personal capacity to give is not a legitimate criterion for election to our board," Howard duly pointed out, sounding as he often did as if he were reading from the bylaws.

"That's fine, then," Clif responded. "I just don't want folks to jump into this without understanding that it'll be a cool day in Hades when Frank Nilsson is in a position to write a check for anything. At least one that doesn't bounce."

No one had an immediate response, but after a brief silence Dalton asked, "Is there any chance, Clif, that Frank's financial situation could become an embarrassment to the board? Aside from whether he can make a gift, are you saying we should be worried that he might get into some public difficulties about his finances?"

After a fairly long pause, Clif said simply, "Could be."

Howard began to chew on the pencil he waved, baton-like, to conduct board business. Julie sensed he was having doubts. Loretta was closely examining the printed agenda that lay before her, and Dalton was looking around the room, as if an answer might be written on the wall. Henry broke the silence: "Perhaps we need to think about all this," he said. "We've been short-handed for a year, so what's the harm in putting this off till next month? Just so we can all think about it."

"An excellent suggestion," Howard said. "It never pays to be hasty."

"But what about Frank Nilsson?" Loretta asked. "If he's eager to become a trustee and we don't proceed now, will that look bad? Will it put Julie in a bad position since she sort of interviewed him for this?"

"Julie?" Howard asked. Julie said she had made no promises and was careful to say the board had a good deal of other business and might not get around to considering new trustees for a while. "Then I think our attorney's remarks carry the day," the chair continued. "I speak for myself, of course," he said in the commanding tones that Julie and the others knew meant that he was in fact speaking for all of them, whether they knew or liked it. "Then let's agree to continue this discussion at our August meeting. Obviously this has been a confidential discussion, and

I suggest to the clerk that the minutes merely reflect the fact that the board briefly and privately considered the prospect of electing additional trustees. No need to spread this matter on the record, I would think."

Loretta moved adjournment, and it was happily seconded. As the trustees headed for the door, Julie looked at her watch: 5:20. If she could clear out of here quickly, she and Rich could still have some time before they had to leave for dinner. When she looked up after gathering stray papers from the table, she was relieved to see she was alone. But as she walked through the door and turned back to close it, Clif appeared. "Don't suppose you've heard any more about the shovels?" he asked.

For entirely different reasons, she assumed, Clif was as interested in those shovels as she was. "No," Julie answered, "but you should probably talk directly to Mike Barlow about them. He doesn't keep me informed about the investigation."

"No, I suppose he wouldn't, but I thought he might return them to the society, not knowing they were mine. If he does . . ."

"I'll be sure to let you know, Clif." Hoping he would follow her lead, Julie began walking away from the classroom and across the exhibit area toward the exit. "I need to lock up and activate the security system," she said when they reached the outside door. "Could you just hold these?" she added as she handed him the sheaf of papers she had collected from the meeting.

"About Frank Nilsson," Clif said awkwardly when he returned the papers to her at the bottom of the stairs.

"What about him?"

"You have to understand how small towns work. I hear lots of things at the bank. I don't go around telling folks everything, but it seemed to me the historical society needs to know about Frank's financial situation. But I wouldn't want him to know where the information came from."

"Of course not. I certainly won't tell him. Like I said, I can just let him know the board has a lot of business right now and won't be electing new trustees till the fall. In fact, Rich and I are having dinner with Frank and Patty tonight, and I can just casually let him know."

Julie smiled and started to move away.

"Up at the skiway?" Clif asked.

"Yes."

"Probably going to use Frank's sauna?"

"He mentioned it, yes."

"Take a bathing suit," Clif said as he turned and walked in the opposite direction.

If she didn't need to set the security system on Swanson House, Julie would have walked straight home and dealt with the meeting papers tomorrow. But she stopped at her office long enough to deposit them and lock the door and set the system. As she walked briskly past the construction site she smiled to see Rich's car turning off Main Street and swinging into the back drive of the house.

Chapter 38

While Rich drove, Julie filled him in on Luke's and Frank's alibis, Clif's comments about Nilsson's financial situation, swearing him to secrecy, and the missing Oakes diary. Then she told him about the two Tabor letters.

"But you knew that, right?" he asked.

"That the Swansons needed the money? Right. But they also refer to bad blood and an old dispute over ownership. They just help to fill in the picture. The Nilssons are up there on the right," she added. "Maybe you should pull in here so we can finish this first. It's just 6:30, so we don't need to rush."

Rich turned into the parking area for another set of condos and turned off the engine. Julie asked what he thought about the alibis. "I think they cancel out," he said. "Nilsson couldn't have murdered Mary Ellen, and Dyer couldn't have broken into your house. And if Nilsson's alibi about being in Boothbay Harbor holds up, he couldn't have broken into your house either. And if Dyer is telling the truth about being at Birch Brook when Mary Ellen was killed, then he—"

"Everything depends on their telling the truth. If one or both is lying, then it's another matter." Julie sat silently for a moment and then said, "We'd better get going."

"Sure you want to?" Rich asked.

"A purely social evening, yet in my role as historical society director."

"Ah, I see," Rich said, nodding sarcastically.

He pulled the car into the Nilssons' driveway. "Nice digs," he said. "Doesn't look like he's ready for debtors' prison quite yet."

Frank Nilsson answered the ring of the bell and greeted them heartily. "Just getting the sauna warmed up," he said. "Nice that it cooled off again. Should feel good."

"I haven't taken a sauna in years," Rich said. "I'm really looking forward to it."

Patty came out from the kitchen, and Frank introduced Rich and led the three of them downstairs and across the room where Julie had looked through the boxes of Oakes papers. "Just out through here," the host said as he opened a door at the end of the room. Beyond it lay a large room that at first appeared to be the unfinished part of the basement. "Sauna's right there," he said and pointed to a cedar door with a long glass panel. "This is where we come to cool off, and over there's the shower and changing room. You brought suits?" Julie held up the canvas boat bag she was carrying. "Okay, you can use the changing room here. Take a shower if you like—some do it before as well as after, but I think I'll wait. We'll go get changed and be right back."

Julie and Rich went to the door he had indicated and changed into their bathing suits. As they reentered the bare basement, the Nilssons came through the other door. Frank opened the sauna door and gestured to Julie and Rich to enter. She had been so busy today that she hadn't thought about the sauna until she stood in front of the door. For a very brief moment she froze, imagining the tight space and wondering if she could go through with it. But when Frank opened the door she saw that the room was quite large—easily ten feet wide and fifteen or twenty feet long. She was amazed and relaxed at once.

Inside, happy that she was feeling so comfortable, she said that the smell made her think of her mother's cedar chest, Frank laughed and explained: "Whole thing's cedar. Resists moisture—and it does smell nice, doesn't it? Here, come try the benches."

A single bench ran the length of the room, and on the two ends were double benches, the lower ones jutting out into the room so you could step on them to reach the uppers. Julie sat on the long one, and Rich joined her while Patty settled onto a lower one on the end. Julie could feel Frank's eyes on her as she crossed her legs. He's checking me out, she thought, and not too subtly either. Maybe it had been wrong to come here.

"Now for the steam," Frank said as he stood up. "I'll start." He walked over to a wooden bucket, dipped into it with a large metal scoop, and splashed water onto the electric heating unit. Steam rushed up at him, and he quickly stepped back. "Have to be careful when you do it. Stand away so the steam doesn't hit your eyes." He ladled out several more scoops of water, and the room, large as it was, was enveloped in steam. Frank sat down beside Julie rather than joining his wife on the bench at the end of the room. "You can add some water in a minute, Julie. I'll show you how when the time comes."

Julie, still feeling the distaste of Frank's ogling, wondered exactly how Frank would show her—helping himself to a few feels as he directed her in the use of the scoop? "Maybe Rich should go first," she said.

"Sure," Frank said. "But we can wait a minute. Smell that? It's not the cedar now. There's pine pitch in the water—nice clean smell, isn't it?"

Julie and Rich agreed that it was. Rich started a conversation with Patty about how often they used the sauna. Patty was as bright and pleasant as she had been with Julie yesterday when the two of them had looked through the boxes of family papers.

"Okay," Frank interrupted. "Time for some more steam. Rich?" Rich took his turn with the water and rejoined them on the bench. They sat in silence for several minutes, soaking in the steam. "Your turn," Frank said in Julie's direction as he leaned toward her. But she jumped up and asked Rich to help her with the water before Frank could offer instructions. She enjoyed splashing the water and stepping out of range of the steam; the smell of the pine pitch was pleasing, and she said so.

"Thought you'd like it," Frank answered. "Now we have to be careful. See that timer? I set it when we came in. It's best to limit yourself to fifteen or twenty minutes for the first round. When the timer goes off we step outside and cool down. Take a quick shower if you like. Then come back for another round. I call it *layering*. It's what really relaxes you."

Rich resumed his conversation with Patty, and Julie and Frank sat quietly until the bell on the timer sounded. "Everyone out of the pool!" Frank said. The unfinished basement seemed freezing now, though it was obviously only the sharp contrast with their body heat that made it so. "You don't want to shiver," Frank explained, "but it's good to get just about to that point before you get back in." They circled around the room, Rich now asking Frank about the house and the sauna.

"Planned the sauna from the beginning," Frank answered, "and I'm glad I did. It's a great family experience, and we enjoyed it with the kids in the years before they left."

Rich inquired about the Nilsson children, and Patty rather than Frank responded, enthusiastically reciting their college choices, their majors, their prizes and achievements. "Ted graduates this year, Sue next. Hard to believe," Patty said. "They're both working this summer. Sue's in Portland and Ted's working for Frank at Boothbay. Ted's staying at our camp there, and Sue will join us for a couple of weekends when I spend the month there."

"Patty," Frank sharply interrupted, "I doubt Julie and Rich share your fascination for our wonderful offspring." Before Julie could counter him, he continued: "Let's do a second round." He held open the door to the sauna while the three others reentered and took up places on the benches. As Frank ladled more water onto the stove, the rising steam filled the room. "Twelve minutes should be enough this time," he announced as he set the timer. "So, what were we talking about?"

Julie was tempted to return to the Nilsson children, not that she really cared but to spite Frank for cutting off his wife so impolitely. Instead, she decided it was a good opportunity to bring up the question of Frank's joining the historical society's board, because with Patty and Rich present she could do it quickly and casually. Although the steam made it hard for her to see his face as clearly as she wished, Julie thought she saw a flicker of annoyance after she mentioned that the board was postponing the election of new trustees until the construction project was well launched. If he was annoyed, his response didn't show it: "Probably smart," he said. "I've got my hands full with Birch Brook anyway, but keep me on the list. Now, speaking of full hands, shall we have some Akvavit, Patty?"

His wife rose obediently and started for the door. "I'll bring it down," she said. "I'm getting pretty hot anyway."

"Akavit?" Rich asked.

"Ak-va-vit," Frank corrected him. "Danish—means water of life or something. Traditional sauna drink—chug down a couple of shots of ice-cold Akvavit and some little sausages and you really understand what sauna is all about."

Rich offered to help, explaining that he, too, was feeling pretty hot. Before she realized it or could act, Julie was alone with Frank. Neither spoke as Frank added more water. Julie was beginning to experience the steamy heat in an unpleasant way, feeling it was wrapping around her like a smothering blanket. When Frank sat beside her on the long bench, she was tempted to move to one of the smaller end seats. Before she could, he put his hand on her bare knee and patted it gently, in an almost fatherly way.

"It must be hard for you, Julie," he said, "to be working with that board of dinosaurs. I was looking forward to coming on, as your friend and supporter. But I guess they're not ready for me."

"It's not a question of whether they want you on the board, Frank," she said, putting her hand on his as if to reassure him and then gently moving it off her knee. "It's just a timing issue: Things are so busy they want to get some stability before adding to the board. I know they're eager to have you join."

"You're a good soldier," he said. He stood, headed to the bucket, and, using the metal scoop, dribbled water across the heating unit. "When the time's right I'll still be happy to get involved," he said as he started back toward the bench, still carrying the scoop. He walked slowly toward her, twirling the wooden handle in his right hand, which made the nine-inch round scoop itself rotate slowly. "I'm sure you've got plenty to do with the project," he continued as he stood over her now, still twirling. "You really ought to keep focused on that. Not worry about other things so much."

"I'm not sure I follow, Frank." Julie shifted away from him.

"Just keep your eyes on the ball, Julie," he said as he held the scoop in front of him. The metal portion *did* resemble a ball. Was that what he was trying to illustrate? she wondered. "The construction project," he added. "If I were you, I'd let someone else deal with stuff like the archives. You were very nice to have a look at Patty's family papers, and I know you keep track of what goes on in the library. But Tabby Preston can handle all that. No need for you to worry about things like the old Oakes diary, or papers and letters and the like. It'd be better for you to let others do that so you can concentrate on the project. Just a word to the wise, Julie—advice from someone who's been around the block."

As he spoke, Frank was looking intently into Julie's eyes. Then he turned and walked toward the heater and replaced the scoop in the bucket. The message Julie got came as much from Frank's look as from the words—or even the scoop that he used like a baton to accompany them. Was it kindly advice? Or a warning? Julie really wasn't sure. Before she could respond, he turned back to her and held up the timer. "Couple of minutes left, but I think I hear Patty and Rich. Shall we try that Akvavit?"

Chapter 39

The Akvavit, icy cold, went rapidly from Julie's mouth to her stomach to her brain. She felt momentarily disoriented, woozy from the steamy heat, unsteady enough to take Rich's arm for support. "Eat some sausages and crackers," he told her. A few nibbles helped, but she continued to hold onto him. Patty noticed and asked if Julie was okay.

"I think so," she said, uncertain if that was true.

"Better stick to one shot," Frank said pleasantly. "Pretty powerful stuff. Why don't you folks take a cool shower and get dressed? I guarantee you'll feel better then, Julie."

The concern for her well-being was so obvious in Frank's words and tone that Julie had trouble connecting what he had just said to what he had said to her in the sauna. Actually, she had trouble connecting much right now and was happy Rich took over. He guided her into the changing room and into the shower.

The pulsing water revived her.

"That Akvavit really hit you."

"I guess so, but I think it was more than that. In the sauna, when you and Patty were gone, Frank talked to me about the historical society, about being willing to join the board later, and then about how I should focus on the construction project and not get involved in diaries and letters. 'Keep your eyes on the ball'; 'a word to the wise.' It was really strange—I think it was a warning. And he was sort of brandishing that water scoop while he talked, twirling it around."

"Threatening you?" Rich asked, alarmed.

"Not exactly. Maybe just a nervous thing, wanting to hold something while he talked. I don't know, Rich—maybe I just got too hot in there and was imagining things."

"Or maybe Akvavit's not your drink," he said, adjusting the water temperature.

"Too cold!" Julie said.

"No, it's good this way—bracing. It'll wake you up."

They took turns standing directly under the shower, but after two turns Julie said she was cool enough. "And wide awake," she added. "I can see how this works—warming, cooling, warming, cooling. Have to admit it's refreshing."

Although the shower hadn't fully washed away Julie's concerns about Frank's comments in the sauna, nor his hand on her leg, which she decided not to tell Rich about at least for now, by the time they had dried and dressed and gone upstairs she was feeling relaxed and actually eager for dinner. After dinner they returned to the family room in the basement, Julie making sure she was beside Rich and across from Frank and Patty. Just before ten o'clock, the pent-up emotions of the last few days, combined with the aftereffects of the sauna and the wine and food, hit her with an almost physical force. She suddenly felt too exhausted to say another word. Rich and Frank continued to talk with animation, now focused on that perennial New England summer topic: the Boston Red Sox's chances this year. If they didn't leave now, Julie thought, Rich would surely have to carry her to the car. Patty sat up alertly when Julie interrupted the baseball talk to say they should be leaving. Julie hoped they hadn't overstayed their welcome, but Frank was pleasant and talkative as he walked them upstairs and out to the driveway. "We'll do it again," he promised as he waved good-bye.

"Nice evening, except the part about the threat," Rich observed as he drove out of the residential area and came onto the access road just below the ski lodge.

"I didn't say it was a threat, exactly. I'm too tired to even talk about it. Sorry I pooped out," Julie said. "Everything just hit me at once. It's been such a crazy week. I'm so glad you're here!"

"Happy to be your guard dog for the night. Think you'll be able to sleep?"

"I'll be lucky if I can stay awake to crawl up the stairs to the bedroom."

She was able, but once she hit the bed she was out instantly.

The alarm clock said 12:25 when she awoke with a start. The memory of Wednesday night flooded in on her, but this time it wasn't a noise downstairs that woke her. What woke her was Frank Nilsson. They were alone in the sauna, and he was wielding a shovel instead of the water scoop, and calmly but menacingly walking toward her through the steam and repeating "a word to the wise," "a word to the wise." The steam was filling the sauna, becoming thicker, covering her like a hot blanket. And still Frank kept coming, getting closer now, and still repeating that phrase. She shuddered and grabbed desperately at the blanket to tear it off her. And that woke Rich.

"Sorry!" she said as she sat up. "I had a bad dream."

"It's okay . . . I'm here. Don't think about the other night."

"I wasn't. I was dreaming about Frank Nilsson. In the sauna. Rich, it was really scary. I mean, when he talked to me in the sauna about staying away from the business of the diary and the letter, I sort of sensed it was a warning, but I wasn't scared. I guess I really was but didn't let myself think it then. But now I'm sure he was threatening me, warning me."

"About?"

"About not trying to put things together, to figure it out."

"This is why I'm so worried about all this, Julie. You may not have any idea what you're getting into. You don't really know these people."

"I know, I know. I'm sorry. Let's finish this conversation in the morning."

When they woke at 6:30 on Saturday morning, Julie felt more rested than she'd expected. They lay in bed and talked quietly,

Julie reviewing her dream and her unease about Frank, Rich mostly listening but interjecting occasional questions.

"And the shovel—did I tell you my idea about that?" she asked. "That definitely needs to be checked out right away," she resumed before he could respond.

"Okay, okay," Rich said when she finished. "Maybe. But I think we need a good long run to clear our heads."

She agreed, and as they did a cool-down walk across the Common, Rich said, "We've earned it."

"What?"

"Breakfast. A big, high-calorie feast, with lots of coffee. Let's go to the diner and indulge ourselves."

"I'm beginning to appreciate the value of running," she said.

The Saturday-morning crowd was different than the weekday customers. No carpenters and plumbers starting their day over coffee and gossip, no businessmen like Frank Nilsson. In fact, at eight when they arrived, the diner was nearly empty. Two young couples dressed for hiking occupied one table, and a woman sat at the counter reading the paper. Otherwise, they had the place to themselves.

"So the shovel does seem to be key," Rich said after they placed their order. "You should just tell Barlow your idea and then drop the whole thing, Julie."

"What idea would that be," a voice said. Julie and Rich both turned to locate the source of the words. "Had a funny feeling I'd find you here," Mike said. "Mind if I join you?"

"Please," Julie said. "How come you thought we'd be here?"

"I saw you running this morning, and when you didn't answer at the house later, I guessed you'd be here. Rewarding yourself for running."

"It was Rich's idea," Julie said.

"But you didn't disagree," Rich pointed out.

"Julie's gotten to be a regular here," Mike said. "Pretty soon they'll be giving you your own mug. Thanks, Doris," he said to the waitress who handed him a cup of coffee. "Like mine—see?" He held up a mug that said CHIEF OF POLICE.

"You were looking for me?" Julie prompted.

"Right. But let me just order." He beckoned for the waitress and said, "The usual, Doris. So," he said, turning to Julie, "I figured you'd be interested in what I found out about Frank Nilsson."

"As a matter of fact," Julie said, "I have something to tell you about him, but go ahead."

"You remember Frank said he spent the night at the camp in Boothbay? I called there—didn't expect an answer, but their son was there, Ted. Seems he's working on Frank's project and using the cabin. I told him I was checking out that famous auto accident we had here, and it turns out his dad came down Wednesday afternoon to check on the project."

"So his alibi checks out," Julie said, with clear disappointment in her voice.

"Did I say that? Matter of fact, Ted says his dad left around seven to drive back to Ryland. Didn't spend the night."

"Wow! That means he lied to you—and that he did it. Or he could have."

"The first thing you said is true: Frank *did* lie to me, and I mean to sort this out with him. As to the other things, we'll have to see. I'm going to go talk to Frank this morning, but the reason I was looking for you is that I wanted to find out more about that diary. Figure it might be useful to bring that up at the right moment, just to see his reaction. So tell me again why you think it's important."

Julie explained that if the Oakes diary did contain information about a survey of the Birch Brook land, and that information was used in settling the dispute in the nineteenth century, then Frank might want to keep it from being discovered. "Patty was surprised it wasn't in the boxes," she reminded him, "and Frank is the one who brought the boxes from the rental storage place. So he could have taken it."

"That's helpful. Just in case. Now I need to find out where he was Wednesday night. So," he added, as he tucked into his eggs, "you said you had something to tell me about Frank."

Julie told him about Frank's comment in the sauna. Recalling Clif Holdsworth's warning about not attributing to him the information about Frank's indebtedness, she confined herself to speculating that the Birch Brook development must be putting a financial strain on both Frank and Luke.

"Typical real estate project," Mike said. "Using someone else's money is the way to go. But come back to last night, Julie. Did you really think Frank was threatening you?"

"He didn't say 'If you do this, I'll do that.' It wasn't that kind of a threat. But it was certainly a warning."

" 'Course, I've done the same myself," Mike said with a laugh. "I think even Rich here has been guilty of trying to keep you out of things, am I right?" Rich quickly admitted his guilt.

"But he really was warning me off, Mike," Julie insisted. "I feel sure of that."

"Okay. I think I'll head up to the skiway to have another chat."

"Have you confirmed Frank's story about being at home with Patty the morning Mary Ellen was killed?" Julie asked.

"Not yet. Maybe I can talk to her, too. Have to see how it goes."

"That might be a problem," Julie said. "Patty is going to their camp this morning. She might already be gone."

"Well, if I can talk to Frank alone it might actually be better. I can always confirm the other story with Patty another time. You going to be around later today?" Julie said she and Rich would be at the house because he had papers to read. "Okay," Mike said, "I'll give you a call if I find out anything you should know. Hope that won't interrupt your work, Rich."

"The only way to read student papers," Rich said, "is with a lot of interruptions. We'll be there."

When the policeman left, Julie said, "Rich, this is it! It's all coming together now. I told you it would. I just wish I could go with Mike when he talks to Frank."

"Settle down!" Rich said. "Finish your coffee and relax. There's nothing for you to do till you hear from him."

"No, there *is* something to do. Remember about the shovel?"

"I thought you were going to tell him that."

"I was, but then after what he said I just forgot. But that doesn't mean we can't check ourselves."

"True, but it doesn't seem right to do that on our own until Mike talks to Nilsson."

"I guess that's fair enough. And it shouldn't take too long. Mike said he'll call. So maybe we should go home and wait to hear."

"I've got plenty to do, Julie—a carload of papers to read."

"What a thrill!"

Chapter 40

Her only teaching had been as a graduate assistant while she was working on her PhD, but it had been enough to make Julie sympathize now with Rich as he faced the stack of papers on the kitchen table. She had transferred the State of Maine puzzle, still incomplete, to a folding table and sat down there just a little away from him.

"You don't miss the academic side at all, do you?" Rich asked as he thumbed through the stack as a way of delaying the hard work.

"Not really," Julie said. "Remember I never taught full-time." She added after a pause, "Besides, I like running things. Oh, I know, Ryland Historical Society isn't the Smithsonian or even a state museum, but it's big enough for me now—and I'm responsible for it."

"Power-hungry!" Rich said with a laugh.

"Right. But you understand—I just can't get excited about standing in front of a bunch of adolescents in a classroom. It's great that you love teaching, but what's exciting for me is actually being in charge and making something happen. Funny, though, my dad said the same thing about me."

"That you're power-hungry?"

"Not quite that. Just that this is a good job for me because I like to run things."

"He knows you well. I suppose this is the conversation where he pointed out what a loser I am, being a lowly faculty member."

"Rich, I keep telling you: Dad likes you, and he respects that you're a teacher, like him." Julie could see from his look that Rich doubted her description of her father's view of him. She continued, more quietly, "We never really talked about that conversation on the hike last weekend. Maybe this is a good time to."

"Distract me from my deep involvement in reading papers?"

"You don't always have to be so sarcastic," she said.

"Sorry. Sure, let's talk. I apologized for blowing up and running on ahead."

"Not quite, not with words."

"Fair enough. I apologize, Julie. I shouldn't have gotten pissed off, but when you brought your folks into the conversation it just reminded me that I don't know where this is going, where we want it to go."

"By *this* you mean us, our relationship? What do they have to do with it?"

"I accept everything you say about your dad's protectiveness, that you're his only child and still his little girl. I really do understand that. But I also realize he doesn't think much of me as a boyfriend, and I guess—this is really hard—I wonder if you, well, if you feel the same."

"About you?"

"Yes. That I'm not really worthy of you, that—"

"That's so Victorian, Rich! What does *worthy* have to do with it—like it's some sort of business arrangement or contract?"

"What's your *it* here?"

She hesitated. He watched her closely. Finally she answered: "Marriage. Isn't that what we're talking about?"

"At some point, yes; or at least I am."

"What's wrong with the way we are now?"

"Oh, shit, Julie—nothing. Everything's *right* about it, at least for me. But where's it heading? Can you imagine marrying me? Can we keep commuting afterwards? Does marriage fit your view of yourself, of your career?"

"I can't answer all those questions, Rich. Not right now. My career does matter to me, you know that very well, but it's not everything. I guess I just don't know how much it counts, how much else there is, how it all fits together."

"I bet your dad would say it counts most."

"Why do you keep bringing up my father, as if I'm a teenager?"

"Because he's such a strong presence in your life, still, even now. And I understand that. I respect that you have that relationship with him. And what he'd respect is that you put your career first."

This wasn't the first time Julie had considered the points Rich was making, but it was the first time the two of them had talked about her family and its influence on her. And despite the underlying tension of the conversation, Julie suddenly realized she was happy they *could* have it, that she and Rich could focus on something so intimate. "Rich, I don't know if I fully agree with you or not—I mean, about my dad and how all that affects me. But I do agree you're right that I have to sort out my career goals and my other goals and figure out how to find the right balance. It's going to take time, but I think we have that, don't we?"

"Yes; whatever it takes," Rich said. He got up from his side of the kitchen table and walked around to where, during the conversation, Julie had moved to sit opposite him. He stood above and behind her and stretched his arms around her shoulders and hugged tightly.

"Thanks," was all she said, but it seemed enough for both of them.

"Think you'll ever finish that puzzle?" he asked.

"Get back to your papers, Professor O'Brian."

She went back to examining the pieces of the puzzle and fitting them slowly into the map, absorbed now in a concrete task, relieved at their talk but eager to resume the ease of just being together, not talking or thinking.

"Listen to this!" Rich exclaimed, "You won't believe how stupid students can be. Can I just read this sentence to you? It'll confirm how you feel about teaching."

Julie looked up and smiled. "Read on," she said.

"Okay. The assignment was to write about the role of Maine in the French and Indian War. Not a trick question. Lots of material in the textbook for them to start on. So this bozo writes, 'Since Maine didn't become a state until the nineteenth century, it had no chance to play a role in the French and Indian War, which occurred in the eighteenth century.' "

"That's it?"

"That's it."

Julie laughed. "Well, maybe he deserves a C for creativity."

"More like an F for being not just stupid but also a wiseass. Sometimes I wonder . . ."

But the ringing telephone stopped his wondering, and Julie leapt up to answer.

"Mike! What's the news?"

Rich looked up from the papers and read the disappointment in Julie's face as she carried on her side of the conversation. After a few minutes, she said, "Well it's not conclusive until you check that out, right?" And then: "Okay, I see. Thanks for letting me know."

"So?" Rich prompted after she put the phone down.

"I don't know if Mike believes it or not," she said.

"I'm sure I don't either, Julie, because I don't know what *it* is."

"Sorry. Seems Frank admitted right away that he didn't stay at the camp. His son is there, and Ted has a girlfriend who's staying over, and Frank didn't want to impose on them. He told his son he was headed home but instead he went back to his office in Boothbay and spent the night there. Slept in his chair, he said. He told Patty he had stayed at the camp because he didn't want her to know about Ted's girlfriend staying over."

"Guys always stick together," Rich interjected.

"Right. And he lied to Mike before for the same reason. Oh, I can just hear Frank saying all that—he's so smooth. I'm not sure if Mike believes him, but it'll be hard to verify that Frank stayed at the office by himself and left before anyone showed up. Convenient."

"Did Mike talk to him about the diary?"

"No, he said it didn't really come up, and if Frank's new story is true it might be irrelevant. But I'm not eliminating Frank. We've got more to do, that's all. Think you can tear yourself away from those papers?"

"That won't be hard, but what's up?"

"The shovel! You know my idea on that."

"Yeah, but how come you didn't mention it to Mike? You said you would after he talked to Frank."

"I know, but let's just go ourselves and not get him involved until we find out."

❧

The drive along the river to Birch Brook took only a few minutes, and when they got to the construction site they were happy to see no other vehicles. Rich parked where he had the week before, and they walked up the rise from the river. The yellow backhoe sat at the top of the rise.

"What if it's locked?" Rich asked.

"It won't be," Julie said. Just seeing the big machine excited her. It had come into her head the night she lay awake at the Black Crow Inn, and during the past day and especially last night the image kept reappearing. Now it was real—right ahead of them.

"What makes you so sure?"

"I just don't think they have locks on construction equipment like this."

They were standing directly in front of the backhoe, and its headlights were so like eyes that Julie's earlier notion of its being some sort of prehistoric animal recurred to her.

"Here goes," Rich said as he moved along the side toward the steps to the cab. He took them quickly and grasped the handle of the door. "You're right!" he said as he pulled the door open and stepped into the cab. "Come on up—there's plenty of room for both of us."

Julie bounded up the steps but stood outside the cab. Rich's idea of ample room inside the cab didn't exactly fit Julie's sense of space: Backhoe cabs were too tight for her. "I'll stay here," she said. "Start looking."

Rich knew what he was looking for, but where he would find it was another matter. He began with a visual survey, carefully examining the cab from top to bottom and side to side. "It's got to be in something," Julie said impatiently. "If it were just lying around someone else would have already found it." Rich bent to look under the seat and then got down on his hands and knees to explore the floor. "Nothing," he said as he stood up.

Julie was peering into the cab from the outside steps. "It *has* to be here," she said impatiently.

"Hey, you want to look?"

"If you come out, I'll try. There's just not room for both of us in there." They traded places, and Julie repeated Rich's search while he looked on from outside. "Step down so I can come out," she said, and then backed out onto the steps and hopped to the ground to join him. "This just doesn't make sense," she said sadly.

"Tell me your theory again," Rich said as they stood beside the backhoe.

"It's so simple that I just know it has to be right. Think about it: This backhoe was sitting at the construction site when Mary Ellen was murdered. If Frank didn't want to walk away with a bloody shovel, he had to hide it—and fast. So he sees this." She pointed to the machine as she continued. "Voilà—a perfect hiding place! No one would check the backhoe, so he puts it inside."

"And walks away?"

"Or runs or whatever. But the point is that the bloody shovel would be safe in the backhoe."

"But he could have already gotten it and disposed of it. It's been over a week, Julie, and the machine has been out here untended."

"I know, but even if Frank removed it already, there would be signs—blood. Did you look for that?"

"I'm not a CSI, Julie. Besides, if someone took the shovel he'd have wiped up any blood."

"Probably, but we need the police to check this out."

"So we'll go call Barlow?"

"I guess so," she said reluctantly.

"Well, at least you satisfied yourself that the shovel's not here."

Rich started down the hill toward the parking area, but Julie stayed behind, staring at the yellow backhoe. "I keep thinking it should be able to *tell* us something," she said with a laugh when Rich, realizing she wasn't beside him, turned to rejoin her.

"I guess you have to be able to speak backhoe," Rich said.

"Not one of my languages. Let's just look around it." She walked in front of the machine, then down the opposite side, slowly and carefully examining every feature as if the backhoe were a historic artifact that with the right reading could reveal something. Rich remained at the front.

"The toolbox!" she shouted. Rich came around to where she was standing at the rear of the backhoe. She pointed to a chrome box affixed to the back of the cab. "Can you climb up there?"

Rich grasped a handle on the side of the chrome box and hoisted himself up onto the small platform behind it. He lifted the lid of the toolbox and looked in. Then he turned to Julie and smiled. "Maybe backhoe is one of your best languages after all. Looks like a bloody shovel down underneath stuff."

"Don't touch it!" Julie yelled.

"Hey, don't worry," Rich said as he straightened up and turned to look at her down on the ground. "You want to check for yourself?" He extended his hand and pulled her up beside him. "See—down there underneath those wrenches."

"And the ribbon's still on!" she said. "We found it, Rich."

"Looks like it. But now what?"

"We've got to get Mike right away. But one of us should stay here, just in case."

"I'll stay. You go call Barlow."

Julie began to trot down the hill toward the car. "Hey," Rich shouted. "Would you like the keys?" She came back to get them.

"I'll be fast. Be careful, Rich."

"Not a problem. I'll go up there and sit under a tree till you get back. But drive carefully; there's no hurry now."

Rich didn't for a minute think Julie would agree, but he felt obliged to say it anyway. He walked toward the higher ground that hadn't yet been logged for the foundations of the condo development and found a shady spot under an oak tree.

He was awakened by the sound of a vehicle down the hill by the river. Could Julie be coming back so soon? The sound grew louder. Cursing himself for dozing off, he stood to walk toward the backhoe to greet her but then saw a black SUV with dark tinted windows coming right up the path from the parking area. He ducked behind the tree. The vehicle kept coming, slowly but powerfully ascending the hill. When it approached the backhoe and slowed, he saw the unmistakable Cadillac logo. It was stopped now, but its engine was running.

Rich made a quick calculation. If he showed himself and walked toward the vehicle, he'd have some explaining to do, especially if the driver was Luke Dyer or Frank Nilsson. And he didn't really relish the thought of confronting someone by himself so far from any passing cars down on the road. If he stayed out of sight, the driver might get into the toolbox and retrieve the shovel. But maybe it didn't have anything to do with the shovel.

The vehicle was still sitting by the backhoe, the driver apparently waiting inside. For what? He didn't know that, either. Okay, he finally told himself, I might as well do it. He moved quickly from behind the tree and then broke into a jog toward the parked SUV. I'll make it up as I go, he told himself, but the main thing is to find out who's in that monster and what he wants. Before Rich could get close, the engine of the SUV roared, and the driver pulled it sharply around and hit the gas. As he got to backhoe, he could just see the back of the vehicle as it cleared the hill. And the license plate. He didn't have a head for figures and wasn't sure he read the numbers right, but at least he got the state.

Chapter 41

Since Rich did most of the driving on the Orono–Ryland commute, Julie had suggested several times that he needed a cell phone. He resisted, telling Julie he found no need to have a phone attached to him 24-7. And, he also, Julie assumed, didn't want to be like seemingly everyone else in Maine, talking on a cell phone while driving and not paying attention to the road. But she had resolved to break the impasse by buying both of them cell phones for his birthday in September. She'd done away with her own upon moving to Maine, but now that coverage was better in the Ryland area, she was ready for one again. As she drove into Ryland she wished she had acted sooner. She wasn't sure if she'd go all the way home to call Mike or stop along the way. Were there any pay phones left these days? She was coming up to the diner when she remembered that there was a phone there.

She fished some change out of the center console and rushed to the pay phone beside the front door of the diner. Two adolescent boys in those baggy pants so popular even in Ryland were standing in front of it, and a third was using the phone. Julie stepped back so as not to overhear the conversation. Then she began to pace, thinking about the shovel and feeling clever that she had thought of the backhoe as its location. Well, not *thought* so much as dreamed—or visualized it, really, Thursday night when she had trouble sleeping at the Black Crow Inn. But if it came to her in such an odd way, there was a compelling logic, she realized—the backhoe was simply the perfect place to quickly dispose of the shovel. As she paced she still wondered why Frank hadn't removed it—he'd certainly had time and opportunity. And so had Luke, for that matter. Well, everything would come clear when it was checked for prints. So why were these kids taking so long?

"You, like, need to use this?" one of them said in her direction.

"I do, yes. I need to call the police," she added.

"Dudes," her questioner said to his friends, "we should, like, let this lady make her call."

"Thanks, I appreciate that," Julie said as the three sauntered off. She couldn't remember the number of the Ryland Police Station and so called 9-1-1 and told the dispatcher she needed to talk to Chief Barlow right away.

"Is this an emergency?" the woman asked.

"Not an accident or something, but I really have to talk to the chief right away."

"Let me see if I can patch you through. What's your name, please?"

Julie listened impatiently to some clicking and pulsing on the line, fearing she would be cut off, but in thirty seconds or so Mike came on.

"I don't have anything more," he said abruptly. "I said I'd call when I did."

"But I have something, Mike: the shovel. We found it!"

"Where?"

Julie explained, omitting the reasons she and Rich had purposely gone to Birch Brook to search the backhoe. "Damn," the policeman continued. "That's the best news yet on this case. Where are you?" She told him. "Okay, stay there. I'm up the highway about two miles. I'll meet you at the diner."

She heard the siren before she saw the pulsing blue light of the Ryland police cruiser. Mike pulled into the parking lot beside her and rolled down the window. "You'd better take your car so you can leave if I get tied up out there. I'll follow."

Julie knew it wasn't logical, but having the cruiser behind her made her drive well under the speed limit. When they reached the parking area at Birch Brook, Mike pulled beside her.

"Up there," she said and pointed to the knoll.

"Hop in. That path looks doable."

As they pulled over the top of the knoll, she saw Rich standing beside the backhoe—waving in welcome.

"It's in the toolbox," she shouted to Mike when they had gotten out of the car. He started in that direction, but Rich stopped him: "There's something else," he said. He explained about the black Cadillac SUV, and his suspicion that its driver had come to retrieve the shovel but had been scared off by Rich.

"Get the plate?" Mike asked.

"I *think* it was 358 266," Rich said. "But I didn't have anything to write it down on. But I do know for sure it was a New Hampshire plate."

"What?" Julie asked loudly.

"New Hampshire. I'm sure of that."

"Maybe Frank borrowed someone's car," Julie said. "Or Luke—"

"Or maybe it was someone else," Mike said. "Let me run that."

Julie and Rich stood by the car as Mike tapped some keys on the small computer on the front seat of the cruiser. "Takes a little longer when it's out of state," he said through the window. "The shovel's not going anywhere, and while we're waiting, Julie, why don't you explain why you were looking in that backhoe."

Julie still felt embarrassed that the idea of searching the backhoe had come to her when she saw the machine in her mind's eye, so she stressed the logic. "I just thought this machine was sitting there where Mary Ellen was killed, and since the shovel hasn't turned up, it seemed possible someone had hidden it in the backhoe. It isn't a place the police would have searched."

"Should have been," Mike said. "I can see that someone would hide it there, but why haven't they retrieved it before now? I mean, this backhoe's been sitting out here for almost a week. Lots of opportunity to . . . oh, there's the read on the plate." He looked down and grinned.

"Myerson," he said. "Bedford, New Hampshire."

"Myerson?" Rich said. "Who's he?"

"Not *he!*" Julie shouted. "Steven's wife Elizabeth uses her maiden name, Myerson. But what would she be doing here?"

"Maybe she wanted to see the site," Rich suggested. "Didn't you say she's in real estate?"

"She's a mortgage broker, but that's different from someone who helps you buy property. But Steven does. Maybe he's using her car and came out to look at Birch Brook for a client or something."

"Is he a broker in Maine?" Rich asked. "You have to be licensed by the state, and he lives in New Hampshire."

"Hold on, you two," Mike said. "Before we get into all that, the important question is why the driver tore off when Rich approached the vehicle. That's what you said, isn't it?"

"Definitely. It just roared off as soon as I started toward it."

"And you didn't see who was driving—man or woman?"

"No, sorry, the windows are tinted."

"Okay. Then the first thing to do is find the vehicle. Excuse me a minute." Mike got into the cruiser and used his radio to put out an alert to stop the Cadillac SUV.

"Think it's time I saw that shovel," he said when he finished. "In the toolbox, you said?"

Julie and Rich accompanied him to the backhoe and stood below while he climbed up and opened the toolbox. "Looks like a shovel with a ribbon all right. I better call for the crime lab—don't want to mess this up by digging in there," he added as he climbed down and pulled the cell phone off his belt to place the call.

Rich took Julie's arm and directed her back toward the tree he had sat under before. "Let's sit down. Wish we had brought lunch."

"How can you be hungry already after that big breakfast? And all that's happened! I can't even think about food."

"Because you're thinking about what all this means."

"That too. I mean, it's pretty telling that one of the Swansons was here, don't you think? And especially that he, or she, drove off when they saw you. That's got to be suspicious."

"Agreed, but—" Before Rich could finish, they heard the crackle of the police radio: "State to Chief Barlow, over." The policeman ran toward his cruiser, and Rich had to put his arm on Julie to stop her from joining him. "He'll tell us," Rich said. But the radio was loud enough so they could hear both ends of the conversation from where they sat:

"You put out a call on a Caddy SUV, black, New Hampshire 358 266?"

"Right. You got it?" Mike asked.

"Sitting behind it, down at Gilson—just inside the line. What do you want me to do?"

"Routine check. Keep it there—I'll be down in fifteen minutes. Kill some time. Do a safety inspection, walk around the car. Say your computer is slow on the registration. Just keep it there till I get there. Who's the driver?

"The owner—Elizabeth Myerson. She's pissed and nervous."

"So it's Elizabeth, not her husband, who came here and then got out so fast," Julie said before the policeman could speak.

"I'm in a bind here. The crime scene officers have to call me back because they said they can't come till Monday, and that's just not acceptable. I told them to get permission for Saturday overtime and get their butts up here. They'll call me back about that. But it'll take at least an hour for them to get here from Augusta once they clear it, and I don't want to leave this site unprotected. I'm going to call in my new officer to cover it, but she's off this weekend. If I can't reach her right away on my way to Gilson, I'll get that statie to come cover until I can reach her. Anyway, the point is—"

"We can stay, Mike, if that's what you were going to ask," Julie said.

"That'd be great. Don't do a thing. Just hang around till the statie gets here. I don't think anyone will come by, but if they do, don't say anything about the shovel—just make sure no one goes up on that backhoe." Rich said they would. Then Barlow said: "Look, there's a small problem here about your being on private land when you found this. I don't want any technicality to screw things up. I gather you two were hiking and came through here to get to the road."

"Exactly," Julie said before Rich could respond. "And we did the same the other day, when Frank and Luke were here."

"And of course they didn't object," Mike said.

"Not at all—told us to do it anytime," Julie said.

"Good. I need to go. Be careful."

Julie and Rich stood by the big machine as the cruiser bumped down the path toward the road. They heard the siren as it disappeared in the trees, heading back toward the highway that led to Gilson.

"Let's go sit down over there," Rich said. "We can keep an eye on things from there."

"I just can't believe it, Rich," Julie said as they found spots under a large maple. "I was so sure Frank Nilsson had done it. That's still just so fishy about his alibi. But it was Elizabeth!"

"You don't know that."

"No, but it looks like it was her, doesn't it? Why else would she be here—and then run off so quickly when she saw you—except if she was coming to retrieve that shovel?"

"Plausible, but maybe she really was just looking over the site—for an investment or something, or to tell her husband in case he had some buyer for a condo."

"So why'd she rush away?"

"She doesn't know me—maybe she got scared that I was some sort of nut. Or maybe she thought she shouldn't have driven her SUV up the hill and the owners were going to chew her out. There could be an innocent explanation."

"True. But you're overlooking a big thing: The shovel is still here. If Frank killed Mary Ellen and hid it in the toolbox, why didn't he come for it before now? He had plenty of time. And so did Luke —even more since he works out here. I just don't see how Elizabeth Myerson fits in all this. What's that?"

Julie jumped up. Rich did the same. "What's what?" he said.

"That noise—it sounded like a car."

They walked to the edge of the hill and peered toward the road. "Get down!" Julie commanded in a whisper. Rich obeyed and dropped down on the ground beside her.

"Holy shit!" she exclaimed. "It's Luke." They watched as Luke walked slowly around his truck and reached into the passenger side and extracted a large leather bag. "With a gun!" Julie exclaimed.

Chapter 42

"He's got a gun!" she repeated, her voice more urgent for its low tone.

"Try camera," Rich said as he extended his arm to point toward the scene below them. "He's taking pictures, that's all."

Luke was walking around the sign for Birch Brook Condos and, as Rich had said, taking photographs of the sign—from the front, close up, far away, and then from each side. He was taking his time, walking and snapping, and Julie began to think she'd never be able to stand up. "This is crazy," she whispered to Rich. "I can't just lie here. Let's get up and go down and talk to him."

They pulled themselves to a standing position, dusted off their clothes, and started down the hill toward Luke. When they were halfway down, he looked up from his photographing and saw them coming toward him. Julie immediately waved and yelled his name in the friendliest tone she could summon up.

"You must have taken a shine to this place," Luke said when they reached him. "Hiking again?"

"Yes," Julie lied before Rich could respond. "It's such a nice walk, we thought we'd do it again this week."

"Ought to wear hiking boots," Luke said as he looked down at their sneakers.

"They're in the car," Rich quickly responded as he pointed to Julie's Jetta. "We thought we'd start at this end today. We were just going to get booted up to go."

"Don't let me keep you," Luke said, and turned his back to them while he aimed the camera to take another picture.

"Using them for promotional materials?" Rich asked.

"For the damned planning board! Excuse my language, but I'm sick and tired of it. The planning board is objecting to this sign, saying it doesn't fit the town ordinance. So I've got to go to a hearing and prove it does. Thought I'd take lots of pictures with me, show them exactly what it is. Lazy fools never came out to look at it themselves, just claimed they had an 'objection' and that I have to prove the sign's okay. Bureaucrats!"

"I heard that from someone else," Julie responded. "Nickie Bennett—she runs that ski shop? She's having trouble, too."

Julie's hope that Luke would take her statement about Nickie as a sign of sympathy and support for his own battle seemed to be achieved. He actually smiled at her when he said, "That so? Guess they're not picking on me, then. Still, it's a pain in the you-know-what."

"I can't imagine how you handle all the details of this project, Luke," she continued. "Everything's so complicated, and you have to be on top of it all."

"That's true." He finished taking photos and was tucking the camera back into its bag. "You can't take anything for granted."

"I gather even the land itself was quite a complicated proposition," Julie said.

"Land always is."

"Didn't your family actually own this area once?" Julie decided that with Luke, subtlety wasn't going to get the job done.

"That's right. If my dad hadn't sold it back to Dan, Frank and I wouldn't have had to pay a king's ransom to Mary Ellen."

"I'm sure Frank wasn't any happier about that than you were."

"Frank? He didn't know anything about all this in the beginning. Why would he? He's not from here. He just figured Birch Brook was a great site for a development. Which is true."

"So Frank didn't know your family had owned this?"

"Not at first. Didn't seem worth telling him about until I did some checking myself. That's why I was looking in those papers at the historical society."

"After Mary Ellen died?"

"That's right. You know when I was in there. We've been through this."

"I hope you found what you needed."

"Can't say I've found what I *needed,* but I may have. Probably too late anyway now—except for the principle of the thing."

"So Frank didn't know about the ownership questions until you told him you were looking at the Swanson papers?"

"That's what I said." Luke stared at Julie.

"Right. Sorry, but like I said before, I'm new to all this and just trying to figure out the local scene."

"Well, it's nothing for you to be concerned about, I'm sure. Anyway, you folks probably want to get started on your hike, and I'm done here and have to get home. Have a nice time."

Luke walked to the other side of his truck, placed the camera bag on the seat, and came back around to the driver's door and got in. He nodded but didn't speak as he put the truck in gear and drove off. "Want to get those hiking boots now?" Rich asked as they watched Luke drive off. A siren could be heard in the distance.

"That was fast thinking."

"Well, you told Mike we were hiking, didn't you? Now *that* was pretty fast, too."

Julie laughed. "I don't think Luke suspected anything," she added.

"He was too pissed about the sign. You sure grilled him—find out what you wanted?"

"I'm still trying to figure it out."

"You think he's involved?"

"I'm not sure. There's a lot of money at stake here, for Luke as well as Frank. But I just can't believe he'd leave the shovel in the backhoe when he had plenty of time—alone—to get rid of it.

And I don't see him as the breaking-and-entering type. He's too straightforward; I think he'd just plain come out and ask me for the copy of that letter. But—"

"Here we go again," Rich said before Julie could finish. The siren grew louder. "Bet there's never been so many cop cars on this road before," he continued as the blue State Police cruiser, its blue lights pulsing, came into view.

It pulled up beside them and a young man emerged, holding his trooper hat in his hand. He put it on before speaking. "Dr. Williamson? Mr. O'Brian? I'm Trooper Stearns. Chief Barlow asked me to take over here till the lab crew comes. He asked me to thank you for all your help. He said he'd get in touch with you later today to take your statements about what you found. Said you were hiking."

"Yes," Rich said.

"Is the backhoe up there?" the policeman asked. Rich said it was, and Julie told him Barlow had driven his cruiser up the rough path earlier. "Guess I can do it, then," the policeman said. "Thanks again for your help," he added as he got back in the cruiser.

They watched him negotiate the route up to the construction site. "It's after three," Rich said. "Have we missed lunch?"

Chapter 43

At home they assembled lunch from leftovers. After they had eaten, Julie cleared the table and Rich settled down with his student papers again. Julie sat at the folding table in front of the puzzle. Instead of working on it she was jotting on a notepad, and she kept rising to walk around the kitchen. After her third circuit, Rich said, "You're not getting very far on your puzzle."

"Just thinking. Sorry. I must be bothering you. I should leave you alone. I can go to the office."

Before he could respond, the phone rang. Rich listened as Julie spoke to Mike. As had happened earlier in the day when Mike had called to tell her about his interview with Frank, Julie became more subdued as the conversation continued. At the end she said, "Now's fine. See you."

"No developments?" Rich asked as Julie paced around the kitchen after hanging up.

"Mike said he'd explain. He's coming over to take our statements now. I assumed that was okay with you?"

"What—interrupt my paper reading again!" Julie laughed and punched him lightly on the arm. "So he didn't say anything about Elizabeth?"

"Only that he'd finished questioning her and she's gone back to New Hampshire. We'll find out more when he gets here."

"Does that affect whatever you've been thinking about?"

"As a matter of fact," she said, "I really wasn't thinking about Elizabeth Myerson. I was thinking about what Luke said this afternoon."

Rich placed the paper he was reading facedown on the pile. "Something tells me this is going to be more interesting than this paper. Tell all."

"I'm still thinking. I just haven't untangled this yet! Let's see what Mike says first. Here he is."

She opened the kitchen door for the policeman. He accepted her offer of coffee.

"I'd better take your statements first," he said. "Then I'll explain."

Julie and Rich repeated their story about finding the shovel, and Mike took notes on his pad. "I guess that's it," he said when they finished. "I'll get these typed up and you can sign them when it's convenient." He closed the leather notebook.

"So?" Julie prompted.

"Not much to tell," Mike began, and then summarized his interview with Elizabeth Myerson.

"So you believe her?" Julie asked when he finished.

"Not sure. But I am sure that I had no grounds to hold her. The crime scene crew can't get up till tomorrow morning, and unless we get her prints on the shovel or something else to tie her to it, well—"

"But you believed what she said about being at Birch Brook?" Julie interrupted.

"Again, not sure—but it's plausible. She's in the real estate business, and if she says she wanted to look the place over, how can I refute that? As to running away like that, well, I can't prove she didn't get an important phone call, like she said she did."

"You can check her cell-phone records, can't you?"

"Yes, and I will. But right now I don't have any reason to hold her. Any chance you heard her phone ring, Rich?"

"No, the windows were up, and I couldn't even see who was driving. So she could have gotten a call right at that moment. It's possible."

"That just seems too convenient to me," Julie said. "She drives up here from New Hampshire to look at Birch Brook—which she could have done lots of other times. Then she gets a call on her cell phone just at the very minute Rich comes out of the woods toward her, and she just has to roar off to go home—without looking the place over. Come on, Mike."

"I know, I know," the policeman said. "It's pretty thin, but I have absolutely no reason at this stage to doubt her. I guess mortgage brokers have to be on call all the time, like cops, and if she says she had a call about a major problem with a closing and had to leave right away to sort it out, well, that's her story. So thanks for the coffee, and the statements. I'm going to go relieve Stearns out at Birch Brook."

"Do you have to stay there all night?" Julie asked.

"Not if I can finally get ahold of my new officer. Anyway, I'll be in touch."

"Julie," Rich said as Mike stood to leave, "aren't you going to tell us what you're thinking?"

Mike stopped to look at Rich, then turned to Julie.

"But you need to get to Birch Brook," she began, "and I haven't got this clear in my mind yet."

"Maybe talking it out will help," the chief said as he settled back into the chair.

Julie began after she poured more coffee for all of them. She stood by the sink while the two men remained at the table.

"There's something new, something I just found out this afternoon." She explained about meeting Luke at the Birch Brook site.

"The planning folks are nuts," Mike said. "I understand why Luke's mad about that."

"Whatever. Let me just tell you what Luke said: that Frank didn't know about the shady aspects of the ownership of Birch Brook until Luke started looking for letters in the historical society and told Frank why."

She paused for dramatic effect, but the two men just looked at her, waiting for more. Finally Rich said, "I sense you'd like a drum roll here, Julie, but I still don't get it."

"Think about it, Rich. You were there when I asked him."

"I was there, but I obviously wasn't applying your puzzle-solving skills to what Dyer said. You're going to have to spell it out—for me, at least. Maybe Mike understands."

"I feel like I arrived in the middle of a movie," the policeman said. "Put me down with Rich as one of the dumb kids at the back of the class."

"Okay, two things: One, it was Luke who put Frank on to the fact that the ownership of Birch Brook was clouded and maybe subject to dispute; two, that happened *after* Mary Ellen was killed." Julie smiled brightly and looked at Rich and Mike hopefully. "You see it now?" she asked to break their silence.

"I think I'm beginning to," Mike said. "But I'm not sure where it leads."

"Give it a try," Rich said. "Anything you say will be illuminating to me."

"I think what Julie is pointing at is that Mary Ellen's murder isn't connected to the letters that show Birch Brook might not belong to the Swanson family. Because—"

"Right!" Julie shouted before Mike could continue. "Look at the dates." She grabbed her pad and made a list:

July 3: Mary Ellen murdered, 2 days ahead of date to back out of deal

July 5: I found out Luke Dyer was reading Swanson papers

July 11: I found Dan Swanson's letter

July 12: break-in at my house; copy stolen; found that original also missing

"You see the problem, don't you?" she asked, looking first at Mike and then at Rich. Neither spoke. "Okay, the first dates have to do with the land sale—but it was another week before the whole business of Dan Swanson's letter came up. I was confusing them, but they're separate. I was thinking the two things were directly connected, and that Luke had to be involved because he stood to gain by disputing Mary Ellen's ownership of the land. But Dalton Scott pointed out that Luke had every reason to make the letter public, not to hide it. It's only Frank who gained by suppressing the information in the letter—and in the Oakes diary, I think, though I'm still not sure what it proves."

"But Mary Ellen's murder?" Rich interjected.

"I think she was killed to stop her from exercising the option to back out. Look at the dates, Rich! If she had lived till July fifth she could have stopped the whole thing, which would have left both Frank and Luke in a pickle because they had borrowed so much—or at least Frank had."

"So both Frank and Luke gained by her dying on the third," Rich said.

"True. And that's part of what confused me: they had a common interest in her dying before the fifth, but if Luke had been involved in that—alone or with Frank—he wouldn't have continued digging in the Swanson papers. He wouldn't do anything to draw attention to himself or the land. Whatever he might have gained financially from bringing the ownership into dispute would have been lost by focusing interest on the sale, because that would have revealed the motive for Mary Ellen to be killed *when* she was. So that's where Luke's interests diverged from Frank's."

"Okay," Mike said. "You're saying Frank killed Mary Ellen to make sure the deal went through?"

"Right."

"I've got a question on that," the policeman said. "Why did he do it at the groundbreaking site, and with a shovel that just happened to be there? That doesn't sound premeditated to me."

"Nor to me," Julie said. "I don't think he planned to do it, and certainly not where and how. My guess—it's only a guess, but I think it's reasonable—is that he happened by the site, saw Mary Ellen, started talking to her about the price. And Mary Ellen, being Mary Ellen, got stubborn and said she had time to back out of the deal altogether. Now *that* would really have scared Frank because he just had to go ahead with this project because of his debts."

"So he panicked and killed her?" Mike asked.

"That's my guess, yes; and walking away with a bloody shovel wasn't possible, so he hid it. And then afterwards he found out from Luke that the ownership might be disputed, which would put him right back where he was—in financial trouble."

"But don't you think he could get back the money they paid?" Rich asked.

"Probably so, or at least probably, eventually. But just imagine the legal mess that would follow if Luke made the various claims public. You know what the law's like—a case like that would keep an army of lawyers busy for years. Frank couldn't wait—he had borrowed heavily and needed to get the project under way. I really think his debts are at the heart of this, dragging him deeper and deeper."

"So he had good reason to steal the letter from the archives and then to steal your copy of it," Rich concluded.

"And to hide the family diary," Julie added.

"I see that," Mike said.

"Me, too," Rich added. "But there's a big problem here, Julie: Frank had plenty of chance to retrieve the shovel from the backhoe. He could come and go whenever he wanted at Birch Brook. Why would he leave it there?"

"To implicate Luke!" Julie shouted. "That's not a *problem,* Rich—it's the *solution.* With Mary Ellen out of the way, Frank thinks the deal is safe. But then Luke starts to dig into the Swanson papers and tells Frank why. If Luke can prove the land didn't really belong to the Swansons because they got it through trickery or blackmail or whatever, he could sue to regain the title—and make himself a lot of money, at Frank's expense."

"So Frank had a double reason to get rid of the letter and the diary," Mike said. "First, the money, and second, to keep us from seeing that Mary Ellen's death was related to the sale. If he killed her to keep her from backing out, he sure didn't want Luke Dyer messing around in the matter and putting everything up for review."

"Exactly! Doesn't it all fit?" Julie said.

"I'm still stuck on the shovel," Rich said. "To implicate Luke, which is your assumption, Frank would have to be sure his own prints weren't on it. That's at a minimum. Better yet if Luke's were—but how would he do that?"

"I'm not sure he had to go that far," Julie said. "I agree it would be hard to do that. But if the shovel doesn't have any prints, the fact is, it's still in Luke's backhoe, and that would certainly make Luke a suspect. Wouldn't you be interested in that, Mike?"

"Sure. Though I guess Luke could argue that if he had killed Mary Ellen, he would have gotten rid of the shovel as soon as he could, and he had even more opportunity than Frank to do that."

"He could argue that, but wouldn't you still be suspicious, Mike?"

"Absolutely. Especially since his alibi for the time of Mary Ellen's death was that he was at Birch Brook alone. Which means no alibi at all. And like Frank, as you said, Luke had a motive—to make sure Mary Ellen didn't back out."

"But even if you'd suspect Luke," Rich said, "that doesn't put Frank in the clear. It just seems to me he's sort of trapped still. If we follow Julie's logic, he killed Mary Ellen and then figured he was in the clear on the deal. Then he found out from Luke about the Swanson papers and the clouded ownership. So he stole them, and he thinks he's in the clear again. Except that Luke can still keep digging, and if he does, the whole business comes out. He's got to do something to keep things from flying apart."

"And you know what that means," Julie said.

"No, I don't think I do," Rich replied.

"*I* do," Mike said. "He's got to kill Luke."

"Exactly!" Julie said.

Chapter 44

"Damned answering machines!" Mike said more to himself than to Julie and Rich, who stood watching as he called Frank Nilsson. "Either he's not home or he's not answering," Mike said, this time in their direction. "Can you find Luke's home number for me?"

Julie pulled the thin Ryland directory from the drawer and read the number out as Mike dialed it.

"Mrs. Dyer," he said with a calmness that amazed Julie, "this is Chief Barlow. I'd like to talk to your husband if I may." He listened silently to her reply. "What time was that?" he asked. And then: "Did he say *where* they were meeting? Okay, thanks, Mrs. Dyer, I can check there. If he does get home before I catch up with him, would you just ask him to call me, please? Thanks. You too."

Julie didn't need to ask for an explanation. "Frank called Luke around three o'clock," Mike said, "just after he came in from taking those pictures at Birch Brook. Said something important had come up and they needed to talk. Mrs. Dyer says Luke left to meet Frank at four. At Birch Brook." He smiled. "They'll be surprised to find Officer Stearns when they get there." He looked at his watch. "Almost four. I better get going." He picked up his notebook and was reaching for the radio sitting next to it on the table when it crackled to life and a voice asked, "Chief Barlow? Stearns here."

"Go ahead," Mike answered.

"Sorry, Chief, but I had an urgent call. Two-car accident on the East Flat Road—sounds serious. I'm on my way, but I wanted you to know I had to leave the Birch Brook site. Maybe you can get someone else out there. It's been real quiet."

Barlow frowned but told Stearns to continue to the accident scene. "I'll head to Birch Brook now," he said. "Anyone else around there?"

"No. Like I said, it's real quiet. You want me to come back after I do the accident?"

"I'll take over, Stearns. Got to go," he said in Julie's direction after he ended the call. "I'll get in touch later."

Before Julie and Rich could say anything, the policeman was out the door, running across the garden toward his cruiser. Rich put his arm around her. "Nothing you can do now," he said.

"I guess not."

"Except, of course," he quickly added, "to tell me what the hell's going on. Why did you say Frank has to kill Luke?"

"You said it, Rich: to keep things from flying apart. Every time Frank thought he had something under control, it came loose. It must have seemed like that Whack-a-Mole game to him: you hit one, and up comes another. If Mary Ellen backed out of the deal, Frank would be in big financial trouble. So he got control of that one by killing her. Then up popped Luke with questions about ownership, so he got that back under control by getting rid of the evidence. But then when Mike interviewed him this morning about where he was last Wednesday night, he realized something else had gotten loose—he was definitely under suspicion for the break-in."

"I follow all that—but not why he has to kill Luke."

"Because Luke could tell *Mike* what he told *us*—that he told Frank about the land problems. And that proved Frank's motive for getting rid of the letter and the diary. So killing Luke brings everything back under control."

"Not everything," Rich said. "What about the shovel?"

"That, too. If Luke's dead, and even if there are no prints on the shovel, the police will assume he killed Mary Ellen and hid the shovel in his backhoe."

"If Luke's dead, doesn't Mike have to find his killer?"

"Not if he committed suicide."

"But you said Frank wants to kill him."

"He does. For all the reasons I said. But he has to make it look like suicide. At least that's what I think he's going to try. I just hope Mike gets there in time!"

The next hour felt to Julie like the longest day she had ever spent. Rich tried to read papers, but Julie's pacing distracted him. He suggested they take a walk, but Julie wanted to stay in the house in case Mike called. He suggested they take the portable phone out into the garden and he'd do some work on it. She agreed.

Julie circled around and around Rich, who was on his knees, pulling weeds.

"I wish we could drive out to Birch Brook, but Mike would kill us."

"Wrong word," Rich said.

"I can't stand this waiting. I just hope Mike gets there in time."

"He'll call as soon as he can, Julie. We just have to be patient."

The phone rang, and Julie answered it on the first ring. "Not interested!" she shouted and hit the OFF button. "Damned telemarketers!" she said. "I hope Mike wasn't trying to call right then."

"You weren't on the line for more than two seconds."

"Maybe three," she said. "It's after five, Rich," Julie replied. "This is taking too long! I just wish . . ."

And as if in response to her wish, the phone rang. Rich watched as she smiled and the smile swelled to fill her face. "I'm so glad, Luke," she said. "I was expecting Mike, but it's even better to hear your voice. No, I understand—it was good of Mike to have you call. Yes, I'm sure he'll be busy. Well, thanks, but really, I don't deserve any credit. Okay."

Julie punched the OFF button and threw her arms around Rich. "Mike made it in time! Luke's okay, and Mike arrested Frank!"

Holding her tight, Rich felt Julie shaking. "Hey, it's okay then." But she began to sob. "It's okay, it's okay," he repeated, and steered her toward the house. "Let's go inside."

Rich stood over Julie as she sat at the table. "Want to talk?" he asked gently.

"Not much to say," she replied between sobs. "Can you get me a tissue?"

Rich took the paper towels from the counter and pulled one to hand to her. "Big towels for a big cry," he said. She laughed and used the towel to wipe her eyes.

"Sorry, but it's just such a relief. That it's over. And it was so nice of Luke to say that—he thanked me for saving his life. Did I say that?"

"No, you haven't said anything."

"Luke said Mike asked him to call since he knew we'd be waiting, and Mike had to take Frank in and didn't have time. I can't wait to get the details, but the main thing is that Mike got there in time to keep Frank from killing Luke."

"Then you really did save his life. By solving the puzzle. Just in time."

"Took me long enough, didn't it?" she said, smiling. "I was all over the place on this, Rich, but I guess it finally worked out."

"No, *you* worked it out, Julie. You should feel very good about that. But just don't make it a habit—solving murders."

"I just hope people don't make a habit of committing murders."

"That's hard to disagree with. How about some coffee?"

"Maybe something stronger."

Rich opened the refrigerator and took out a bottle of white wine. "I was saving this for dinner, but, hey, why not?"

Julie said she wasn't really hungry because of everything that had happened, but Rich said he was *always* hungry, and insisted on fixing them an asparagus and leek frittata he had seen a recipe for in the newspaper. When she smelled it and then saw it, Julie said she was glad he had insisted, and found she was much hungrier than she had realized.

"So now that it's all over," Rich said between bites, "what about those letters from the doctor?"

"The Tabor letters. You mean the two that mention Swanson in the Depression?"

"Right."

"They don't add much, do they?"

"Probably not to the case against Nilsson, but they do add to what we know about Ryland."

"My 'Down and Out in Ryland, Maine,' you mean?"

"Exactly. You're going to keep on with it, aren't you? Here you've got those great letters with lots of local detail and all. It's a treasure trove."

"I know, I know. But finding time to really do historical research—well, it isn't easy with my job. Maybe you should look at them. Hey, that's an idea. We could collaborate. You're the real historian, and I could sort of help out with stuff about Ryland."

"I'm a colonialist; what do I know about the Depression? No, it's your project. And right now, I think it's time to call it a night, after I get the kitchen cleaned up."

While he cleared in the kitchen, Julie fell asleep in the chair, and so when Mike called at 10:30, she practically jumped up at the sound of the phone. He apologized for calling so late and said he just wanted to be sure that Julie had heard from Luke. Julie told him Luke had thanked her for saving his life. "But you were the one," she added. "You got there in time."

"Thanks to you," Mike said. "I'll fill you in later; we'll talk tomorrow."

With that welcome prospect, Julie announced she was going to bed, and Rich was happy to join her at once. She slept better that night than she had in weeks.

Chapter 45

Rich gently rubbed her shoulder to wake her.

"What time is it?" she asked as she sat up and tried to focus.

"It's eight-fifteen. Barlow just called. He wants to get together at the station. You want to return his call?"

"I didn't even hear the phone ring."

"I figured you didn't. You seemed to be sleeping so deeply. I woke up about a half-hour ago and sneaked downstairs. I didn't want to bother you."

"Sorry to phone so early," Mike said when he heard her voice. "I figured you'd want to get this over with. I need you to identify some things, and sign those statements from yesterday. Later's okay if you want to have breakfast first."

"Now's fine. We'll meet you at the station in, say, fifteen minutes. See you." She hung up and asked Rich, "okay if we have breakfast later?"

"Somehow, I don't think that's a real question," he answered as he started to dress. "You thinking of giving Barlow a thrill, or do you plan to dress, too?"

Julie rang the buzzer outside the door of the Ryland Police Station exactly fifteen minutes after the phone call.

"Which one of you is the stickler for promptness?" Mike asked as he looked at his watch while opening the door. "Come on back," he said, and pointed toward his office. "Coffee?" Julie and Rich sat at the worktable in Mike's office while he went to the coffee machine in the main office. "Didn't think you had time for any at home," he said as he handed cups to each of them.

"Thanks," Julie said. "Guess we're just eager to hear."

"Figured that. Okay, you know I can't go into all the details."

"Just tell us what you can."

"Well, as you know from Luke, you were right on the mark about what was going on. Frank got Luke out there to kill him. Had a handgun. It was real quiet when I got there—Luke just standing, staring at Frank, Frank holding the gun. Honestly, I don't know what would have happened. Maybe Frank would have just backed off, maybe not. Who knows? But when I saw them I hit the siren and started up the hill, and I guess that scared Frank. When I got out of the car, the two of them were still just standing there, looking at each other. Frank handed me the gun and then just started talking. I had to stop him to give him the Miranda, in fact, but it didn't slow him down. He admitted basically everything you guessed at—about Mary Ellen, putting the shovel in the backhoe, stealing the letter, and then breaking into your place to get the copy. He was planning to put Luke's hand on the shovel—after he killed him, I guess. 'Course, he didn't know then that we already knew about it. And then—well, I really can't go into the details, but there was one thing we didn't know: Frank and Luke had a contract that transferred 75 percent of the ownership of Birch Brook to the other partner in case one of them died."

"Wow!" Julie exclaimed. "Remember, Rich, when we talked to them out at Birch Brook, and Frank said something about 'protecting' everyone in a partnership. That must have been what he meant!"

"You actually remember that?" Rich said. "You're incredible!"

"I agree," Mike said. "If Julie hadn't figured this out, Luke would be dead, and I don't know if we'd have been able to nail Frank. I didn't want you involved, but I guess I should just say thanks again."

Julie blushed and nodded. "Anyway," she said, "did Frank say anything about the diary?"

"You don't let go, do you?" Mike said, and laughed. "Matter of fact, it was in his trunk—with the letter and the copy. He just turned it over to me. I'm still not exactly sure what it's going to prove, but I assume you'll help me out on that."

"I can't say till I read it, but I'm willing to bet the diary will show the land survey in 1883 had been faked. And that someone found that out and threatened a scandal, which is why Dan's father sold Birch Brook cheap in 1933. And then Dan himself found out from the papers that maybe his father had been blackmailed. So *he* did a little blackmailing and got Luke's dad to sell it back cheap to him and to keep the whole thing quiet!

"Remember the Oakes and Swanson families are related. Frank Nilsson had to suppress the diary—as well as Dan Swanson's letter—to make sure Luke didn't stir up the ownership issue and kill the deal. Frank has too much money at stake and can't afford to have a long legal battle."

"What a mess!" Rich said. "But I still can't understand why Frank was so, well, crazed about this. If Luke disputed the ownership, surely they could have worked something out."

"You'd think so," Julie said, "but I think Frank was just in so much debt that he saw everything unraveling—his whole career, the way he saw himself as a successful developer. Remember that he has another big project going on the coast, and I'd be willing to bet that the financing on that is somehow tied into this. I know—" Julie paused because she didn't want to attribute this to Clif Holdsworth, "well, at least I'm pretty sure Frank had borrowed way, way beyond his means. When it looks like your whole life is collapsing, I guess you just see things in a weird way and some kind of self-preservation instinct kicks in. And, as Mike said the other day, land is a blood sport in New England."

"Blood and money," Rich added.

"That's right. And then when everything started to unravel again for Frank—and when he was actually face-to-face with Luke and pointing a gun at him and you came along, Mike, well, he must have just crumpled."

"*Crumpled* is a good word for it," Mike replied. "I think he was actually sort of relieved. You know, everything was so fragile—once he got one problem settled another one popped up."

"That's just what *you* said, Julie," Rich added.

"You can't go on that way forever," Mike continued. "Eventually it gets to you, and I don't really think—I know this sounds crazy under the circumstances—but I don't think Frank is a really evil guy. He just got in over his head—way over his head—and he had to keep going, doing one more thing to try to get his head above water. Anyway, it's a real tragedy." Mike paused and looked around the room, as if seeking an answer somewhere up on the wall as to why things happen the way they do. "So," he said to them, "want to sign those statements now? I've got to go down and meet the assistant DA and present all this stuff. Statements are right here."

While Mike stood and gathered some papers from his desk, Julie asked, "One more thing, Mike—about Elizabeth Myerson?"

"What about her? Here, you should read these through. Just make sure it's what you told me. And make any additions or corrections right there in ink and initial them."

"About Elizabeth?" Julie prompted.

"Elizabeth—yeah, I need to check those cell-phone records, but frankly, I think they'll support her. There's no reason to think she had anything to do with any of this."

"What about the boy on the bike who saw a blonde woman at the construction site when Mary Ellen was murdered?"

"That was all BS! I told the damned staties that before. That kid's just got a good imagination—and a desire to make trouble. Anyway, I'm going to talk to him again myself. But Elizabeth is out of this. Frank confessed, and everything adds up. Just like you said. So go ahead and read those statements. I've got to do some work in the other office. Take your time."

Rich and Julie did as he directed. Rich finished first, signed his, and sat quietly, staring at Julie as she worked through hers, making notes on the pages. When she finished and signed hers, she noticed his gaze. "What are you thinking?" she asked.

"About Elizabeth Myerson, as a matter of fact."

"You think she *was* involved?"

"No. Just about her name. Would you keep your name if you got married?"

"I haven't really thought about it. Why do you ask?"

"Oh, no particular reason," Rich said with a smile. "Shouldn't we be getting home? You've still got some of that puzzle to finish."

Julie looked at him quizzically.

"The map of the State of Maine," he explained.

"Oh, *that* puzzle!"